Time

Out of the Box, Book 19

Robert J. Crane

Time
Out of the Box, Book 19
Robert J. Crane
Copyright © 2018 Ostiagard Press
All Rights Reserved.

1st Edition

This book is a work of fiction. Names, characters, places and incidents are products of the author's imagination or are used fictitiously. Any resemblance to actual events or locales or persons, living or dead, is entirely coincidental.

The scanning, uploading and distribution of this book via the internet or any other means without the permission of the publisher is illegal and punishable by law. Please purchase only authorized electronic editions, and do not participate in or encourage electronic piracy of copyrighted materials. Your support of the author's rights is appreciated.

No part of this publication may be reproduced in whole or in part without the written permission of the publisher. For information regarding permission, please email cyrusdavidon@gmail.com.

1

Nagasaki Prefecture, Japan
Now

The sun sank low in the sky, falling gracefully into the Sumonada Sea, heralding the passing of another day. The man sat in lotus position, watching the orange hue light the clouds as the disc of fiery red glowed at the close of eve. Japan was behind him, the sea and sky ahead. He was an island—and on an island, miles from the Japanese mainland island of Kyushu. Sitting on the fourth floor of a decaying building, he saw only the endless horizon stretched out before him.

All of that blended into the background, though, for the man. His focus was solely on the sunset, heralding the end of the day. He had long ago lost count of how many sunsets he had watched. An endless succession of them. He watched the sun set from here; he could watch the sunrise less than a hundred feet away, as he stared out over the sea back toward Kyushu, and some of the outlying suburban shore of Nagasaki.

This was how he bookended his days, these endless days. Sunrise, sunset. He marked the passage of time with both, sitting on the hard, cracking concrete in the decaying building. Summer rains had washed away the roof long ago, and now the walls too were beginning to collapse under the cruel weight of time, its mission to reduce this building back to its component parts and wash it into the sea.

It was working. Nature was winning, now that man had given up the fight. For he took no part in that struggle, performed no maintenance, tended nothing. He was a stone in the river. Water flowed around him, and he took no notice of the small eddy his presence made.

Unnoticed by men.

Unseen by time.

Unstopped by all.

And so the man sat, watching the sinking sun fading into the west as the sky turned purple above him. He let out a little sigh, the cool prickles of night settling upon his skin beneath his suit. This was what he did every evening, marking each day as it passed, though he had long since lost count of how many he'd witnessed.

The sigh marked the end of his silent meditation, and he stood, brushing the hint of dust accumulated during his vigil from his black jacket sleeves and the back of his pants. A flick of his hand, and the dust was gone from him, had never been there, as though time itself had turned back to the moments before he sat. It was a simple trick, one he could initiate as easily as controlling his breath. He had come to mastery of both through long practice.

The sun was gone, the day was done. Night loomed, darkness clouding the skies over him as the last light faded away.

It was time. Again.

With another small sigh, the man turned from the sky, and the sea, and all the signs of the passage of time. Here in the wreck of this building, where nature's slow, inevitable war against the progress of man was being waged, he began his day anew.

As he had every day for ... so many, now.

And yet, it was not new. It was the same. For he himself was in a war against nature, wasn't he? The thought troubled him, when he dared to consider it. He might not be fighting against the decay brought by rain and earth and greenery, but he fought his own unending battle against the laws of nature nonetheless.

His brow puckered, and he dismissed the thought once

more. This litany of days, this endless string of them … they could not stop now.

Not now. Not ever.

He stared into the darkness of the rotting building, inhaling the smell of decay and mouldering walls. He scarcely remembered the scent of dew in the morning, but this smell—this mix of mildew, crumbling concrete, and damp stone—this was ever-present for him.

It was time to begin again, and he steeled himself for it as he made his way through the ruin of this building—of this island … and of so many other things …

For today was simply another day for the man on the island. Dread attended him as he descended the stairs into the interior. It was shrouded in darkness, and yet every step was familiar from the long practice of walking it daily.

Another day.

Just the same.

Forever.

He would see to that, he resolved, though somewhere deep within, he could feel the slipping … nature reasserting itself somewhere beyond him … and the dimmest trickle of fear made its way down his spine as he wondered, if maybe—just maybe …

Something was soon to change.

And that thought terrified him as little else did.

2.

Sienna

Whoever said time heals all wounds probably hadn't ever had souls ripped directly out of their body. Because it had been months—months and months, really, almost seven by now, since Rose Steward, Redhead McHellface, had held me down and ripped mine out, and time—

Time hadn't healed shit.

I was staring out the window of a diner on the coast of Oregon, an expansive glass screen between me and the ocean beyond, a troubled grey sky hanging overhead. For the last two months since I'd come to this town, it had been pleasant sunshine and the occasional rain, a little chill in the air as winter gave way to spring. The kind you could feel dance across your skin, sneak into your underclothes in the morning, give you a little tickle that made the bumps rise on your skin.

And now ... there was this grey crap. Blegh.

I didn't need sunshine and daisies every day of my life, but neither did I like the feel of storms on the horizon. Storms meant I'd feel compelled to spend the day indoors.

But at least ... not alone. Probably.

I glanced down at my coffee, black, then let my eyes flick back up to the picture window. It spanned the length of the place, which was ... pretty lengthy. A couple hundred feet of length, actually, and I was one of a very few people here. It wasn't tourist season in Cannon Beach, which was why I was here. I go where the people aren't, because I was still a wanted fugitive.

"Sorry for the delay," my companion said, sliding into the booth across from me. He favored me with a quicksilver smile as he did so, perhaps sensing that my mood was as dark as the gathering clouds outside.

"When you gotta go, you gotta go," I shrugged and looked back at the thunderheads looming over the Pacific Ocean. The beach was empty, not a soul brave enough to go out in this impending mess. Far to the north, probably half a mile, there was a mighty rock that jutted hundreds of feet out of the ocean like some immense, foreboding evil tower. It was a perfect location for a supervillain to build a lair, and I'd kinda been waiting for one to do just that so I'd have someone's ass to kick. I'd been here for two months and I still hadn't learned its name. "Future Supervillain Hide-out Rock" sounded better than anything someone else could have come up with, anyway.

"Still daydreaming about some great evil rearing its head here in peaceful, small town Oregon?" Harry Graves asked, taking a sip of his coffee and leaning back with a knowing look. Always the knowing look from Harry, because he could read the future. Or at least read the odds of events happening in the future. It was creepy on occasion, but also ... "Here," he said, and held out a piece of candy, a little toffee that looked yum, "I saw this by the cash register and thought you might need it."

I eyed the brightly colored candy, extended like a peace offering. I reached out and took it, unwrapped it, and popped it in my mouth. "Mm," I said, unable to control myself. It was really good. And it hit the spot. Not enough to totally disperse my bad mood, but ...

I eyed Harry a little suspiciously. He was really good at defusing me, like I was an ever-pending bomb, ready to blow up. Sometimes it was doing something as simple as bringing me a piece of candy. Sometimes it was more complicated.

And sometimes ... there wasn't a damned thing on earth he could do to make me feel better when I was down. He was usually smart enough to volunteer to "Go to the store" during those times. Seeing the future had its advantages, I suppose, and knowing your girlfriend was about to have emotional blowout and do some weeping? Well, what guy wouldn't want a heads up before that happened so he could leave town for a spell, come back when the pieces were all put together again?

"You might need to go to the store later," I said, picking up my coffee and taking a sip.

"If you want me to," he said, seeming to hesitate just a second.

I could feel a storm building in me too, not just out on the horizon. It had nothing to do with Harry. You couldn't ask for a kinder, more conscientious ... guy companion person. He could anticipate all my needs before I had them, and was ready in advance with—well, whatever was appropriate for the situation. He'd brought me roses, gift baskets, presents—you name it, he'd brought it to me these last couple of months. He'd stayed with me ever since we got here, and ...

He was great.

In every way, he'd given me all I could have asked for and more. He even gave me space on the days when I needed to just lose it without anyone watching. Because nothing would have pissed me off more than if he'd stuck around to watch me at my lowest. That was the stuff of real intimacy, I supposed—and we weren't there yet. I'd confided in him more than anyone else of late, but this last thing ... it was like a wall between us, one I couldn't just let him hurdle over. He'd seen me at my almost worst, let me cry on his shoulder before, but lately ...

I just couldn't let him in that last door. Which ... was par for the Sienna course. The only thing he couldn't give me was the damned thing I needed most. The thing I didn't let him give me.

Well ... maybe there were two things.

"You don't want to talk about it?" he asked. I could tell by the stiff manner with which he asked the question that he didn't love the options he was being presented with in terms of my replies.

I took a little pity on him. "No," I said. He didn't need me dumping my sadz all over him. Besides ...

"You sure?" His eyes were filled with concern. So sweet.

Too bad he couldn't give me a heinous supervillain to build a lair out on the rock. I don't think it would have made me happy exactly, but that grinding emptiness that always seemed to reveal itself whenever I had too much empty time? It would have been nice to submerge that under some straightforward action. Damned fugitivity. Messing with my ability to solve crimes and save the world. Didn't these people know that if I didn't stop this stuff, the wheels would fall off the damned car that was everyday life?

Also ... I'd probably lose my effing mind.

"Hey, Paris," a guy said at the table across the way. I turned my head to look. It was an old guy, probably a regular, talking to the waitress who was coming over to him.

"Hey, Jimmy," Paris said to the old guy, a kind twinkle in her eyes. "How's the world treating you this morning?"

"Like a dog treats his own junk," Jimmy said, causing Paris to chuckle. She had a carafe in hand, and started to move it toward his coffee cup.

"I'm sure," I said, turning back to Harry and forcing a tight smile of my own. He had that look again. The one that suggested a mixture of regret that he couldn't fix me, worry that I was losing my mind or at least unspooling under the weight of all this unresolved trauma (I wasn't. Probably.), and that strangest of all emotions, the one I wasn't quite used to yet ...

Desire.

Harry Graves wanted to be with me, I was pretty sure.

Weird.

"Okay," he said and stirred. "I paid the tab, so we can—" He started to get out of the booth—

Then he just stopped. He was partway between standing and sitting, one hand braced on the table, the other on the back of the booth, plainly poised to get up, but—

He was just hanging there, unmoving, mouth partially open in mild exertion.

I stared at Harry, who stared at the ground. It was one of

the strangest things I'd ever seen, as though he'd just ... frozen. But without the benefit of any ice holding him in place.

"What the hell—?" I started to ask, turning back to Jimmy and Paris and their ongoing repartee, but when I turned my head, I found them both ...

Frozen. She was pouring coffee, filling his cup as he watched, steam in a small cloud rising out of the cup but—

It wasn't moving at all. Neither were they.

It was as though every particle in the diner had stopped all motion.

Except mine.

I moved my hand, just to be sure I could. I got to my feet tentatively, half-expecting that long-awaited supervillain to come flying in from the rock. I checked, just to be sure—nope, no massive hideout had appeared up there in the last few seconds—or second, singular, given that no one else was moving. I walked hesitantly over to the restaurant's passage to the kitchen ...

The cooks inside weren't moving, either. They were standing there at their job stations, one of them looking like he'd just told a great joke that had another guy roaring with laughter over a skillet that was filled with scrambled eggs.

I looked back to Harry, still stuck in place in the booth, somewhere between standing and sitting. I made my way back over to him, glancing out at the dark clouds on the horizon.

A single spot of water marked the place on the flawless picture window where the first drop had hit.

With a rush of motion and sound, everything snapped back into movement. Paris the waitress pulled up the carafe, the coffee stopped pouring, the last of the steam cloud dispersed, leaving just a hint wafting off the coffee cup that Jimmy took in hand, letting out a satisfied sound as he brought it up to his nose and gave it a sniff. "The world's heading toward its proper shape now," he said to Paris, responding to some question I'd missed, maybe, or just generally proclaiming something that was ...

Not right ...

TIME

At all.

"What the ...?" Harry asked. I was standing in the middle of the room, some twenty feet or more away from where I'd been a moment earlier. His brows were knitted close together, and he stared at me, slightly openmouthed, cringing in ...

Pain?

Whatever had just happened, it had startled the man who could see the future.

"Oh, shit," I said, a little tingle running over me. And I tried to contain the feeling that welled up within me, along with the totally normal fear and worry that I should have felt when the entire world stopped around me. Because those were definitely there, if only in trace amounts.

But I kept that other feeling to myself, that ... more unseemly one, the one that was way, way out of place when the world was in crisis. "Come on," I said, hurrying over to Harry and brushing past him. "We've got to go."

"What the f—?" Harry was looking around, bewildered. "I didn't see—any of that—what—what is going on here, Sienna?" he asked, hurrying to keep up with me as I shot through the makeshift gift shop that covered every surface of the entry to the diner.

I darted out into the spring air, got hit by my first droplet, then another, then another as the sky opened up in a total downpour. My hair was soaked in seconds, and still I just stood there, taking it all in.

No rain was going to kill my mood right now.

Because now—after months of just sitting here, wallowing and being liked by Harry and accepted and doing frisky stuff and killing time—

Now, NOW, *FINALLY!*

I had a case.

3.

Jamal

"I always thought being a PI would be cool," Augustus groused, his head against the driver's side car window of our rental. He sounded like a child who'd opened up his Christmas presents to find rat crap or something instead of ... I dunno, whatever kids are into nowadays. Hatchimals, maybe? "But if I'd known it was like ninety-nine percent boredom and one percent excitement ... dude, I'd have thought about going into something that has a little higher action to boredom ratio. Like being a greeter at Wal-Mart."

"Yeah, I think they kinda work security there, too," I said, staring out the window into the grey day ahead. The skies were not clear over Cleveland, Ohio, where we currently found ourselves sitting. In a rental car. Watching a warehouse.

"That's what I'm saying," Augustus lifted his head off the window. "You know that at least a person a day tries to shoplift at Walmart. So you'd be seeing action every day. I could be in the thick of it, stopping the pretty criminals before they get out the door. Bringing them to their knees with my superpowers."

"Mmm," I said, kinda listening to him but mostly numb because we'd been sitting out here all night. "I doubt they'd be pleased if you ripped up the entry to their store to stop a shoplifter from walking out with a pack of gum. How much damage do you figure that'd do, having to replace concrete floors and—?"

"I'd just leave a pile of dirt next to the door and bind 'em up in that," Augustus said, waving me off with a dismissive hand. "Hell, as amped up as I am these days, I could almost do it with a handful. I've been practicing. And I'm gonna tell you something, too—whenever I got to Walmart in winter in Minnesota—" He mimed the motions of being cold, like it triggered some subconscious memory for him. I could sympathize; Minnesota was cold like nowhere else I'd ever lived. "—they got all kinds of dirt on those floor mats, tracked in with the soaked-ass snow that melts everywhere. Everything's so damned dirty all the time up there, it's gross, you know? Like—"

"We got movement," I said, sitting up a little straighter in the passenger seat.

"Yeah, awright," Augustus said, sitting up, too. "To be continued."

I frowned at him. "We really got to continue the discussion about the dirt content of Walmart entry mats in winter time in Minnesota?"

"Yeah, because I ain't done griping about 'em yet," Augustus said. "*Every* store in Minnesota in winter. Every one. It's terrible. I hate winter. I wish we could have drawn the assignment for Louisiana this time. Why'd Friday and Olivia get the one in the Deep South while we get stuck with Ohio?"

"Personally, I'm wondering why Olivia drew the short straw and got stuck with Friday at all," I muttered under my breath, trying to watch the minimal action ahead of us. "What'd she do to Reed to piss him off and get paired with Friday?"

"I think it's a random rotation," Augustus said. "Like, he keeps a list of all of us, and sometime your number just comes up, you know? Like the worst lottery you can imagine. Maybe worse even than the Shirley Jackson one."

"You think being paired up with Friday is worse than being stoned to death by your friends and your family?" I paused. "You may have a point there."

"That's what I'm saying." And he turned back to the scene before us.

Under the grim Cleveland morning we had a light industrial warehouse-district scene, painted in the greys of late winter. No fresh buds on the trees, nor any trees at all; the only green was a few ragged spikes of grass sprouting from cracks in the sidewalks. The aged warehouses before us had been around back when Cleveland was a little pre-industrial powerhouse, and definitely before it all went to hell and manufacturing left in droves in the last thirty years.

It was seedy. Sketchy, even. I'd seen a good half dozen junkies pass through in the last twelve hours. You could tell by their thinness, by the glazed look in their eyes. They were miles away, even though they were here. Our rental car might have been in danger of losing its hubcaps if Augustus hadn't peppered the kid who tried to steal them with pebbles until he left. Just kept pinging him with them like little BB's until the bastard gave up and went home. Didn't even notice us inside, watching him, giggling every time he took a hit, swatting at himself like he was getting eaten alive by mosquitoes.

"Yo, I think this is our guy," Augustus said as my phone buzzed in my pocket, the light vibration triggering me to jerk slightly.

"Mm-hm," I said, fishing for my phone. I extracted it and lit it up, and a text message was waiting for me. Unknown Number.

You're looking in the wrong place.

"Cryptic," I muttered. *Who is this?* I answered back, my finger communicating directly via 1's and 0's.

"He's just standing there," Augustus said. "Why's he just standing there? Oh. Lighting up a smoke."

I glanced up; sure enough, there was a skinny white dude up there blazing a cigarette, the fire-red glow of its tip lit, and he was putting his lighter away. I grunted acknowledgment, and waited a second.

My phone buzzed again: *Only a year, and you've already forgotten me? I thought I had made a bigger impression.*

"The hell?" I muttered.

A second later, the phone buzzed again, this time with a photo. It was the blurry black and white of a security camera shot, grainy and low-res, but there was a person standing in the middle of it ...

And they had a drawn-on digital skull face over a trench-coated body. The photo lasted only a moment, the skull face looking straight out at me, then the photo disappeared as though it had been yanked out of the digital memory of my phone.

"Holy shit," I whispered.

"He's just sitting there smoking," Augustus said. "Just sitting there. How much more boring could this be? Do something already, gangsta. I been sitting out here all night waiting for you to incriminate yourself, and you can't even get your lazy self moving until it's getting toward lunchtime. The early bird gets the worm, and you know what your sorry ass is going to get? Nothing. Nothing, you hear me!"

"I hear you," I murmured, and texted back. Augustus didn't need my attention right now anyway, not really. He'd be ranting until this guy decided to do something. *ArcheGrey1819?*

So you do remember me, the phone buzzed again a moment later, lighting up with her reply.

You're not an easy person to forget, I replied. *Being the best hacker I ever met.*

"Just sitting there. Like the laziest-ass white boy east of the Mississippi. I ain't saying they get lazier out west, but—you are lazy, boy. You're so lazy they make a whole line of chairs with your name on it. Just do something, you piece of sh—"

Flattery will get you everywhere.

I paused. Why had she decided to text me now, of all times? *You said I'm looking in the wrong place. For what?*

The buzz was near instantaneous. Either ArcheGrey had magical thumbs or she was interfacing directly with an electronic device. *Oh, you know. That thing you've been looking for in your spare time. That thing we talked about. Before.*

"Ambition, son. 'Early to bed, early to rise.' I mean, I don't care for the supervillain type, but at least they got ambition. Taking over the world means you don't roll your ass out of bed at the crack of eleven and think it's all going to work out, you know? And they be getting on with their evil promptly. Not sitting smoking a cigarette in a crackhead-ass neighborhood after spending their evening doing not a damned thing while my ass is stuck watching you and pelting idiot hubcap stealing kids for my own kicks—"

I was blazing back to her, interfacing directly with my phone to send quickly. I tended to get away from the habit in times of low stress, trying to disconnect more often. *You mean the video file of you know who?* In this case, I meant Sienna.

Maybe, she replied. Took a little longer, too, like she was teasing me or else thinking about how best to reply. Teasing me either way, I suppose.

Where's the right place to look? I sent back.

"... this is the kind of villain that would think robbing a Chuck E. Cheese is the path to wealth. Can't even be bothered with sticking up a Pizza Hut, no. Blinded by the bling bling of thin crust pizza and gaming, you go strutting your meta powered ass into a frigging kid's game and pizza parlor on a Sunday afternoon and bring the thunder down on your ass—Thunder and Lightning, that's what they should call us—"

"I don't make thunder," I said absently as I awaited Arche's reply. "And neither do you."

"Rocks rubbing together sound like thunder," Augustus said. I could hear the heightened agitation in his voice. He was working himself up, but I didn't pay much attention, because I was waiting for that text to come back.

Where it actually is, she replied, helping me precisely not at all.

Where is it, actually? I shot back. This was the thing; the holy grail in our question of late. *Please,* I added a second later.

And he has manners. For this, I will reward you.

"That's it. That's it!" Augustus said, breaking into a shout. "I've had all I can takes, I can't takes no more!" And he threw open his door.

"That ... was a grammatically ridiculous sentence," I muttered, still engrossed in my phone and ArcheGrey1819. The fact he'd thrown open his door and was getting out was lost on me for a second or so after he'd left and was driven home by the slamming of said door. "Whut?" I looked up.

Augustus was striding across the street toward the skinny-ass white dude smoking the cigarette, and my mouth fell open as I stood there, my phone in hand, trying to figure out what to do about it.

You should probably get after him, my phone buzzed, delivering this message to me. *We can talk later. After you have a chance to think about whose interests you're neglecting to consider.*

I stared at that a quarter second longer than I probably should have, trying to figure out what she meant, when a shout cracked through the street like that thunder I couldn't actually make. And not like boulders rubbing together, either, but like my brother, all worked up into a fearsome head of steam.

"HEY, YO!" he shouted at the man smoking the cigarette, and I sighed, throwing open my own door.

"Here we go again," I said, hurrying out after him to catch up before it all went to hell.

4.

Sienna

"What the hell is going on, Sienna?" Harry asked, hurrying to catch up to me. We were staying in a rental house not two minutes' walk from the restaurant, which was fortunate, because now the rain was pouring down and I was striding on through it, in a hurry to get back under cover.

"Action. Adventure. Excitement," I said, not bothering to turn back. "You know, the usual." The rain was colllllllld, and I wanted to get out of it. Action, adventure and excitement were one thing, but my hair that I'd spent time straightening this morning getting completely frizzed by the downpour? Not so cool.

Harry caught up a few seconds later, feet splashing in the small puddles that were already beginning to accumulate on the pavement. "I did not see you disappearing and reappearing—it was not even an option available in the future until you did it," he sputtered, clearly discombobulated, "and now—what the hell is going on?"

"You didn't see it?" I asked, my cheeks pelted with rain. Another concern, because I was wearing makeup. I know, bleehhh, but it was part of my disguise, you know, looking like a normal person, and not Sienna Nealon, fugitive at large. "Time froze, Harry," I said as he came alongside, jaw hanging a little low. I'd never seen Harry Graves flabbergasted before. I couldn't decide whether to assume it was a good sign or a bad one. "The waitress just hung there, coffee paused in mid-pour—"

"You mean she stopped pouring." He sounded like he was asking for reassurance.

"No, I mean the coffee stopped mid-pour. Steam hung in the air, unmoving. Total cessation of particle motion," I said. "Like someone hit the freeze-frame on life. The pause button on the internet video of my saga. Which would explain a lot, if my life was actually an internet video. I wish it was a cute one, with wombats, but no, it's some sort of Netflix original series gone completely off the tracks, superhero awesomeness one minute, then maybe a thriller for a little bit, and into a horror film the next. Now we're going into, I dunno, sci-fi, maybe—"

"What the hell are you talking about?" Harry exploded, stopping in the rain. "My powers, Sienna! They didn't work! At all! I can see the freaking future and—"

Wow. Harry was freaking out. In the months we'd been together and all through our acquaintance before that, he'd never shown so much as a crack in his cool facade, even the time we'd been literally shot out of a plane over the Dakotas.

"—my powers are broken!" He paced in front of me, rain drenching him, his eyes shifting back and forth desperately. "I—I —"

"Time froze, Harry," I said, keeping a little bit of distance between us. Sure, we'd been together for a few months, but ... were we really *together* together? Calling our relationship for what it was, giving it a name, I'd have to say ... early stage boyfriend/girlfriend. Maybe a little frozen there, too. "Time stopped. Everybody around me stopped. For minutes. That's why your powers got effed. The probabilities changed while you were trapped in time and I was moving around freely."

He stared up at me, blinking furiously, trying to put it together, hair completely soaked down, clothes clinging to his skin. "What?"

"It's like this," I started to say, but stopped when the rain quit.

No ... it didn't quit. It stopped moving. In midair. A

thousand, a million drops, still hung there, motionless, in front of me.

The world had quit moving again. The usual crash of the waves upon the beach just a few hundred feet away? Silenced, utterly. The faint, constant hum of traffic and electricity through the town of Cannon Beach? Gone.

"Oh, Harry," I said, looking at his face paused in time. He was watching me attentively, clearly trying to get a handle on his freakout. I tried to imagine being a guy whose power was knowing what was going to happen next, always, for the last hundred, two hundred, however many hundred years. (I'd never asked his age; there's a point where the cradle-robbing gets Edward Cullen creepy, and I liked Harry too much to want to work through that psychological hurdle in addition to all the others I was laboring with.)

I looked at the frozen grey sky above me, unmoving and felt my shoulders sag. This was not good. Time was skipping a freaking beat every few minutes, and—

Everything surged back into motion like someone had pressed play on the world, and Harry's eyes nearly bugged out of his head as he swung it around, meta-speed, trying to account for the fact that I'd moved a few feet closer to him while time had stopped, feeling like I should brush his skin or something with a sleeve, try and give him a little pat on the head or something to make him feel better.

"What the f—?" He stared bug-eyed at me when he caught up with my motion. I'd have to have moved way beyond meta speed to be where I was, nearly up in his grill, and he nearly tripped over his feet in surprise at my sudden appearance next to him.

"You're kinda cute when you're freaked out, Graves," I said.

"How can you be calm about this?" Harry asked, hand on his chest like he was about to have a coronary. Good thing metas didn't have those, but I would have to guess this series of events was probably elevating his pulse in a way that Harry Graves had maybe never experienced outside of cardio. Which he did not do. Still had a great body, though. "The world is coming off its freaking axis, time-wise—the—

the—" He was sputtering violently, talking with his hands expressively, but the only thing he was expressing was being completely freaked out. "—This—is not right! The world—is—"

"Coming off its axis, yes," I said, heading him off on that one.

"And you're ... completely calm about it," he said. "Look, I know you're really into projecting the aura of how awesome and experienced you are, and how you've been through enough ringers by this point that everything seems totally normal even when it's coming apart at the seams—"

He froze again, mid-gesticulation. He had a point, and I pondered it during this hiatus in which my hair was no longer getting soaked by the rain. In fact, I took a moment to wring it out, and watched the water droplets freeze the moment they left my hair. They just hung there, as I stepped away, brushing aside the ones occupying the space I moved into. They were shunted aside, losing their downward appearance as raindrops. I pushed a few together, made a little ball of liquid, shaped it, made a little game of it. It stayed in place, didn't wobble, didn't shudder. I shaped it in midair until I had a little water ball, like a snowball without the cold.

It was kinda neat, being able to do this, separate from time. I thought about what Harry was saying, and took my little water bomb and moved around behind him, carefully placing it just outside his collar, then moving to his side where I could stand in his peripheral vision field.

Time started again a moment later, and the bomb of water slid down the back of Harry's shirt as soon as gravity got hold of it. "—but really, this is—" He stopped mid-rant, like time had frozen again, and I watched his expression change as he realized two things: one, I wasn't in front of him anymore, I was standing at the side, smiling to beat the band, and two—

He'd just gotten about a quarter gallon of water poured down the back of his collar, and it was not warm.

"Gah!" he said, doing a little goose step away from me. "What did you do?"

"Acted my age," I said, a little impishly. "Listen, Harry—I'm not freaking out right now because time's not stopping on me. I mean—it's stopping, and I can see it stopping, but it's not messing with my powers—"

"Oh, well, if it's not messing with your powers, then everything must be hunky dorey," he muttered.

"I didn't say that," I said. "I'm genuinely concerned about what's going on here."

"You just used a time freeze to put water down the back of my shirt!" He did not look as pleased by my juvenile prank as I was. "How does that display your concern?" He was hitting some mighty octaves there. "Shouldn't you be, y'know—working on a solution?"

"Can't work up a solution until I get there," I said.

"Get wh—" He paused, and I assumed he was reading ahead in our conversation. He did that all the time. "Why are we going to—"

Time froze once again, and rather than wind him up more, I just stood there and waited for it to start again. It took a few seconds by my reckoning, and I composed the rest of the planned conversation in my head outside of his ability to read it, waiting for him to surge into motion again.

"—Japan?" he finished, and then looked like he'd been slapped. "Did time just ... stop again?" He blinked, surprise etching itself along the lines of his forehead.

"We're going to Japan because I think that's the origin of the trouble," I said. "With a guy named Shin'ichi Akiyama. We'll find him on an island off the coast near Nagasaki." And I calmly turned away, heading back toward our rented house, cold water streaming, again, from the sky, soaking me. I felt warm anyway.

"How do you know all thi—" He started to ask, and then he must have caught the answer without me having to say it.

"Because I've been waiting for this moment—or something like it—for almost seven years," I said, with a little buzz of anticipation.

It was time.

5.

"I don't understand," Harry said when we were back in our apartment. I'd already started packing my limited wardrobe. I didn't want to have to do any shopping once we got to Japan, and I was mentally working through how best to make this happen. Only a few years ago, when I'd had access to private jets or could fly myself, it had seemed like it'd be pretty easy to get to there when this day came. No planning necessary.

Now that I was an international fugitive, I doubted customs in the land of the Rising Sun was going to happily stamp my passport. Especially since I could no longer fly in under the radar, sans plane, this complicated things.

"That's because I'm not bothering to explain things as yet," I said, throwing a pretty nice halter top that I had yet to wear into my suitcase. It was black, and exposed just enough skin to actually kill people and also make the Oregon spring seem far too chilly for even this Minnesotan. I wondered what the weather was like in Japan right now, and decided it was probably not all that different from here.

"Which is another thing that's driving me slightly nuts," Harry said, pacing behind me. He'd packed in about two seconds once he'd seen me do so, and I was pretty sure he'd forgotten his toiletries in his haste. Men. "How long have you known this was coming? This time freeze and whatnot?"

"I didn't know it was going to be this, exactly," I said, folding the halter top clumsily and putting it in the suitcase.

"But I've only seen this time control power on display before from one type of meta. There's only one of those still alive on the planet that I know of, and we have a destined meeting, ergo this is probably Shin'ichi Akiyama, and the time has come for us to, y'know, meet for the first time." I blinked. "Well, his first time. My second."

Harry's voice sounded like a plaintive squeal. "What the hell does that even mean? First? Second? This isn't explanation, this is like an Abbott and Costello routine."

"Today is the catcher," I said, "Tomorrow is the pitcher."

"I like that you get that—" Harry started to say.

"My mom was into the classics."

"—but this is not helping allay my concerns, which are many and varied," Harry snapped, and I sensed he was about to blow a gasket. What do you get for the guy who's always been able to see the future and quietly reveled in the control that gave him?

Uncertainty. Change. I suspected I could have been with Harry all the days of his life and not seen him as freaked out as I was seeing him right now. He was trying to hide it, now that he'd had a little time to try and calm himself, but he was still about two seconds from losing his shit, and I didn't need future-predictive probability powers to see that.

"Relax, sweet cheeks," I said, probably a little too condescendingly, "this is all going to work out in the end."

"How do you know this?" Harry asked, with some fervency. He just couldn't quite keep a lid on his freakout. And he had pretty good reason.

"Because it all worked out before," I said, slamming my suitcase closed and zipping it.

Harry's head sagged into his hand. "This doesn't make any sense."

"Yeah, time travel is confusing like that," I said, picking up my suitcase. "I gotta grab a nap."

"It's nine o'clock in the morning," he said in a strained voice. This was not going well for him, but God bless him, he was trying. This was probably already the most strenuous year of his life just based on the last hour.

I probably wasn't helping with my reaction to it all, but I

figured he'd catch up sooner or later, provided time didn't skip him past my explanation. "Yeah, but I gotta line up my ride to Japan." I paced over to the bed, which was a saggy double. We were staying in someone's part-time home, Airbnb-ing it in the off season.

"Will you please just stop for a moment and at least consider explaining this to me in a manner that isn't—" He stopped, eyes moving back and forth like he was reading invisible text. Which he wasn't. He was reading the future, and my responses to his slowly unspooling sanity as he searched for answers. "Who's Weissman?"

"He was a huge tool and a buddy of Sovereign's," I said. "At the close of the war with Sovereign, he was the second in command of Century and was running the extermination of our people."

"And he could control time," Harry said, reading along with me, but not jumping ahead as he usually did. That told me how freaked out he was. He was more solidly stuck in the near-term present than I'd ever seen him, unable to look forward very far at all. He'd told me that his powers were based on his ability to basically stay calm and calculate, but this was proving it beyond a doubt. He was like a computer most of the time—just calmly chunking along, reading the most likely probabilities as he went, seeing a few minutes ahead in time and measuring the probabilities of the various outcomes of the paths we could choose.

But now his head—his Random Access Memory, where he stored all the current thoughts and considerations—was jammed up by panic for the first time in his life, and he couldn't hold enough data in his head to see more than a few seconds out.

"Yeah, Weissman could control time," I said. "Stop it, start it again. He was basically invincible, and he would have completely annihilated every metahuman on the planet, happily, except—"

"Except there was someone out there with his same power," Harry said, "and that made them immune to his abilities. Shin'ichi—"

"Akiyama," I said with a nod and a tight smile. "More

powerful than Weissman, and apparently keeping an irritable eye on him from afar. They had an agreement. Akiyama let Weissman play with time some, provided he didn't push it or freeze it, whatever—too much. He had limits, imposed by Akiyama—"

"Like your big brother telling you that you could only play with his toys for thirty seconds at a time," Harry said, eyes still dashing back and forth as he tried to make sense out of stuff that honestly didn't make a ton of sense, even when you'd lived through it like I had.

"If my big brother tried to do that, he'd get his ass kicked." Well, he would have before. Now that he was more powerful than me … pfft, I'd still kick his ass if he tried dictating to me. And I bet he knew it.

"But—you're saying this Akiyama didn't leave his island—" Harry started. I hadn't said that, obviously—he was reading ahead in the conversation again.

"He hasn't left his island in years," I said. "Hundreds, for all I know. All the big deal metas in the world know about him and leave him way the hell alone. Even Century didn't mess with him, because he could have killed every last one of them without breaking a sweat. He can freeze time," and I gestured around me, "and so, obviously—"

"He's the one doing this," Harry said. "But how do you—" He paused, blinking. "How did you meet him? You just said he hasn't left his island in years."

I let a subtle cringe escape. This was where things got complicated. I moved my suitcase to the door while I contemplated how best to explain this without losing Harry, and it occurred to me that I was going to have to jump ahead. "I met his future self. After he left the island."

Harry just stared at me, his eyes very still, which I took to mean he was firmly in the moment with me and had stopped trying to understand what the hell was going on seconds and minutes ahead. "My head hurts," he said, and sagged onto the bed.

"When I met him almost seven years ago, it was the future Akiyama I encountered, coming back in time to … thank me or pay me back for some great service I had done him in the future," I said, putting the travel bag down and working my way slowly back to Harry. "I'm guessing here, now, that it's finally time for me to perform said service. In return, he came back in time to seven years ago and allowed my mother to kill Weissman, making the war ... winnable." I felt my voice take a slightly scratchy quality. "She sacrificed herself to end him with Akiyama's help, and ... she couldn't have done it if he hadn't suspended Weissman's powers, so ..."

Harry had a hand over his mouth and was blinking furiously again. "So ... it's coming time to ante up for your favor ... that came seven years ago? And resulted in the death of your mother?" He gave me a wary look. "Forgive me, but that does not sound like a great favor."

I shrugged. "It saved the world."

"At the cost of your mother's life."

"Shit happens. People die." My voice was suddenly very scratchy.

"So you think this is Akiyama." Harry looked around the room. "This time skipping thing. That the time has come to pay—or pay back—or forward—or whatever—this shitty debt of yours to him."

"Seems like, doesn't it?" I asked.

"I don't know," he said, putting his face in his hands. "The future, the past, the probabilities being askew ... none of this makes sense to me."

"It's okay," I said, taking a couple steps over to him and putting my hand on his back, which was still soaked from the rain. I'd changed before I'd packed. Harry, on the other hand ...

Well, his head was elsewhere. Understandably.

"How do we even get to Japan?" Harry asked, clearly too frazzled to look ahead the ten seconds it'd take to get the answer. Then he looked up at me, sighed, and said, "Greg Vansen? That's not going to work. Your sleep schedules are too far apart, you won't be able to get ahold of him for at least forty-eight hours via dreamwalk, and if you try to contact him conventionally ..." He concentrated hard. "Yeah. Ninety nine point nine percent chance the cops come crashing down on us. There's no path to Japan that way."

"Shit," and then I was furiously reconsidering. And then,

after a minute, I said, "Okay, plan B."

"Oh. Geez." He lurched forward, catching his head in his hands. "For the sake of a—"

"Will it work?" I asked, as he buried his face in his fingers, not looking up. He didn't move, just sat there, looking as ... hell, I dunno, I'd never seen this kind of a thing from Harry before.

"Insult to frigging injury," he muttered under his breath. "Of course it'd be—" He lifted his head out of his hands and blinked at me for a few seconds, sighed, and said, in a voice that sounded drained of life, "Yeah, that'll work—but only if I can keep my head about me and steer you through customs and all the snares that are going to be coming. It's a pretty tight path we'll have to walk."

"I'm good at following instruction," I said with a tight smile, and watched his frustration evaporate to be replaced by something mildly amused—and maybe a little annoyed. "Well, I *can* follow instructions ... from time to time ... when I see a reason to."

"Uh huh," he said, pushing his face back into his hands. "I don't mean to put any pressure on you, but you should probably get to sleep if you want to pull this off. Your window for a nap and catching—"

"Yeah, yeah," I said, getting in bed and closing my eyes. As if trying to oblige me, time seemed to have stopped again, the sound of rain tapping at the roof ceasing into silence. Even Harry had frozen, though his face betrayed ...

Worry. And hints of ... something else, his forehead lined heavily, his eyes staring off past me in contemplation.

I stifled a yawn as I pressed my cheek to the soft pillow. Maybe if I hurried, I could get to sleep before time started again.

With that in mind, I cleared my head save for thoughts of one person, in particular, whose help I needed. A vision of them carefully in mind, I tried to relax, and a few minutes later, before time had resumed its course, I drifted off in the lightest of naps.

6.

Jamal

"You lazy, no good, after-market, shit-level, made in a fourth-world-country-sweatshop-quality supervillain," Augustus said as he stormed up on the guy smoking his cigarette, eyes wide at the big black dude stomping toward him. "You are going to get off your lazy ass and get to work on this petty crime shit you got going on or I am gonna put my foot up your ass—"

"Augustus!" I shouted, trying to catch up with him as our mark just stared, cigarette dangling from his lips in shock. I wasn't sure how the cops would view this scene if they saw it play out, but I had a feeling the law wasn't technically on our side if my brother kept carrying on like he'd lost his damned mind, trying to entrap our mark into something more illegal than smoking on the sidewalk.

"When I haul my ass out of bed in the morning, I expect a certain level of commitment from my criminals," Augustus said, now up in the guy's face. He flicked the cigarette right out of the dude's bulging lips. Our mark watched it sail through the air, ash flicking loose as it twisted in a slow arc down onto the pavement. "I expect them to get their ass to work robbing stores or shaking people down, and then I expect I'm going to have to kick their ass senseless, drag them to the nearest authorities, and then pull their sorry ass back to the Cube where they can spend some serious time thinking over all the bad shit they've done. You feeling me, here?"

The guy just blinked. "Who ... who are you?" He sounded a little scratchy, like maybe he was still strung out.

"My name is Augustus Coleman, and I'm going to be your arresting officer for today," my brother said, all thinly restrained and polite.

"What ... what did I do?" the guy asked, smacking his lips. I think he hadn't quite put together that his cigarette had been knocked free. Even though he watched it happen.

"You know what you did!" Augustus thundered, becoming the substitute teacher from the Key and Peele sketch before my very eyes.

"Augustus, I'm not so sure—" I started to say, and my phone buzzed. I raised it up to look at it. *You're looking in the wrong place. Again.* "That's not very helpful," I muttered. I looked up, searching for nearby cameras. There weren't any obvious ones, but for all I knew, Arche could have hacked every cell phone nearby and was watching this play out in real-time.

"I ... I don't know what I did," the guy said, very subdued, meek, eyes still glazed over. "Was it bad?" His voice was cloudy, and I wondered if he even remembered Augustus's approach, let alone anything he might have done in the last twenty-four hours. To say nothing of going further back. "Was it bad?" He sounded genuinely curious.

"Was it b—can you believe what he's asking us?" Augustus shot a look at me. "Are you hearing this?"

I was torn, trying to look away from my phone, which I hoped would buzz with something less cryptic and more helpful, given that I was caught between trying to talk my brother down from a foaming-at-the-mouth frenzy and a conversation I really wanted to have. "I'm—yeah, I hear it. I don't think this is our g—"

"What did you do?" Augustus asked, getting eyeball to eyeball with our subject, who had paled a good dozen shades just in the last few minutes since we'd rolled up on him. The guy looked like he wanted to retreat but didn't know quite how to. "I'm asking you," Augustus said, "what'd you do? I know you remember."

"I ... I ..." the guy's voice wavered. He was pitifully thin, still smacking his lips, and he gazed past Augustus, staring into space, "... I ... got high ...?" He ended on a somewhat comic note, like he was simultaneously seeking approval and also confessing.

"No shit you got high," Augustus said, and ripped the guy's sleeve down to reveal a ton of needle marks. My gaze caught on them as my brother lifted his arm up. "It wasn't even a question that you got high. The question was—what'd you do while you were high—and what are you going to do now, motherf—"

"Augustus," I said, raising my voice loud enough to cut him off. "This ain't our guy."

My brother rounded on me, still holding the junkie's arm up. "What are you talking about? He's admitting—"

"He's admitting he's an addict," I said, and nodded at his arm. "But he ain't much of anything else."

Augustus brandished the guy's arm. "How do you think he's getting his drugs? Paying for them?" He spun back to the junkie. "How do you pay for your drugs?"

"Uhm ..." The guy stared into space. "I ... sell stuff sometimes."

"What stuff?" Augustus was like a dog on a bone, unwilling to let anything go. I didn't bother to break in and inform him that there was a pretty obvious reason this was not our guy, not our case.

"Uh ..." The guy stared into space, his voice taking on a dreamy quality. "... Stolen ... stuff?"

Augustus turned back around to me with triumph in his eyes. "See? You see that? Stolen stuff. He's our thief." I shook my head. "What are you shaking your head for?" my brother asked. "He just admitted it."

"His arm, man," I said, nodding at the track marks. "Look at his arm."

"Yeah, I see them," Augustus said, still pouring out his annoyance. "That just tells me—oh." And just like that, all my brother's thunder petered out. Metas healed too quick to even develop bruises, and they damned sure didn't display track marks from repeated use, regardless of how dirty their needle might be. "Well, damn."

"Yeah," I said, and looked back to my phone. *Good catch,* Arche had texted. *Watch your head.* I frowned. What did that mean—?

The wall behind Augustus exploded, and he dodged by a mere second, pulling our new junkie friend down with him. A car came flying over us as I dropped to my knees as well, an old sedan stripped down to the frame crashing past and rolling sideways into the street from where someone had hurled it at us.

Lucky thing my brother had gotten a power boost a year or so ago, because otherwise that flying sedan would have turned him into a pulp hero rather than just an overzealous one. Dust filled the air around us and I sprang to my feet the moment the car cleared me, leaping after them.

I emerged from the cloud after a short hop through the wall and into a warehouse. The dust hung heavy in the air, but even over the slight ringing in my ears produced by the aftershock of a car being hurled through a concrete block wall, footsteps were audible in the distance, retreating rapidly. I caught motion out of the corner of my eye and took off at a run.

A shadowed figure ducked into a doorway. Other figures were strewn about the room. The warehouse was an abandoned old place, glass ventilation windows up top all knocked out and providing the only light in the interior. Whatever this place had been, it was a hell hole now, piles of discarded brick and refuse all over the place, between the dozen or so junkies that were using this place to squat and do their business.

I knew the person I was chasing was the one responsible for chucking that car at us because they were the only one who was getting a move on in this mess. Everybody else was still trying to shake their high. Hurling a car? Not on their list of priorities, and definitely not through a wall at people they couldn't even see—but probably could hear, if they had meta hearing.

Rounding the corner into a narrow hallway, I almost got

leveled by a punch. I saw it at the last second and it just clipped me across the cheek instead as I slowed my roll and tried to dodge. My quarry had ducked behind the corner, figuring on knocking my ass out in ambush, and they damned near got me, too.

My phone buzzed in my hand, and I loosed my powers a little, enough to electronically translate the message through my finger into my brain: *Watch out.*

"Still not helping!" I announced as I took another hit due to ... let's say distraction, but it might have had a little to do with me not being much of the fist-fighting type.

I lashed out with a clumsy kick that my opponent dodged. They put a fist at me that I ducked. It shot past me into a wall, dashing concrete and releasing another cloud of dust into the air.

My foe was skinny, that much I could see. Wearing skinny-ass jeans with a hoodie to give them some bulk. They seemed to be swelling even as I stood there, and I groaned as the skinny jeans ripped a little along the seams. A huge fist shot at me, twice the size of the one I'd dodged seconds earlier.

"Okay, I'm not going to win a fistfight with a Hercules," I said, falling back down the hall, cradling my phone in one hand and holding out my other like a peace offering to slow them down. Didn't work; I couldn't see the shadowed face on this hulking brute, not in this lack of light, but they were coming at me hard. "So ... don't expect me to even try."

I let loose a blast of lightning that went straight from my fingertips into the outreached fist of my enemy, jolting them hard and tearing out a high-pitched scream from ...

From *her* lips. Which I could see once my lightning flashed in the hallway.

Shit. I was fighting a girl.

"Oh, damn," I said, my lightning dying down as my quarry—my female quarry—struggled back from the hit. "I'm so sorry, Miss—"

She raised her shadowed face and then her damned ham fist again, coming at me with another punch. I let out a little scream—probably almost as high pitched as hers—and shot off another bolt of lightning, harder this time, maybe a little bit motivated by panic.

My opponent was lit by the flash once more, and I saw the pain flash over her face, which was ... weird. She was all swole up, and I had to guess she was usually petite, which made her look really grotesque, like her head hadn't caught up with her muscle growth. Her pained look turned into a feral snarl, as my lightning only made her madder, and she started to push through it ...

At me.

"Oh, shit, oh shiiiiiiiiit!" I shouted and juiced her again as I tried to fall back in a hell of a hurry. She was snarling, pissed, my electricity not really doing the trick to put her down. I was afraid to juice her too much for fear I'd kill her, but as she raged down the hall, smashing through the walls by lashing out in anger, I realized I was running really short on time. All my choices—flee, capture, contain—were reduced down to one as she closed the distance between us to about three feet, hand out, reaching for me like she'd be grabbing me by the neck and shaking me into a pudding.

My phone buzzed, and the digital connection between my finger on the charging port and my brain put it directly into my mind, another "helpful" message from Arche. *Don't be so gentle. Your life is in danger.*

"Sorry," I said, and let loose.

The walls flashed with bright blue as I poured all the electricity I had into the charging behemoth of a Hercules. She took it right in the hand and—I shit you not—her hand exploded like a hamster in a microwave. The lightning coruscated down her arm and into her chest, and she jerked, letting out the most pitiful and plaintive scream I'd ever heard in my life—and this counted the people I'd killed. She spasmed as my power was grounded out by her connection to the floor, and she keeled over, faced down.

"Oh, damn," I said raggedly, my breath coming hard. She twitched, but I barely saw it as the spots in my vision from the blinding flash slowly faded.

Footsteps echoed at the end of the hall where she'd ambushed me, and my brother appeared from around the corner. "What happened?" he asked. "I heard a girl screaming."

"Yeah," I said, trying to get my breathing under control. "Yeah ... ah ... our villain ... it was a woman." I nodded at her, noticing for the first time that her shoulders and back were moving as she drew regular breath. Smooth and steady, like she was unconscious. Whew. Not dead.

"Is that so?" Something in my brother's voice sounded a little guarded. "Hm. I just figured you got scared. Cuz your voice gets high when you get scared, you know."

"So it's like yours when you see a spider, huh?" I snapped right back at him.

"Hey, man, spiders are scary things," Augustus said seriously. "Eight legs. Fangs. All hairy. Some of them are poisonous—"

"Which wouldn't affect you because you're a meta," I said, taking a knee next to my downed foe and rolling her over. Her hand had definitely exploded under the lightning, flesh peeled back from bone. I didn't want to check, but I was guessing the soles of her feet were probably similarly affected given that they were the exit route for my lightning. I touched her wrist, and she didn't stir, but her pulse was low and regular. "You got any suppressant on you?"

"Yeah," Augustus said. "Why? You scared of this little thing?" He reached into his jacket as he came over and nudged her with his foot. She didn't stir.

Now that I got a look at her, she was probably only a hint over five feet tall, and ninety pounds on a day when she'd eaten every calorie she could lay her hands on. "She was a lot scarier a few minutes ago," I said, taking the proffered needle out of Augustus's hand, popping it right into her neck, then pushing the plunger.

She took a long breath, gasping, and then settled back down into slumber, unstirred. She seemed to shrink another inch or so, or maybe just curled up into a ball. She looked like a china doll, pale, waxy, dark hair and—shit, *tiny*. She couldn't have been more than eighteen.

"That little thing?" Augustus scoffed. "Man, she don't even weigh as much as a parakeet, and she's got you screaming.

Pffft."

"Wouldn't have happened if my brother had just waited to make his move until we had an actual line on the subject," I said, and in the distance I could hear the sirens coming this way. They were a long ways off; I was guessing cops didn't bother to come down here much. "Patience."

"Hey, I got her drawn out, didn't I?" Augustus scoffed.

"And we damned near lost our heads for it. Which, admittedly, would be a bigger tragedy for me than you."

"It all played out all right," Augustus said, and he pulled dust out of the air and pieces out of the concrete block around us to bind her up, just in case the suppressant didn't work. That done, he lifted her into the air by the earthen grip shackles he'd constructed for her, pulling her up like a marionette. "What are you squawking for? We got her now. Mission accomplished."

"Yeah," I said as he started to parade her back outside, to the car. "Mission accomplished." And I remembered my phone, still grasped in my hand, and re-established my link with it.

There was a message waiting. Simple. Quick.

Nice work. Now chew on this:

At the end of it was a link that I immediately clicked, by instinct. I followed Augustus, on auto-pilot, my mind already forgetting the fight I'd just fought ... and already on the one ArcheGrey had just put in front of me.

7.

Sienna

I stood under a building overhang as the rain drizzled down around me. The Pacific Northwest was really living up to its reputation as a precipitation-heavy place today, which was funny, because it had been pretty dry overall since I'd gotten here. Now I was cold and wet and should have been generally unhappy.

But I wasn't. I was just staring straight ahead, humming to myself. Because I had something important to do.

"I understand why you're happy," Harry said next to me, chafed from the wait. Or maybe because of the cold and/or being soaked to the skin. I was trying not to let that get to me. "But you might want to tone it down just a smidge, otherwise people—not me, obviously, since I know you—might get the idea you think it's really swell when shit's going all to hell."

"It's not that I *like* it when things go bad, per se," I said, brushing some of my now-red hair back behind my ear, "it's just that ... uhm ..."

"Beating bad guys is the thing you live for," Harry finished for me.

"No," I said, trying to clarify, "it's that ... if I don't solve the meta problems no one else can ... what's the point of me?"

"Ahhhh—and I'm just spitballing here—you could try and

be a normal, non-fugitive person."

I gave him a pitying look. "We both know I'm not a non-fugitive person. And let's just give that 'normal' thing a wide berth, cuz I'm pretty far from that, too, as the awkward precautions required for our romantic interludes should have made clear by now."

"It's a little weird the lengths we have to go to in order to keep my soul from being absorbed," Harry admitted, "but I've met a lot of people in my life, Sienna. You're not so different from any of them, once you get past the physical contrivances associated with being a succubus. You want things—well, you want to be needed, anyway. That's a pretty universal human desire."

"I really prefer to focus on my special weirdness, Harry," I said, giving him a frown.

"Everyone wants to be special in some way," Harry said. "Even if it's minor. I don't blame you for wanting to focus on the part of your identity that makes you unique, but—"

"Why is it that anytime someone pays me a compliment they follow it with a 'but' so big that Sir Mix-A-Lot would drool over it?"

"I don't know what that m—oh." He must have read my explanation of it out of the probabilities. "Nice reference. You know you weren't born until 1994, right? Meaning after that song was released?"

"You know my primary exposure to culture until I was seventeen was my mother, right?" I tossed back. "Followed by TV and books, then music, most of which was not new."

"It all starts to make sense now," Harry said, "you're an old soul because your mother didn't let you associate with the cool kids. Or any kids, really."

"I mean, I do my best to fit in with your normies who have been socializing and associating with other people all your lives," I said, trying to play it cool when in fact Harry had touched on an area of pretty deep insecurity for me. Being cavalier about it was my only defense. "But ... you know, I was playing a heck of a game of catch up when I left the house."

"I feel like my point got lost in all this."

"Then it probably wasn't worth making," I said, "because it was basically just a paean to how I'm totes 'normal,' which I'm really not, Harry. And I'm not saying that in an, 'I'm so super special!' kind of way. I agree that when it comes to genetic code or whatever, I'm probably 99.9% like other human beings. But those differences? Killer in terms of how we experience life." I raised a hand. "Not being able to touch like a normal person? Pretty key defining feature of the Sienna experience."

"I'm not saying it's not different for you," Harry said, looking, if anything, even more impatient and still clearly flustered that he wasn't reading as far into the future as he normally did. "What I'm saying is, your joy at being needed to save the world—or in this case, save me—"

"Huh?" I blinked at him. "Oh, because it messes with your powers." I hadn't really thought of this job as saving Harry.

It only took him a second to pick up on my unspoken answer, and his eyes narrowed. "If you weren't thinking of this in terms of helping me, what the hell are you charging to Japan for?"

"Well, time's freezing, Harry," I said. "And even though I'm the only one who can see it, I don't imagine it's a healthy thing to be happening. You know for the, uhm ... space time continuum or whatever. Science ... stuff."

He didn't appear impressed by my whipping out the 'space time continuum' bit. Which made sense, because I didn't know what the hell I'd just said. "You're just running into this because—"

"Because I have a fated date with Akiyama," I said, "and to help you and stuff. And because the world will probably need my help on this one before the end." I forced a smile that was super fake.

"'The world will need'—Sienna, the world can't see this time break thing happening."

"Yes," I said, "but mark my words—the world will need my help on this before it's all said and done. I have a sixth sense for danger, and this? It reeks of it, like douchebags stink of Abercrombie and Fitch colognes." I settled back against the edge of the building and stared pensively out across the airport tarmac as a private jet came rolling up. I hadn't even noticed it landing. Must have been caught up in the argument. "Do you think my succubus powers to reach into souls count as a sixth sense? Because if so, I guess detecting that the world is coming to danger is probably a seventh sense—"

Harry let out a low sigh, a groan under his breath that lasted a few seconds, and he looked up at the plane rolling our way warily. "I wish we could have found a different way to do this."

"It's a private plane," I said, "it's going to be totally kittens."

Harry stared at me blankly. "... What?"

"Never mind," I said, glancing away. "It'll be fine."

"I hope you're right," Harry said, "I'm just, ah ..." The plane taxied right over to us and rolled to a stop. The door started to open a moment later, stairs built into it lowering almost to us. Curbside service. Couldn't beat that.

"It's called nerves, Harry," I said. "And I know why you're nervous." He cocked his head at me curiously. "I remember what you said at Midway Airport. You've got ... history."

His face froze. "You're not, uh—"

"I don't care about your past," I said. "It's the future that's concerning me at the moment, anyway." And I started up the ramp the moment the stairs finished folding down.

"Hey, you guys!" came a bright, enthusiastic voice as I ducked into the plane, past the flight attendant who was waiting at the top of the stairs, trying to stay in so the rain didn't pepper her. I didn't have to duck to squeeze through the door, but Harry did, just a little, after me. I stepped into the Gulfstream jet and managed not to shake myself like a wet dog. I settled for dropping my baggage with the flight attendant, who took it wordlessly. I headed down the aisle to where my host was waiting. Harry followed a moment later, and I could sense his hesitation.

I plopped into a seat across from the girl—woman, I supposed, though she only occasionally acted like it—across from me, who was eyeing me brightly. "Hey," I said, settling back. "How's it going?"

TIME

"It's been such a dynamite year so far, Sienna," she gushed as Harry eased up, taking a seat a couple rows ahead of us. There was only two seats per row, and they could be rotated like an office chair. He sat down in his and then rotated it halfway toward us, so he could listen to our conversation and not appear totally rude, but also not look like he was deeply involved, either. "Hey, Harry," she said, a little uneasily.

"Klementina," he said, a touch uneasily himself.

Our host blushed, red replacing the usual tan of this California girl's skin around her cheeks. She forced a tight smile, at me, then to Harry, and said, perfectly polite, "I don't really go by that anymore ... Please ..." And she smiled a lot more genuinely, "... call me Kat."

8.

We were airborne in minutes, streaking across the sky and going "feet wet" over the Pacific Ocean. The flight attendant was kind enough to bring me an apple juice (I nicely avoided the alcohol; two months sober and counting) and I settled in, tempted to sleep my way through the flight, or at least as much of it as I could.

Unfortunately ... there was a big obstacle in the way to that.

"... And he says to me—can you believe this—he says to me," Kat was talking, non-stop, "'I'd love to take you out sometime if we can find some mutual overlap in our schedules.'" She just stared at me, like she'd thumped down two big stones filled with Commandments or something, I dunno. After a few seconds of my silence, she asked, "Can you believe that?"

I paused the apple juice halfway to my lips. Damn. I'd been just about to drink it to postpone answering, but now I was caught midway there. Should have meta-speeded it to my lips. Although that would have the unfortunate effect of tossing all the juice directly into my face. On the other hand, it'd have given me a primo excuse to go to the bathroom and get the hell out of here without answering.

"I ... cannot believe that," I said, hoping that was the right answer. "How could some pretty boy Los Angeleno douchecanoe actor possibly hit you with that ... uhm ... terribly weak come-on?" I didn't feel that really needed the question mark at the end. A better question, in my experience, would have been, "How could he not?"

"Exactly!" Kat thrust a finger at me. "Guys in LA just do not know shit about how to play outside of Tinder or whatever. I'm right in front of your face, dude. You can't swipe left here, you have to actually talk to me." And she made a motion waving at herself in a concentric circle. "I hate to sound old, but flirting is becoming a lost art outside of the internet or text messages. It's like all these young guys are afraid to talk to a girl IRL."

"That's amazing," I said very neutrally, though what I was thinking inside was, *This is the greatest news I've ever heard in my life!* I didn't like being hit on in person, and since I lacked an email account or other internet methods of contact, this sounded like nothing but wonderful to my misanthropic ears. Not that I'd been hit on a crazy disproportionate amount or anything, but I'd had enough weirdos mack on me with no game or in bizarrely inappropriate ways that I didn't feel I was losing much if in-person flirting was going the way of the dodo.

"It's terrible," she said, pulling out her phone and firing up the screen. "Sign of our times, you know?"

I stared at her staring at her phone screen, then took a very small sip of apple juice. "You don't say."

She glanced up at me. "I just—I hate to say it, because it's so stupid but—'I can't even,' you know? It fits, in this case."

I started to say, "You're really becoming an old lady, Kat," but it seemed so wrong to crap on her, especially since she'd dropped everything and chartered a private plane on her own dime to come to Oregon to pick me up. I shut my mouth on that one, and especially tamped down on the desire to say something snarky like, "I can't believe people are becoming unable to communicate with others except via those annoyingly ubiquitous phones cemented to their hands!" Mainly because again, as a social outsider who didn't really want to talk most of the time, this was all benefit to me.

"So, what's the deal with this current crisis?" Kat asked, apparently satisfied that whatever was going on in her phone was of less interest than whatever problem I'd brought her—

at least for the moment. "I had to tell your brother 'pass' on a ripe assignment he wanted to hand me and Veronika, would have been good fodder for a TV episode built around it, I think—but you know, whatever. Fate of the world. Totally more important."

Harry guffawed from his seat, and I avoided rolling my eyes at him, though Kat shot him a strange look. "Also, why are you hanging around with this geebo?" she asked.

"Ouch," Harry said, not looking back at Kat. "Coming from you, that carries an especially stinging sting."

"So weird," Kat stage whispered, pointing a thumb at him, as though he couldn't hear her with perfect clarity.

"He's my—" And I tried to find a word that encompassed what Harry had become to me. "Uhm. He's my ... bitch?"

"I saw that answer coming ... and I couldn't avoid it," Harry said, talking to the bulkhead, not even turning to face us. "Still. Ouch."

"Well, you kind of are," I said, shrugging, a little apologetic. "He's like halfway between my bitch and my boytoy."

"That's kinda messed up," Kat said, really trying to get her head around it, confusion peppering her fine features. "Sweetly messed up, maybe?"

"He's really nice," I said, "and good to me."

"And ... not so creepy as when he's around me?" Kat asked, brow all tightly pinched in question.

"Oh, for crying out loud," Harry muttered.

"I don't think he's that creepy around you," I said, "but no, safe to say, he's totally fine."

"Really?" Kat asked. "Because he sets off my weirdness detector like nobody else. Total heebie jeebies."

"A polite person might keep that observation for later, when you're in a private conversation," Harry said, still talking to the bulkhead. "But you keep blazing your own crazy trail, Klementina."

"Ugh, stop calling me that," Kat said.

"Sorry," Harry said, "not sorry. That's how the kids say it nowadays, right?" He looked at me with this.

I shrugged. "I think?"

"If you're so old that you don't know," Kat said, sweetness

gone, mean girl replacing her, "you shouldn't be trying to pull it off."

"Says the woman who has celebrated a centennial and doesn't even pretend to acknowledge it," Harry lobbed back.

"Hey guys, can we not—" I started to say.

"Okay, weirdo, that's it," Kat said, unsnapping her seatbelt and rising to her feet. "I've tried to be polite—"

Harry looked around dramatically. "When? Did I miss it?"

"—but I'm just going to say it: your creepy old man, 'I know you, little girl' act is so thin it makes a girl who hasn't had a carb since age five look thick by comparison."

Harry shrugged, still not looking at Kat. "Just because you don't remember me doesn't mean I have to pretend I never knew you."

"Ugh, everywhere I go I have to deal with this bullshit," Kat said, as angry as I'd ever seen her. "From Scott until he grew up and got over it, from Janus—and now this bizarre frigging guy who looks like an aging eighties action star reject—"

I had my eyes closed when she stopped talking. The hum of the plane engines had suddenly disappeared, and so abruptly I knew something was wrong. I opened my eyes and blinked; Kat's mouth was open, her finger frozen in midair.

Harry, for his part, had turned his head and was looking toward the cockpit, where the flight attendant was paused in the middle of bringing us a tray of drinks. His eyes were closed, too, and though he was turned away from Kat so she couldn't see, there was no mistaking the look on his face.

Pain. He was taking what she said to heart, and it was … hurting him.

I tried to swallow my dismay at this turn of events, because the stoppage of time was probably more important than the thin thread of jealousy that suddenly burned in my stomach like excess bile, but … it was there. I moved past him, and tried to ignore it.

"Uhh, guys?" I asked the cabin, since no one in it could actually hear me at the moment.

Nothing.

No movement.

No sound.

Nothing.

After the first hour, I started to worry.

By the end of the second ... trapped in an airplane with unmoving people somewhere over the Pacific Ocean ...

I started to panic.

9.

Jamal

I read the article Arche sent me, twice, before we got through explaining everything to the Cleveland cops. There was just no way to cause the amount of property damage we had—car flung through warehouse wall into street, lightning being hurled all over the place, even to an abandoned building—without someone getting the law involved. Besides, they were the ones who were paying us to get this Hercules under control, though admittedly we hadn't known she was a Hercules going in. It would have been hard to tell that just from the security footage we'd seen. She'd never hulked out, after all. All we'd known was that we were dealing with a hoodied thief.

Well, now we'd caught her, and in the flurry of activity that accompanied her being taken into custody, I managed to pick through Arche's reading material. I was sitting in the rental car thinking about it real hard when Augustus got back and slammed the door, pronouncing, "Boom. Done." And then he started the car.

"I think you mean, 'Boom. My big brother just got it done, and I nearly got him killed,'" I said.

"You ain't been bigger than me since puberty, son."

"And you haven't been smarter than me, ever."

"Somehow I've avoided murdering anyone, though,"

Augustus said, a little gleam of pissed-off triumph in his eyes as he went low. "So there's that."

"Yeah, well," I said, going even lower, "that's because you haven't lost Taneshia. If someone went after her like what happened to my girlfriend—I bet you'd go full Sienna on them."

His eyes flared, and he started to say something, but then the fire died away in his big pupils like someone snuffed it down to coals. His desire to say whatever shitty thing he'd been about to faded, and he looked at the steering wheel, head a little bowed. "How do you suppose she's doing?" he asked instead of hitting me with what I was sure was bound to be a hell of a snap.

"No idea," I said, looking straight ahead at the field of cop cars, lights flashing red and blue all in front of me. "I don't track her because I'm afraid someone from the government might hit on my searches."

"Pffft, ain't nobody from the government got the skills to do what you do," he said, shifting the car into gear by virtue of a little knob that reminded me of the circular ones on our mother's oven. It clicked into reverse, and he started to back us down the street, away from the still-ongoing operation and cleanup in front of us. They were parading some seriously strung-out people into paddy wagons.

"I wouldn't be so sure," I said, picking up my phone and brandishing it, the screen lit so that he could see the article I'd been reading.

He stopped the car and peered at it. "What the ...?"

"And that's just the headline," I said as he tilted his head to look at me.

"I read more than the headline, fool," he said.

"Not that fast, you didn't."

"Yes, I did. You have no idea how fast I can read."

I rolled my eyes and pulled the phone back. "Oh, yeah? How far'd you get?"

"Far enough to know there's a family of metas with your power working for the government," Augustus said, now clicking the car into drive and executing the second part of his intended three-point turn. "That the article you're showing me is one of those new puff pieces about how 'out' metas are contributing to society in positive ways." His eyes flashed as he finished the turn. "Like we didn't know that. Gravity up in New York, the whole group of us—don't people have some examples to look to by now?"

I shrugged. "I don't mind. Especially given how much of the press goes to Sienna, and a hundred percent of it is negative."

"You got a point," Augustus said grudgingly, backing the car up again so that now we were facing the opposite direction, all set to leave the scene of our ... uh ... crime, sorta. "Still, this kinda shit drives me nuts."

"You don't like the headline?" I deadpanned.

"I told you I read more than the headline—"

"You didn't read much beyond it—"

"I know what it's going to say without reading more, okay?" Augustus snapped, then raised his voice to an annoying, childlike octave. "It's another touching, aspirational story of a little meta who could. How this perfect little family with big dreams overcame all the obstacles thrown in their path by a hateful world and achieved everything they've set out to do ... by becoming the head of IT for a shit-ton of congresspeople. Basically by becoming servants to the powerful." He bobbed his head as he put the car in drive and started us away from all the flashing lights. "Big whoop de frigging do. I'm more impressed with Robb Foreman becoming an actual senator as a metahuman."

I frowned. "He's not in the Senate anymore, number one, and number two, he didn't run as a meta. I don't even think he's technically 'out' at this point, and he's retired."

"Yeah, it probably wouldn't go too well to tell everybody that the last presidential election was actually two metahumans running against each other," Augustus breezed, getting a little chuckle out of that thought. "I don't care how many aspirational articles get written, most humans ain't ready for that one."

"We don't know even know if that's the first time it happened," I said, looking back at my phone's screen. "I mean—"

"Yeah, I could imagine Abraham Lincoln as a—I don't know, a laser-eyed destroyer with fire powers. He drops down in the middle of the Battle of Gettysburg and calls out, 'I must destroy you!' and then nukes off—"

"'I must destroy' you sounds like something a Rocky villain would say—"

"That's 'I must break you,' fool. How are you older than me, lacking all this important wisdom?"

"Not sure *Rocky IV* counts as 'important' anything, let alone wisdom—"

"There you go again, showing yourself to be a 'damnfool,' as momma would say—"

"You're missing the point," I said, holding up the phone again. "This article—these people," and I flashed down to the picture, "saccharine or not, this got flagged and sent to me by ArcheGrey—"

"Ooh, your girlfriend texted you?"

"She's not my girlfriend."

"Is this how you two interact? Because most couples text each other sexy pictures, not boring-ass puff pieces."

"Yeah, well, being something of IT experts, I guess we know better than to send nudes into the cloud. Will you pay attention here for a sec? This is important."

He glanced at my phone. "How is an article about people who work tech-weeny jobs for Congress in any way important to us?" I reached over and grabbed his phone out of his jacket pocket, to which he replied with a scalding, "Hey!"

I interfaced with the phone, running my fingers over the charging port, and accessed the programs within. Sure enough, there it was. "You got RAT'ted," I said as I switched it off.

"Pfft, only one of us in this car is scrawny enough to look like a rat, and it ain't me—"

"RAT," I said again. "Remote Access Trojan."

Augustus frowned. "I usually rely on Durex."

I slapped myself in the forehead. "A Trojan is a program someone puts on your electronic device to grant them access, like the Trojan horse into the gates of Troy. In this case, someone's been surveilling you through your GPS and your camera and microphone."

Augustus's eyes got wide. "Someone's been watching me?" He paused, blinking. "And now that I think about it, Trojan is a terrible name for that product. It's kinda like they're saying, 'Hey, we let the bad guys in,' which you do *not* want—"

"Get your head in the game," I said, trying to dig into the guts of the program. It was pretty simple, but lacked any of the signature that suggested Arche was responsible—even though it was entirely possible she was using my lunkhead brother's phone to unknowingly surveil me. It could have been anyone, though—Cassidy Ellis was right at the top of that list since I knew she'd done something similar to various electronics in our office months ago, though this also lacked any hint of the programming triggers she'd suggested she'd placed in said program to flag her name. It could have been done on the server side, but—whatever.

"You weren't serious about the cloud being vulnerable to hacking for like … pictures, were you?" Augustus asked, his voice a little off.

"Yeah, I was serious," I said, still scanning my way through the Trojan on his phone and barely paying attention to his inquiry to give it any actual thought. "Don't you remember when all those celebrities got hacked not that long ago?"

"Shit," Augustus said quietly. "Taneshia's going to kill me."

That made its way through the semi-permeable barrier of concentration I was putting up as I worked. "What?" I asked, then shook my head. "Oh. You idiot. Delete that as soon as possible."

"You aren't looking, are you?" He nodded at his phone in my hand.

"I don't want to look," I said, "but I've been seeing your naked ass since you were a baby, and one of the happiest facts of my being an adult is I don't have to see it anymore. So no, I'm not looking at your picture collection. No chance in hell."

"Hey, man, it ain't me I'm worried about you seeing naked in there."

I left that one aside, too. "Ugh," I said. "Taneshia's like a sister to us."

"Except she's not," Augustus said, "which is why I'm dating her and probably going to marry that girl."

"Smart move," I muttered under my breath as I traced the feed—where the Trojan was sending its data. It was, of course, an IP address that led to—where else? Of course. "Hmm."

"What?" Augustus asked. Now that his ass—or photos thereof—was on the line, he was all ears.

"The Trojan in your phone is feeding its data to a server in Revelen," I said. "Good firewall. I can't just push past it."

"Revelen?" Augustus asked. "Yo, is this your girlfriend's doing?"

"Not necessarily," I said, still picking at the firewall. No, it wasn't going to be an easy task. Probably a little too Herculean for me, in fact. "Revelen's a hotbed of IT meta activity and spying. Hell, this could be a VPN masking—"

"I don't know what you're saying," Augustus said. "Bottom line it for me."

"Bottom line? I don't know who did it."

"What the hell is the point of you, then?" he asked, full-on crabby.

"Keeping your ass from getting crushed by a car you deserved to catch in the face, mostly."

"Why did you grab my phone?" Augustus asked, looking more than a little beside himself. "How did you know there was one of those LifeStyles—"

"Trojans."

"Right. How did you know one was on there?"

"I didn't," I said. "But I was about to tell you why Arche sent me that article, and I didn't want anyone else to overhear it." I regarded his phone carefully. Now that I'd deactivated the Trojan, there were only about a dozen more devices in this car that could potentially be hijacked. None of them carried a microphone, fortunately, so we were probably okay.

"Oh, yeah?" Augustus asked. "Why'd she send you that article, anyway? After—what? A year of radio silence?"

"Because," I said, "she was pointing me in the right direction on something."

"Oh, you trust her to do that, do you?" he asked, eyes wide, looking at me like I was an idiot. "She's a super trustworthy person?"

"Not necessarily," I said, trying to avoid getting into an argument about Arche's honesty that I couldn't possibly win, "but ... she knows stuff. And this might be something she knows."

"About what?"

"About ... Sienna," I said quietly. "About finding that evidence you mentioned. The kind that would exonerate her."

Augustus didn't freeze, exactly, but there was a definite moment of pause before he answered, and his tension ratcheted up another notch. "Oh?"

"Yeah," I said, and pulled up the family photo on the article. "Because what Arche is saying ... is that these folks?" I stared at the Custis family as I showed them to Augustus. There was an older man with greying hair, his wife of about the same age, and their grown kids all spread in front of them like some sort of grown-up family Christmas photo, "They're the ones holding the lock and key on the evidence."

10.

Sienna

Things to do when you're stuck on a private plane in the middle of the Pacific Ocean and everyone around you is frozen in time:

Try the internet and discover that the wi-fi is not working. Because time is frozen.

Talk to the people around you, who show as much reaction as statues. Because time is frozen.

Go to the bathroom and realize the toilet won't flush. Because—well, you know.

Try the TV—no signal or replay or whatever.

Attempt to make your electronics work—not a chance, they're as stuck as the people around you. Can't even trigger the lock screen.

Look through the luggage of everyone else on board until you find a very aged paperback copy of Richard Stark's *The Hunter* and settle down to read it while frantically glancing around every few minutes in hopes that time has resumed its normal course.

Spoiler alert: It hasn't.

Feed yourself from the limitless bags of peanuts and chips in the steward's galley, until your blood has the same approximate salt content as the water somewhere far, far below you.

Consider breaking your two-month sobriety with the

approximately ten gajillion miniature bottles of liquor in the galley. Who would even notice? Or give a damn? Pass on that, mostly because drinking has never, not once, ever made me feel better.

Reach the middle of *The Hunter* and realize you've seen the movie of this, and it had Mel Gibson, and was maybe less mean in some places and yet meaner in others. Nervously glance around, hoping time has unfrozen.

Still a no.

Pace endlessly, probably wearing down the jet's carpet. Take particular care in moving for fear that imparting too much strength to any particular motion will end up destroying the entire plane when time unfreezes—*if* time unfreezes—like Quicksilver speed-beating the shit out of people in the X-Men movies.

Begin to question whether this is *it*. That time is now frozen, forever, in this state, and that I will live out the rest of my days with a toilet that will not flush and eventually be forced to resort to cannibalism of people who won't even feel it when I kill and begin to eat them.

I miss you, Wolfe.

"—but dresses like he dropped out of *Leave It to Beaver*," Kat resumed, picking up right where she left off. I jumped so hard I threw *The Hunter* into the bulkhead with enough force that it exploded in a cloud of bindings and torn pages. Kat jerked her head to look at me, now on a small sofa behind her, and saw the pages of the book floating down around me. "What the ...?"

"It happened again," Harry said, all memory of Kat's insults apparently forgotten as he stood, wobbly-legged and looking kind of haunted, eyes vacant and searching. He touched his temple, closing his eyes for a second as though he'd just experienced a headache of the sort Kat used to cause me on the regular.

"Yeah," I said as the flight attendant walked carefully up the aisle, looking at me as though I'd just managed some sort of miracle. Which I had. When she'd started from the galley I'd been in my seat; now I was twenty feet away, standing up from the little sofa. "It did."

"This is what you called me for?" Kat asked, taking a drink from the attendant's tray without even looking at her. Harry did the same and gulped down whatever she'd brought him in one good slug.

"Yes," I said, and looked at the attendant, then made a shooing motion with my hand, which she got the hint on and started back up the aisle toward the galley. I moved closer to them and whispered, meta-low, "I've been stuck out of time for the last—I don't know—a day, maybe? It was hard to tell without clocks or phones or—"

"Ewwww," Kat said. "I hope that never happens to me. No wi-fi? Sounds like my version of hell."

"Sounds like my version of heaven," Harry muttered, passing his empty glass to the attendant as she went by.

"It's terrible," I said. "I was reading that book," and I chucked a thumb at the remains of the novel, which was just coming to rest over a several square foot space next to the bulkhead, "and that was basically all I could do."

"I wonder if your powers would work while time is frozen …?" Harry asked, still seeming pretty glazed.

"Why does that matter?" Kat asked.

"She might need to defend herself in a time freeze when we get to Japan," Harry said with a shrug. "Just thinking ahead."

I was pretty sure that was not what he was thinking of, but kudos to him for coming up with a graceful answer on his feet. "That's not a bad point," I said, "I—"

"Whoa," Harry said, blinking, now staring straight ahead again. "That … is not good."

"What happened now?" Kat asked, turning to face him. "Did you accidentally set off the creeper alarm in here?"

And a point to Kat for unexpected spiked sarcasm delivered with a straight face. She usually wasn't good at that; Harry seemed to really bring out her mean streak. "No," he said, seeming to take no notice of her flippant cruelty, "I'm looking forward—trying to see—" He was speaking quickly, frazzled, and I recalled the time he'd come to me in Chicago, seeking my help because of something about to happen that was the end of the metahuman world. He hadn't seemed this shaken then. "It's so much worse," Harry said, still staring blankly at the bulkhead. Slowly, he turned to me, eyes wide and haunted. "So much worse ... there's ... nothing ... in three days ..." He quivered, staring empty-eyed at me.

"In three days ... what?" I asked, trying to wrap my head around this.

"In three days ... it's all over, Sienna," Harry said, still staring at me, horror creeping into his gaze in a way that wrenched my stomach, "in three days ... the world—the whole world ... time ... it just ... stops."

11.

"Well, that's grim," I said after giving Harry's world-ending pronouncement a moment to settle. It felt like someone had popped a window and sucked all the atmosphere out of the plane. Kat stared straight ahead, blinking a few times. Harry, for his part, said nothing. "Time just stops? Forever?"

Harry nodded. "It all ends. No more forward motion, no more probabilities after that. It's going to happen, 99.9%—unless somehow we get you where you're going by then." He latched on to me, put his hands on my shoulders, eyes wild. "You're the only one of us in this plane that has a future beyond that."

"Well, having just spent what felt like days absent your company and that of anyone else," I said, "trust me when I tell you I'm going to do everything I can to stop this. And not just because I accidentally destroyed the only thing I had to read."

"Please, Sienna," Harry said, and he wrinkled my shirt as he grasped me, "you have to. You have to save us from—this."

"Dude," Kat said, putting a hand on Harry's shoulder and trying to pry him away from me, "you need to relax, okay? Do you want a Valium?"

Harry swung his head around at her as though she were out of her mind. "What are you doing with Valium?"

Kat shrugged. "I lead a stressful life, okay?"

Harry stared at her, thought about it a second, and said, "Yeah, okay. Maybe I could use one." He slumped back into his chair, all the strength gone out of his legs. "There's nothing to do until we get to Nagasaki anyway."

Kat froze halfway to her purse and cocked her head to the side. "Nagasaki? I thought we were going to Tokyo?"

I glanced at Kat. "No. We need to get to Nagasaki."

Harry's eyes darted around. "Oh, shit. We're on track to Tokyo."

I bit off an angry reply that would have scorched the air. It wasn't his fault his powers weren't fully working, or that he was so stressed he was likely to strain a muscle just sitting in his seat. Harry wasn't used to things falling apart around him, at least not without being able to see a clear path around them. I remembered when he'd walked me out of being surrounded by almost the entirety of President Harmon's military and FBI task forces in Salt Lake City, Utah, placid as a sunny spring day the whole time.

It was a stark contrast to the sad, sweating Harry who was sitting in front of me now. He really did need that Valium.

"That's fine," I said. "We can just change it up. Tell the pilot we need to go to Nagasaki—"

"You can't do that," the flight attendant said from just outside the galley. She'd leaned her head out to talk to us. "He already filed the flight plan. We're on track, and we can't change it now. But we can still get you to Nagasaki—after we land in Tokyo and clear customs, refuel and have some crew rest."

I stared at her. She had a pretty sunny disposition, as you might expect someone who was charged with dealing with the uber-lux wealthy celebrity set. A huge part of her job was probably customer service. "How long do you think we'll be on the ground for … refueling and crew rest and all that?"

"Probably overnight," she said. "We'll be landing in the late afternoon local time. The crew rest period is—"

"That's not going to work," I said, putting my hand into my hair and bowing my head. "Crap."

"We're going to need to catch the bullet train," Harry said, almost croaking at this point. I wondered how much more stress he could take. Kat offered him a couple pills, her arm at maximum extension, presumably so as not to get too close to him. "Thanks," he said, as she nearly dropped them outside his grasp. He had to work to catch them, too, but he downed them without anything to wash them down. "Then we can charter a boat. That'll get us there quicker than waiting for the plane."

"Ooh, traveling Japan like one of the little people," Kat bubbled. "Sounds like fun!"

"Yes, being crowded on public transit in one of the most populous per-square-mile countries on the planet sounds like a real joy," I said, "especially among those gropey guys who use it as an opportunity to get handsy with strangers. Sounds like a real great time—for Harvey Weinstein."

"Nobody gets handsy with me and gets away with it anymore," Kat said dismissively. "Broken fingers are a big price to pay."

"Wow," Harry said, looking up at her, his drink drained and all the color from his face gone with it. "That's very ... Sienna of you."

"She taught me well." Kat flushed a little then glanced at me.

I frowned. "That does seem a little less Kat than I recall. Remember when that douchecanoe producer guy was taking full advantage of you?"

"That was the catalyst for my change," she said. "You held up the mirror and showed me how I was being taken advantage of. So ... y'know ... no more. I'm powerful ... and stuff—"

"You come off as stronger if you don't have to say it," Harry mumbled. "Also, 'and stuff' undermines the power of your statement."

"Good for you," I said, nodding along, ignoring Harry, who I suspected was beginning to feel the liquor portion of his drink already. I kinda felt like once the pills hit home he'd crash out, which would be a good thing given his current state of disaster and the length of our flight ahead. "So—about this alternate route to Nagasaki—"

"I'll get on it," Kat said, heading back to her seat, bag in hand. "I'll figure out the train schedules and get it planned. You guys just chill for a bit." She frowned at Harry.

"Especially you. Go full icebox, please." And then she sat, phone in hand, browsing the net, lips puckered in concentration.

I moved to sit next to Harry, and caught a whiff of gin that made my eyes burn. "What the hell did you get? A gin and no tonic?"

"Tom Collins," Harry said, not quite slurring but getting a little close. He held up his glass, which was a tallboy. "Extra Tom, low on the Collins."

"Is the Tom alcohol and the Collins the ... what, club soda?"

"For the purposes of this metaphor?" He smiled. "Yes."

"Harry," I said, lowering my voice, mostly for the sake of not having the flight attendant hear, since I would have had to go beyond meta low to keep Kat from overhearing us, "I know you're a little ... out of sorts because—"

"Because time is going to end? Yes," he said, "I am out of sorts. Of all sorts. The sorts of patience and sanity and —" He stopped and stared at me. "Wait. This is how you people feel every time the world ends."

I thought about it a second. "Yeah, probably. Sort of, anyway. Stress, panic, fruity notes of worry and fatigue—"

"Oh, God." Harry sagged in his seat. "Seriously. You feel this way every time?"

"I don't think I've ever felt quite as desperate as you look," I said, and he sagged a little more, like I'd let the air out of him. I took a breath, and tried to find a better answer. "Okay ... yeah, I've felt that way before. Once. Maybe twice." He kept staring at me. "Maybe a few times. But I never let it get me down for too long, Harry."

He stared at me with these worshipful eyes. "That's why you're the hero, Sienna."

"Oh, screw you, Harry," I said, turning away from him.

"No, I'm serious," he said, and when I looked back, he wasn't making anime eyes at me.

He was totally sincere.

Naturally, this made me hideously uncomfortable, so I changed the subject. "Can I get you another drink?"

"Why does it bother you that people think you're a hero?"

Harry asked, dimestore psychoanalyzing me.

"Because I'm used to attaching my feelings of self-worth to being a terrible criminal," I lobbed back, easy, with a smug smile. "My whole identity is tied up in it."

"Bullshit," Harry slurred. "I saw what happened to you in that bar back in Minneapolis. The woman who came up to you, thanked you for saving her granddaughter—and that was back before you'd even decided to really be a hero. It was in ... what, your Directorate days? When you were just hunting criminal metas. Before Sovereign, even—"

"What's your point?" I asked, feeling suddenly very restless, and jonesing—just a little—for time to stop again, at least long enough for me to escape this conversation.

"When time stopped," he stared at me, all self-serious, "you were so excited about charging into this because you had something to do. A problem to attack, a potential villain to outwit ... but every time I talk to you about heroics, you start poo-pooing it—"

"I do not poo-poo—"

"Everybody does it, sweetie," Kat murmured from across the aisle. "Even you."

I rolled my eyes. "If you're gonna eavesdrop, Kat, you could at least get more than that part of the conversation." I shifted my focus back to Harry. "Look—"

"I'm looking," Harry said with a grin, already buzzing, no doubt, and the look on his face was ... well, he was looking right at me, and not blinking. It was, uhm ...

I squirmed a little in my seat. "*Look*, not stare awkwardly."

"You really have problems with people who pay you the compliment of great attention," Harry said, still grinning. "Come on, Sienna. We've been together for months. When are you going to accept that I genuinely—" I tensed, fearing the last word he'd throw in there. "—*like* you?"

I unclenched. Slightly.

"Maybe someday," I said, trying to breeze past all that. I wondered if, given that his digestion was meta-enhanced, maybe the Valium would be sped into his bloodstream soon.

"You're a hero," he mumbled, putting his head back and breaking that intense eye contact that felt like it had lasted an eternity. "The sooner you accept that ... the better off you'll be." And he turned his head away from me and closed his eyes, looking like he might finally go for some crew rest.

"He's not wrong, you know," Kat said, not looking up from her phone. "You've got real problems dealing with people who actually like you, who admire you. Remember that chick by the fountain in LA who practically worshipped you?"

I searched my memory. "Not really, but in my defense ... I've kinda been through hell since then. Maybe several hells."

"My therapist says—"

"Please don't—"

"—that sometimes we have trouble accepting parts of our identity that we grapple with," Kat said, now looking up at me. "And that maybe ... inside ... there's a segment of us that's self-loathing and struggles with the idea that we're worthy of love."

I stared at Kat, suppressing eight hundred thousand sarcastic responses to that. It was a miracle, frankly, that none got through, and I wished that I was on a flight that provided cookies because I felt I deserved one after this amazing performance. I allowed a simple, "Is that so?" to slip through. Vaguely sarcastic, but not terribly malicious.

Maybe I was a hero after all.

Okay, that was sarcasm.

"That *is* so," Kat said, either missing the irony or ignoring it in favor of skewering me with her overwrought, ham-handed point. "You are a person worthy of—"

"Please stop," I said.

"—love. Say it with me: 'I am a person worthy of—'"

"Please stop. Please make it stop."

"—'love.'"

I waited after that came out. "Are you done?" I asked, staring at her through slitted eyes, like I expected another bomb to drop.

She shrugged and looked back to her phone. "For now. We'll talk more later, when you're in a spirit of acceptance and not defensiveness."

"If I'm defensive, it's because I'm used to being attacked,"

I pointed out.

"We'll work on that," she said.

I started to snap my answer, but settled for a slightly bitter, "You do that. I, on the other hand, am going to work on fixing this world-ending mess, which seems to be of slightly higher priority than me embracing some hippy-dippy mantra that won't actually fix a damned thing."

"Except allow you to feel a sense of self-worth," Kat singsonged, a smile on her lips, "and, eventually, lo—"

"For the love of Zeus, stop—"

She snickered under her breath. "I'll get you to say it by the end of this." She glanced at Harry. "Hell, I was sure you were going to have a stroke when you thought he was going to say it a minute ago."

I looked at Harry. He was snoring gently, already out, lucky for him. He needed a nap to lower his blood pressure. "Harry doesn't love me," I said, feeling a great tightness from my back all the way through my core—chest, stomach muscles, everything between. "He's just, y'know, bored. Looking for someone to keep him entertained. I'm a convenience."

"You sure about that?" Kat asked.

Harry's face was relaxed, his jaw slightly slack, that look of intense worry thankfully gone—again. He looked a lot better without it. "Pretty sure," I said truthfully.

"Okay," Kat said, and she didn't sound so sure. But thankfully, she went back to planning the next leg of our trip, leaving me to sit in silence, as though I'd been restored to the moment of frozen time that I'd lived for hours. Time went on, though, as evidenced by the noise of the engines, thrumming in the background, carrying us through the night. And somewhere, over the vast and seemingly infinite Pacific, I, like Harry, fell asleep.

12.

I woke up as the plane touched down in Tokyo, and I was back to the land of the fully conscious by the time we'd taxied around to the terminal. I was yawning fiercely. Light streamed in from outside, as it had the entire flight, though here we lacked the heavy cloud cover that had formed a grey ceiling over the Pacific Northwest we'd left behind.

"You guys are so cute when you sleep," Kat said, now letting out a yawn of her own. She unplugged her phone and tossed the charger in her sleek, pink backpack. It was one hundred percent Kat, that thing.

"Did you not get any ...?" I asked, stifling another yawn. Harry was stirring to life again in front of me.

"Nah, I usually don't crash until the early morning," Kat said, yawning again. "Which ... it probably is now, I dunno. Cuz I'm feeling tired. Maybe I can sleep on the train."

I grunted an acknowledgment as the plane taxied slowly around. The flight attendant came down the aisle with coffee, and I gratefully took one, as did Harry. Kat waved her off. It was, fortunately, cool enough to drink, and I took a big slug down immediately.

"We'll be pulling up in just a moment," the flight attendant said. "Have your passports ready."

"Sure thing," I said. She'd checked our passports right after takeoff and hadn't detected that mine was, in fact, an immense fake that was guaranteed to be detected at customs. Harry had seen that much before his powers most recently went flippety-askew. I looked at him now, and he was blinking awake. He caught my look, seemed to discern my intent, and nodded once, which I took to mean he was at least competent and awake enough to guide me through these dodgy next few minutes.

Harry slipped his bag over his shoulder once the plane stopped, and I grabbed my own. When you traveled as light as I did, one bag was almost more than you needed. But I had a feeling most shops in Japan weren't going to carry much in my size, so this was pretty necessary.

"Okay, you guys," Kat said, very seriously, "so, I've done some digging—"

"Can this wait?" Harry asked, and his voice was filled with tension. "These next few minutes? They might be kinda dicey for Sienna."

"Oh! Sure," Kat said. "We just need to get to Tokyo Station to catch a bullet train."

"That's easy enough to remember," I said. "Got it. In case we get separated for some reason—"

"We're not going to get separated," Harry said tightly. "We're going to follow my instructions carefully, and waltz right through the back corridors of the airport, free as birds."

"Yeah, okay," I said, not dismissing him, but definitely throwing a little shade on his assertions about how easy it was going to be to bypass the customs service of Japan and airport security.

The plane came to a stop, and Harry tensed. "All right," he said, as the flight attendant worked the door. "Get ready."

"For what?" I asked.

He smiled again, tightly. "As soon as the door opens, let Kat go out and soak up all the attention."

I looked at Kat. "So ... do what we do every day?"

She looked distinctly unamused. "Oh, yeah, no, I totally don't disappear when I'm in a room with Sienna Freaking Nealon, who has—without doubt—the broadest brand recognition on the planet."

I frowned at that. "What the hell is my 'brand'? Chaos? Screaming? Death?"

Kat gave it a second's thought. "Probably some combo

platter of all three of those, to be honest." She paused, staring at what must have been my annoyed expression. "What? I didn't say it was a *good* brand."

Something occurred to me that caused me to leave aside Kat's little snap. "Hey, is it going to be tough to navigate here without any of us speaking Japanese?"

"It'll be fine," Harry said. "I speak enough to get by, and Klementina over there is fluent."

"What?" Kat asked, doing a double take at him. "I am not!"

She'd just made it to the ramp, where a waiting worker bowed to her like she was royalty and said something in Japanese. "*Konichiwa*," Kat replied in flawless Japanese. "*Yoroshiku onegaishimasu*." She promptly did another double take at Harry before her lip curled in disgust. "That's really creepy. I didn't know I spoke Japanese."

"Well, as the kids say nowadays," Harry said with a slight smile, "There. That's a thing you know now."

Kat made a little *humphing* noise as she preceded us down the ramp onto the tarmac and into the building ahead, shepherded by the airport employee that she had greeted. The lady was being incredibly solicitous to her, bowing deeply and showing deference well beyond what I would have considered necessary, even for my famous friend Kat.

Kat soaked up all the attention this woman lavished on her, bowing back—though not as deeply—and responding to her in fluent Japanese. I did my best, with the aid of a pair of overlarge sunglasses that Harry had handed me, as well as a baseball cap that said N7 for some reason (Reed had given it to me), to keep myself anonymous.

We were led into a terminal area, which made me sigh a little. I'd been hoping to do a quick bypass of customs, but apparently that wasn't in the cards. Here we joined busy throngs moving through, going to and from gates, eyes forward, moving with the purpose and bustle I'd come to expect from airports the world over. You know, when I used to actually have to fly commercial every now and again.

"I need to use the little girl's room," I said, as loud as I could, to Kat. She made a strange face at me, probably wondering why I didn't use the one on the private jet, but she shrugged and asked her envoy where the nearest restroom was. She got a bow of the head and we were led just a couple hundred feet to a restroom that was marked clearly enough that even I could have picked it out if I'd bothered to put in the effort.

But that was fine; I wanted to draw a little attention to my need to go to the bathroom, especially since this was where I was leaving Kat behind.

"I'll wait for her," Harry said casually. "You go on. We'll catch up."

Kat shrugged and motioned to her guide to go on. I had no idea who this poor woman was that they'd assigned to this thankless duty, whether she was an airport employee or just some rando who had been handed off to Kat by some local studio or something, but as they walked away I could hear Kat asking her something in Japanese, and I wondered if it was as trivial as her usual English questions. Maybe something like, "Where is the nearest Brazilian wax parlor?" or "Do you know where I can find a low-carb maki roll?"

"Be right back," I said under my breath to Harry, and disappeared into the bathroom. I kept up appearances for the sake of the other people—holy Moses, there was an abnormal amount of flushing going on in there. I slipped into a stall, hung out there for a few minutes even though I actually had used the restroom before we'd deplaned, did a few extra flushes just to blend in, and then I slipped out and met Harry. Kat was long gone.

"Okay," Harry said, falling in next to me, "this way."

He led me through a long stretch of terminal before finally coming to a side door that was probably marked something like "EMPLOYEES ONLY," but in Japanese script. It even had a keypad, which Harry punched quickly and surreptitiously. It beeped, the door opened, and he ushered me inside.

"Okay, we need to do this exactly right," Harry said, pausing to concentrate once inside. The corridor ahead of us was empty, not a soul in sight, thankfully. "This way."

He led me forward into the dimly lit hallway. It was a twisty warren inside, surprisingly so for a place that seemed like it would be pretty straightforward. He beckoned me on as we took a turn, then another, then yet another, and went down a flight of stairs. "Pause here," he said, pulling me off to the side, gripping my arm and swinging me around in front of him as he stooped slightly, pushing his face almost up to mine.

"Hey," I said, frowning as he got all up in my grill. I wasn't that keen on PDA, but his lips were paused about an inch or two away from mine, and I started to say something else but soft footsteps behind me caused me to freeze.

I didn't dare look back, and he put a hand on my cheek anyway to keep me from doing so. I held position, locked in place, and he removed his hand after a second or two to keep from getting his soul ripped out of his body. Harry always wisely removed his hand before things started to burn. It wasn't bad at first, because it got progressively worse the longer you touched my skin, but even at its lowest, a succubus soul-burn wasn't exactly straight-up fun. I could now vouch for that by hard experience.

After the footsteps behind us faded, Harry smiled. "You thought I was going to kiss you right here, didn't you?"

"It occurred to me that you might use this inopportune moment to do a little macking," I said, looking behind me. The corridor was empty, the intersection in the hall now clear.

"Well, I would, but I'm kinda busy keeping us out of trouble," Harry said. "Come on," and he put a hand on my upper arm and hustled me forward, "this next part, the timing gets tricky."

"Oh, good," I said, "I love added risk and difficulty."

We took a few turns, then slowed. I let Harry set the pace, his hand still clamped lightly on my upper arm. I just followed his pace and kept up. When he ran, I broke into a run; when he walked, I did too. It wasn't difficult, playing this non-verbal game of Harry Says, except just following his motion cues. Following other people was never my strongest suit, but now that I was in a strange land and already dodging the law, I was suddenly keen to be a follower.

We reached the last stretch of corridor before a door similar to the one we'd entered the employee-only corridors by. Harry tensed. "Now, just bear with me, because things are about to—"

And then, he froze, mouth half open, words stopped mid-sentence, hand still stuck on my upper arm.

"Oh, hell," I muttered, his grip like concrete banded around my bicep. "Talk about bad timing."

I struggled against his hold, weakly at first. There was no one in the corridor, and his grip was like cold steel, unmovable, around me. I stood there for a short interval, hoping time would just start back up again, but I got impatient after, I dunno—an hour? Or maybe thirty seconds? And claustrophobic shortly thereafter.

"Sorry, Harry," I said, and figured out the weakest point of his grip, adjusting my arm. Once I'd lined myself up right, I yanked as hard as I could toward the direction where his fingers and thumb overlapped.

The reaction was immediate; his hand snapped open and I was free. I stumbled back a step and Harry stayed right where he was, not so much as a flicker of expression. His hand, I noticed when I looked at him, had moved, albeit subtly. I'd probably yanked it forward a good foot by my escape efforts, but the rest of his body was wholly unchanged. I shrugged it off; no big deal.

Looking at the door we'd been headed toward, I wondered if maybe this wasn't a perfect chance for me to make good my escape from customs. Harry, after all, would be just fine; he could just follow his powers and leave anytime. Hell, even if he got pinched by the cops, he'd be able to perfectly calculate an escape route, like he had some sort of temporal GPS—"When this police officer walks past you, take a right." I was not so fortunate.

"To hell with it," I muttered. I needed at least something to do, especially if I was going to be stuck in time for hours again. I jogged to the door leading out of the hallway and froze.

It had a damned keypad on this side, too.

"Shit," I muttered. I stared at it, hard. There was no real

way for me to defeat that right now, since time was frozen. It wasn't like it'd even accept inputs at this moment, because the CPU or whatever was suspended in time, like everything else. It probably wouldn't even register my button presses—assuming I knew which buttons to press. Which I didn't.

Writing that off as a failed idea and deciding that a worse one would be kicking down the door (which I totally could have), instead I started making my way back to Harry. I was already starting to feel antsy, especially since the one thing I'd had to entertain myself during the previous time stop was shredded back in the plane. And I'd been wondering how Parker was going to get himself out of trouble back there.

I was about halfway back to Harry when time sprung into motion again, and I do mean *sprung*. It wasn't like a normal, gentle snap-back to time resuming; no, this was harsh, at least from the only frame of reference I had, which was Harry.

The moment time resumed, Harry lurched forward like someone had yanked him by the hand—the same one I'd escaped moments earlier, oops. He was jerked forward and slammed into the wall opposite, knuckles first and the rest of him following shortly—and sharply—thereafter. Bones cracked, concrete wall thudded, and somewhere in the midst of it all—

Harry let out a short, sharp scream of pain.

He bounced off and recovered his balance a moment later, but was clutching his hand, nursing it with the other as though someone had just hit it with a hammer. He was cringing, too, his cheek red where he'd slammed into the wall. He looked unsteady on his feet, and he caught a glimpse of me down the hall, one eye closed, and tilted his head like he couldn't quite comprehend what he was seeing. "What are you—?" he actually asked, then stopped.

It took me another second to figure out why he was stopping. The noise reached my ears first—soft electronic chirping of someone pressing a keypad, then the sharp buzz of an electronic lock releasing. A moment later, the door behind me—the exit—started to open, and somehow I knew that Harry's scream of pain had changed the course of events in our escape—and now the look on his face—pure panic—suggested to me that ... well ...

I'd screwed up now.

13.

Jamal
Washington, DC

We hit Bethesda, Maryland, by evening, crossing into McLean, Virginia, and eventually over the Potomac again on Interstate 66 via the Theodore Roosevelt Bridge. The route may have been circuitous, but it offered a pretty commanding view of our nation's capital, or at least of certain parts. It had a kind of majesty about it, the Washington Monument and the Lincoln Memorial both right there off to the side. Sure, DC lacked an official downtown with the tall buildings I'd come to expect from major cities, but it had its own charms.

"Man, I don't want to be here," Augustus muttered under his breath. The traffic going against us was prodigious, and I had a feeling once we got into the actual streets of DC, we'd be stuck in at least some of it.

"You want to help Sienna, though, right?" I asked, keeping one eye on the GPS and the other on my brother.

"Yeah," he said grudgingly. After a few seconds of silence, he asked, "What's the move?"

That was his way of saying, "What do we do next?" But of course my brother had to say it the trendiest way possible. "I don't know, exactly—" I started.

"We just drove seven hours, and you don't have a plan yet? What the hell you been doing this whole trip?"

"Telling you what to do," I shot back. "It's a full-time job. If you don't believe me, ask Taneshia."

"Smartass," he muttered.

"I'm thinking it over," I said. "Trying to decide how we approach this. If this family are metas like me—and the article suggests they probably are, complete with electrical command of any device you can imagine—coming at them like a hacker is a bad idea, because they outnumber me four to one. They'll slap down my attempts to bypass their safeguards like Momma knocking the bacon out of your hand when you snatch it off the plate while it cools. But I don't know that walking up and just introducing myself is the way to go, either."

"How about we go up to one of them, beat the living shit out of them, and just get the info?" Augustus asked.

"I'm not really keen on getting charged with assault and battery and probably kidnapping, if we end up dragging their ass anywhere to question them," I said. "Keep in mind these people look like law-abiding citizens—" Augustus snorted, and I frowned at him, "—at least as far as anyone else knows. We can't just walk up and throw down, you know?"

"Pffft. I can throw down with anyone, anywhere, anytime."

"Oh, yeah?" I asked, and pointed into Washington ahead. "Why don't you just stroll on up to Gondry and give him a whack across the cheek, then?"

Augustus had a dark look flash across his face. "You know that isn't what I meant."

"This family works for a lot of Congressional people," I said. "Reps and senators on different sides of the aisle. You want to throw down with them?" He shook his head no, and I went on. "Yeah, neither do I, because you go kicking that wasps' nest and we're going to get stung all to hell. We need to think, we need to plan." I settled back in my seat. "And we need a place to work from, so find us a hotel while I kick some ideas around here?"

"What kind of ideas you thinking about?"

I hesitated, mostly because I was coming up blank thus far and had been for the entire drive. "Well," I said, "here's the big one—how do you pry something you want out of the hands of someone more powerful than you—"

"Kick their ass. It's Sienna 101."

"—*without* getting tangled up with the law," I finished, patience dragging pretty close to annoyance. "Again ... these are powerful people. They're the spearhead of a conspiracy to keep Sienna's innocence hidden. We try and shake them down like that junkie this morning and it's going to have a different outcome." I thought about it for a second. "I mean, walls might still get busted down and my ass might still take a little bit of a beating—"

"Acceptable exchanges, I say."

"Because your ass was cuddling back with the junkie while mine was chasing after a lady who could just about beat me to death with her pinkie finger." I shook my head. "We need a solid plan. Something that keeps us on this side of the law."

Augustus slapped the wheel, smiling. "I got it. We wait till they're at work, and then break into their house and check things out. No need to do your hacking thing, we just take their computer hard drives and bust into them at our leisure. Mission accomplished."

I stared at him dully. "You miss that part about us staying on the right side of the law?"

"Hey, man, when you're dealing with bad guys, they use every means they have to produce the outcome they're looking for, including sheltering in the shadow of the law," Augustus said. "That's probably Sienna 102."

"I figure the coursework there is similar to Knuckledusting 301," I cracked. "'Beating in the Faces of Your Foes.'"

"And Property Damage 501," Augustus said with a chuckle. "Advanced Destruction of Anything in Your Immediate Vicinity."

Our humor died, sobriety crashing back in as the reality of what we were dealing with came back to me. "I don't really want to land our asses in jail by breaking into these peoples' houses," I said. "They probably live in a nice suburb where the cops come rolling down the street every five minutes whether someone called them or not, and the grandma next door dials 911 if her cat gets stuck in a tree. And the whole damned department shows up, because what the hell else have they got going on?"

"Pretty different from our upbringing," Augustus said. "All right. I don't want to go to jail. What do we do?"

"It's a good question," I said, still thinking it over. There wasn't a lot I could see us managing that didn't involve some sort of federal felony—hacking if I went straight for their internet footprint, breaking and entering if we tried to get into their house, kidnapping and assault if we went the full Jack Bauer and tried to wring the answers out of one of the meta famiglia. "I think we also have to assume that even if these people don't know us on sight—"

"Lots of people know me on sight these days," Augustus said. "I'm getting to be a pretty popular metahuman hero, you know."

He was no Kat, but there was truth to what he said, so I didn't argue. "Even if normal folks on the street wouldn't recognize me," I said instead, "there's a good chance that any conspiracy aligned against Sienna is bound to know us on sight. In fact ..." And I pulled up my phone and tried to imagine where someone would put a search program that would look for my face or Augustus's. There were databases for that sort of thing, perfectly legitimate ones, all over the world.

But there should only be one traffic camera system for Metro DC.

I used my phone to weasel in, and it only took about five seconds or so to pass the firewall. I buzzed around in the background code, seeing who was looking at this info regularly. The usual suspects were tied in—federal law enforcement agencies, local PDs in the Washington Metro as well as nearby Baltimore. They were all expected, though, legit with their own doorways in ... some of these I followed, on a hunch, back into their own servers. US Secret Service was a predictable one I gave a swift glance to, deciding not to bother cracking their firewall yet. Capitol Police, though ...

"Huh," I said, under my breath, as the electricity danced in small, small voltage amounts between the tip of my index finger and the power connector to my phone.

"What?" Augustus asked.

"I was just browsing to see who all was tapped into the DC traffic camera feeds. And I found all the usual suspects you'd expect, traced 'em back to their home systems. One of which was the Capitol Police. I decided to follow that one back on a suspicion, and ... sure enough, there seems to be a tap in the backdoor of their access, a little barely-there program that's running facial recognition on all the District's traffic cameras."

"That's ... special, I guess?" Augustus asked. "But how does that affect us?"

"Because," I said, my stomach sinking like it had been lined with lead and tossed into the Potomac, "it means that the Custis family and their friends ... probably already know we're here."

14.

Sienna

There was a Japanese man in a serious, official guard uniform standing not ten paces from me, at the door to the exit from the employee service corridors. It was my gateway out without having to pass customs, my escape with no need for an international incident that would result in my arrest and/or laying an epic, metahuman-level asswhooping on the Japanese equivalent of a customs service guard.

Fortunately, as a succubus and a woman, I was uniquely suited to handle this problem.

"Hi, I am sooooo sorry," I said, doing my best imitation of Kat and hoping my currently red hair would sub nicely for her blond, "we are sooooo very lost." I Valley Girl'd the hell out of that accent, hoping it'd work.

It didn't, at least not fully. "Stop right there," the guard said in heavily accented English. I suspected he'd dealt with more than his fair share of stupid American tourists. In fact, I was counting on it.

"Yeah, sure," I said, and put my hands up. He strode toward me with self-assurance, probably very certain he'd caught another couple moronic Americans in his dragnet. Idiots wandering through, completely unaware of what we were doing.

When he was only a foot or so away, though, I disabused him of that notion by reaching out and seizing him by the hand, then cupping a hand over his mouth before he could scream as I forced him against the wall with meta strength. I didn't hurt him—much—but he thumped against his back and skull, and his eyes were wide like I'd yanked them open myself.

"Mmmmmmphm!" he squealed beneath my hand. I had my pinkie on his jaw and was keeping his mouth shut so he couldn't bite me. The last thing I needed was to lose a finger to an angry, frightened guard. Those took time to grow back, and they hurt the entire time. While Kat might have had some pharmaceuticals that could have helped me, I didn't see any reason to go there if I didn't need to.

"Shhhhh," I said, not that he could say anything. He tried to strike me, but I rebuffed the hit with a forearm block, knocking his blow aside like it was a feather duster. "This will only take a second, pal. Just chill."

My fingertips started to feel the burn, my power beginning to work on his face. His eyes got wider, if such a thing was possible, alarm going from the ten he was currently at to an eleven, or twelve, maybe higher. He struggled, but it didn't do him much good. My feet were firmly planted and he lacked the height and strength to do something like lift and chuck me away.

The burning was a little like a rush of good drink, blood flow in my skin running straight to my brain and making everything feel heightened. The world floated around me as I shot into the guard's mind, like I'd been speed injected straight into him. That was a hell of a rush, but I kept focused on the one job I had right now.

I found the memory of Harry's scream, making its way out to him through the exit door as he had been walking past. It had perked his ears up and of course he'd felt compelled to investigate. A few more seconds and he'd have been clear of the door, clear of the scream, and everything would have gone according to Harry's foreseen plan.

But then time had to go and stop, and someone had to get impatient with being caught in Harry's grip—I don't see any need to toss around blame or whatever—anyway, the point was, shit happened.

Now I had to deal with it.

"Sorry," I said, my voice hissing in my own ears as I stripped this memory from my victim. I took it all, from the present all the way back to just before he'd walked past the door and heard the scream. All told, it was less than a minute of his life I'd just yanked out of his head. He'd stir back to wakefulness standing up in this hallway, wondering what the hell had happened, but not really that much worse for the wear.

I felt bad anyway.

"Harry," I said, flashing out of the guard's mind for a second and beckoning toward the door. "Come on."

"Way ahead of you," Harry said, and his voice came from the behind me, near the door. A series of beeps came from outside my vision of the guard's memory that I was now absorbing, telling me that Harry was on the digital keypad, about to open the door.

"Sorry," I whispered again as I turned loose the guard, pushing him forward down the corridor. I retreated, as quietly as I could, out the door with Harry, and let him shut it quietly with a grimace, his left hand all balled up and misshapen, presumably from where I'd—accidentally—broken it.

"You apologizing to him or me?" Harry asked through gritted teeth. His knuckles were way out of whack, and a couple of his fingers were pointed in grotesquely wrong directions.

My eyes felt like they popped out of my head like a Looney Tunes character. "Holy hell, Harry," I whispered, casting a frantic look around. We were a couple hundred feet past the exits from customs, and I could see a sign indicating the baggage claim and taxis were down the way to our right. "I'm sorry."

"Oh, was that one to me?" Harry asked, a little excess aggravation popping out.

"Yes, I was apologizing to you that time," I said, stopping myself just before I took his hand in mine. My gloves were in my bag, and I didn't want to drain him, so I held off touching his hand. "I'm sorry. Time froze and I got antsy.

Didn't mean to hurt you."

"And yet," Harry said, clearly in pain, clearly pissed off, and clearly holding me to account for his busted hand. It was ugly, too, the kind of damage I frequently caused on purpose but seldom inflicted on people that didn't deserve it.

"Let's get out of here," I said, putting an arm around him.

"What are you doing?" Harry asked, looking down at me. "My legs are fine, You broke my hand."

"Just trying to help," I said, disentangling my arm from his waist. His hand was pretty much shattered. It was a good enough reason to be crabby. I mean, I'd have been in a worse mood than he was exhibiting if I was just hangry. Really, being a little pissy with a wrecked hand wasn't unreasonable, though it did sting my feelings a little hearing him lash at me like that.

"Oh, I think you've done—" he started.

"Enough?" I asked, stealing his sentence-finishing schtick as I started back down the terminal toward the baggage claim and exit.

He squinted at me, which was probably an indicator of how off his game he was that he hadn't seen my smartass answer coming, and couldn't come up with a good reply. Instead he let out a little growl and said, "Let's go."

We made our way down to the baggage claim, though we had no baggage to claim. "Come on," I said, keeping a wary eye on the guards around us, half-expecting them to surge into motion and come after us at any second, "let's get an Uber."

"A what?" Harry asked, and pain was showing on his face, little beads of sweat on his forehead. He was holding his hand stiffly to the side, trying not to accentuate it, since anyone who tossed a passing glance at it would see that it was obviously and terribly shattered.

"Never mind," I said, remembering that I didn't have a phone anyway, "we'll just get a cab, old man."

"Way to add insult to injury there," Harry said. "Primo job."

"I'm sorry, Harry," I said, rolling my eyes and probably not sounding that contrite. "I didn't mean to hurt you … but hey, y'know, if you play with fire—"

"You are not fire," Harry growled as we stepped through sliding doors into the taxi area. A line of compact yellow taxis waited at the curb. "You are a human—or metahuman—being with the capability to make decisions like a big girl. You could have chosen an easier path than smashing my hand to tiny pieces—"

"I did not *smash* your hand, okay? The wall did. I was just trying to get your claw-like grip off me so I didn't have stand in one place during the time stop."

"Whatever," he said, still growling, and hunching over slightly. I figured the discomfort was getting to him, and I wondered how fast his healing would work once we had a chance to reset the bones. Hopefully quickly, but not as swiftly as his passive-aggressive sniping would come to an end. It occurred to me that much like not being able to see the future coming at present, Harry probably hadn't been physically harmed that often—or maybe ever—in his life. He could dodge punches like a champ, after all, his precognitive powers letting him see them coming miles away. My little hand-breaking might have been his first real wounding of the type I dealt with ... well, perpetually.

I got in the line for the cabs, a universal airport staple, and was in the back of a tiny one (there seemed to be no other kind here) before Harry had much more than a chance to grumble under his breath. "Tokyo Station," I said, slowly and clearly, hoping the driver would understand. Apparently he did, because he nodded, and then we were off, the driver focused on the road and me with the freedom to now turn my attention to Harry's misshapen hand. "We gotta fix that," I said.

Harry just grunted, keeping it close to his chest.

I tossed a furtive look at our driver, whose attention was totally on the road, which was logjammed with more cars than I'd ever seen in my entire life. Once I knew he wasn't paying attention to us, I dropped my voice meta-low and dipped down, unzipping my bag and rustling through it until I came out with a pair of gloves, which I slipped on. "Come on, Harry," I whispered, "give me your hand."

TIME

"This is not how I pictured holding hands with you in Japan," he muttered, extending the broken extremity to me in some form of pained surrender, like he knew this was lesser of two agonizing options available. I'd had these kinds of injuries before, and setting the bones tended to speed the healing. I'd done it the other way, too, especially when I had Wolfe's insta-healing, but the agony was much fiercer—and the progress slower—when your body had to combat broken bones going in the wrong direction and warring with each other while it was trying to piece you back together.

"I know, this hasn't been a very romantic trip thus far," I admitted, then got his attention with a hand motion to indicate I was about to reset a knuckle. He closed his eyes, gritted his teeth, and nodded once, which I took as his assent to do it so I cracked the bone back into place and he let out a very, very low whimper that almost sounded like the engine had moaned.

"Well," Harry said, sounding like he was a little out of breath, "when you tell your galpal that you're not even really sure what we are to each other, it kinda kills some of the romance." And at this he looked pointedly at me. And a little pained, too, because I hadn't set the bone gently. Not that there was a gentle way to put a broken metacarpal back into place.

"Oh, for crying out—are you actually upset about that?" I asked, getting ready to do another number on his hand. I put my thumb on a broken bone, ready to pop it back into place. "I was talking to Kat—"

"Who is a friend of yours."

"—it was just talk, Harry. Don't take everything so seriously."

"Why would I take a couple of months of relationship seriously?" he asked, showing me the surly side of Harry. It was new. Almost cute, if it had come at a different time.

Then again, Harry was pretty put together all the rest of the time. He always had control, one way or another. Now I was seeing a side of him that probably nobody had seen before. I didn't love it, but if this was Harry at his worst, it wasn't terrible.

"Look," I said, holding off on cracking that bone back into place, "I don't know what to say about ... this."

"I'd say it's a broken hand," Harry said snidely.

"If you know me," I said, trying to keep from snarking back, "then you know that my relationship history is ... tangled ... Maybe more like a burning train wreck ... No, maybe more like a refinery fire that's undergone multiple massive explosions. Not much is left, that's the point I'm trying to get to—"

"Artfully done."

"—and then, in the midst of—y'know, my darkest hour—along comes you, Harry Graves." I was still holding his hand gently, still holding off on setting the bone. "It'd kinda been a while since my last boyfriend, and even that wasn't—uh—well, it didn't end in what you'd call a satisfying manner—"

"I get it," Harry said, backing off about an inch. "You haven't had a lot of luck in love."

"Oh, I have," I said. "All of it bad. And some of it not luck. Some of it was just me doing stupid shit. My first boyfriend started our relationship because my boss wanted him to watch me. And that one ended in death. The second guy? I ended up not able to deal with things going sour, so I stole his memories of us. The third guy—"

"Let's just leave out that chain of one night stands, huh?"

I rolled my eyes. "You want to talk about the ins and outs of your relationship with Kat-mentina?"

He opened his mouth to reply then changed course, shifting his eyes to his busted hand. "You wouldn't believe me if I told you."

"Try me sometime," I said, acutely aware that now was not the moment to deflect from my own wrongs. "Anyway ... every actual relationship I've had has gone down in flames. And not low temperature flames, like maybe you'd find in a smoker. Epic, Veronika Acheron plasma that will scourge your limbs from your body flames, that's the kind my relationships go down in, Harry. And since my entire life has gone epically to shit, first with the entirety of the world coming after me and then all my ... my souls and a shit-ton of memories getting ripped out of me, costing me my powers and ... seven friends ..." I looked down at stared at the places where his skin rippled across broken bones. "Yeah ... I'm still a hot mess. So ..." I looked up into his eyes. "... I'm sorry ... if I don't know how to define our relationship in the wake of all that. Or maybe I'm scared to, because ... you've been great to me, Harry. Better than I had any right to expect. Better than I deserve, for sure. For the first time since everything went to hell with Harmon, you've made me feel safe. And if I didn't want to call you my boyfriend in front of Kat, it's not because ... I don't want you to be my boyfriend." I swallowed heavily. "It's because I'm scared shitless that I'll say it, and then you'll be like, 'Nah, that ain't me,' and bail. Or worse, it'll all go down in blue superhot plasma flames—again. Now hold on." And before he could manage a reply to that, I cracked his scaphoid back into place.

Harry nearly screamed, but he managed to hold it in at the last second, and when his eyes opened again from the hard flinch, he scowled at me. "I was going to say something really nice, too, until you did that without so much as a second's warning." He took a couple breaths, then said, back to calm, "I'm not bailing on you, Sienna. Not because of you saying we might be what we have obviously become to each other over the last few months. Hell, I specifically sought you out during this time. And I didn't even leave you last time, after South Dakota and Washington and Harmon and all that. You left me behind, remember? Along with everybody else? You isolate yourself."

"Yeah, I know," I said, bowing my head and keeping my eyes on his hand as I tried to smooth out some of the ridges where bones were still out of place. Harry made a little groan as I did so, and I stopped once I got them good enough. "Because

'down in flames,' obviously. Remember? 'Down in flames' doesn't just happen. It's an inside job most of the time, and I'm the one at the controls. Or at least I'm a strong co-pilot on it."

"I don't think you're co-pilot much of the time," Harry said, lifting his hand and looking at it. "I don't think you like to surrender control enough to second seat for anybody, even in a relationship."

"Well, I let you lead me through an airport just now, so there's that."

He let out a gentle guffaw. "Yeah, and that turned out great for all involved." He cringed as he flexed his hand. "Gah."

"How's it feel?" I asked, and now the genuine contrition came out.

"Like someone slammed it in a door and then thrust it into a meat grinder," he said, settling back in his seat now that the difficult work was done. He closed his eyes and tilted his head back as tall buildings passed by on all sides. "I don't want things between us to go down in flames, Sienna. And they won't ... if you can just ... keep yourself from indulging in your darker instincts."

What the hell did that mean? I wondered, but didn't think this was the moment to ask. "Uh, okay," I said instead, settling back in my own seat and looking out the window. "I'll try."

"That's all I can ask of you," Harry said. He delicately put his uninjured hand on mine, threading his fingers lightly through my own. Lightly enough I'd be able to free mine in a pinch without shattering his other hand. "That and, you know ... being a little more gentle."

"Gentle ... is not really a strength of mine," I said, afraid to look over at him. "So far, at least. I'll ..." I took a breath, staring at the falling darkness outside, the lights beginning to glow as night fell over Tokyo. "I'll try that, too."

"Trying works," Harry said, and looked out his own window. His features were still pinched with pain, but we held hands—lightly, of course—as the cab made its way through the crowded city streets toward our rendezvous with Kat.

15.

We got out of the cab outside Tokyo Station, an old-fashioned brick building that would have looked way more in place somewhere like London, but felt a little out of step with the bustling, glassy, futurist neon vision that was Tokyo. It even had a clock tower complete with white-faced clock on the facade. I gawked at it while Harry, gentleman that he was, paid the cabbie.

Stepping out onto an insanely crowded street instantly triggered my agoraphobia, which was totally a thing, but fortunately not a debilitating one. "Ugh," I muttered, looking around. We were about a solid thirty-second sprint to the station across a fairly open square, but there was a restaurant on the ground floor of a glass skyscraper behind us, which I took note of as the crowd streamed past us in all directions. Tokyo was, by far, the most crowded city I'd ever been in, especially at this time of day.

People were thick on every sidewalk, everywhere, but fortunately not so much in the middle of the street. No randos picking their way across in jaywalking fashion. There was an orderliness to the scene, a feeling of calm in the crowd that set it apart from, say, New York City, where the chaos was unmistakable.

"Klementina is this way," Harry said, and I followed him without question through the throng. My skin still crawled at the presence of large knots of humanity as I stepped into the swirling flow of people, trying to work my way through to the entrance to the restaurant across from the station.

"Why do you call her that when you know it irritates her?" I asked, feeling a little irritation myself at the flood of people around me, packing in tightly around me, as if I was a rock in a creek and everyone else was the water rushing past.

"Because the other things I would call her would freak her out even more," Harry muttered, almost beyond meta-low. I caught it, though, beneath the noise of the crowd, and it felt like a subtle stab to the heart.

Harry pulled me forward, and while he had a grip on me this time, it was much lighter than the last occasion. My guess was that he'd learned his lesson and didn't want to suffer any more broken bones due to my impatience. I let him lead me, trying to put those last words he'd said out of my mind.

I wished for a time stoppage as I moved through the crowd. There were so damned many people around me it was insane. Nobody was violently pushy, but there was simply no way to have this many people moving through in one direction while you're moving perpendicular without some physical contact along the way. It was brief and blessedly non-gropey, but it was there, and it felt like I could almost reach out and start ripping some souls from the crush of people rushing past.

Harry held the door open for me and I stepped inside, finding the interior of the restaurant only marginally better than the street in terms of crowd. The noise in the place was a little lower than what I would have expected from a similar crowd and restaurant size in the west. It still gave me a little bit of a headache from the volume, and I worked my jaw because I felt like my ears were still stoppered from the flight.

"See if you can pick out Klementina—or whatever—in here," Harry said with thinly laced amusement as he stepped up next to a strange display with all the food apparently on offer in the restaurant modeled within the case. He was looking around, over the heads of the crowd, which, in most cases, were at about his chin level or lower.

"You are really aiming to antagonize her," I said, rubbing

my forehead and concealing the fact that he was antagonizing me a little as well. It didn't help matters that the volume around here was crazy, and someone was pressing—gently—against my back, trying to get inside. I didn't deign to look, because I had a feeling this proximity was just part of life in one of the most densely populated cities in the world.

"That's not even in the top five when it comes to ways I could aggravate her," he said stiffly, and turned away, somehow leaving me a little more heartsick.

"Yeah, well," I said, my eyes half closed, partially from how he was making me feel but mostly because there was just too much sensory stimuli in this place. There was wasabi in the air, a few different kinds of perfumes and colognes, the volume combined with my ears being stuffed was giving me a headache, and someone was pressing on the person behind me, and I was nearly all up on the person in front of me, making me feel a little too squished for comfort. We were standing in a line to get to the counter, but even past that, in the dining area, it didn't look any more open. The tables were packed close together and anyone trying to maneuver had to squeeze through, close to the other patrons. "It's not very nice to completely mess with someone's identity, or whatever." I wasn't sure how to put it, since Kat had no memory of being Klementina, and had frankly shown the opposite of interest in learning about her past. Antipathy would probably be better description for her feelings about the good old days, like she wanted to run away from it all and embrace being a youthful little minx.

"I'm not messing with her identity," Harry said, a little stiffly. "She lived a long life before she became ... whatever she is now. I'm just trying to remind her of it."

"She doesn't want to be reminded of it," I said, about ready to throw an elbow at the lady who was pushing up against me from behind. "Just let it go, man."

Harry looked at me a little cockeyed. "It's not making you jealous, is it?"

I froze in place. "Me, jealous? I—"

There was a disturbance across the crowd, rippling through

from somewhere in the dining area. I turned to look, and through a set of double doors that led to an entirely different room, I saw a flash of blond hair.

If that wasn't Kat, I reflected as I looked across a sea of ebony heads (with the occasional blue or pink shocker), I'd be very surprised.

"Excuse me," I said, shoving someone out of my way—lightly. I crossed under the rope that separated the line from the dining area. "Get me a plate of sushi," I called back to Harry. "You'll know what I like." I didn't know what was going on with Kat, but I needed to separate myself from this crowd before somebody ended up getting murdered, most probably at my hand.

"Hey, wait—" Harry called back as I cut through the crowd through the double doors into the other dining area. It was packed with people, tables filled all through the restaurant with so little distance between them that a US fire marshal would have thrown a shit fit at the mere sight. Hell, for all I knew, a Tokyo fire marshal would have, too.

As I came into the dining room, I got a closer look at the blonde I'd seen from the line. It was definitely Kat, and someone was leaning over her table, talking to her. I could see long, dark hair, lank and hanging around his shoulders. The guy had a thin frame, and was wearing a black suit with a white dress shirt beneath it.

"She's got fans everywhere," I muttered, pushing between two guys in chairs that were backed up right to each other. "Excuse me. Rude American coming through." And I shoved them both out of the way, because they could have shown an ounce of consideration and maybe not put their chair backs two inches from each other. Stagger them, guys. It's called courtesy for your fellow humans who want to pass through.

"I can't help you," Kat was saying, and I caught a glimpse of her face now that I was only a couple more tables away from her. She was in a booth on the far wall, a small one, admittedly, the kind that would seat two people in the US but might have been designed for four or six here, for all I knew. I saw four people in the one that backed to hers, and they were the same size. Crazy.

"You don't understand," the man said, with a thick Japanese accent. He brushed his dark hair back over one ear, and I caught a sideview glimpse of his face. "I need this. You must help me."

"I—no," Kat said, and her body language told me everything I needed to know about the situation. She was all pressed up against the back wall of the booth, and if she could have made like a slug and crawled up the wall to get further away from this guy, I would have bet she would have. "There's nothing I can do for you. Please leave."

"You must help me," he said, leaning further over. "This is my request. Please honor it."

That was an interesting fragment of conversation. A lot of guys made "requests" of Kat, and not the honorable kind, either. She was strong enough to make clear to them that she wasn't interested, but she was also way more polite, restrained and sociable than I was, which was probably a large part of why she wasn't a wanted fugitive right now. Kat's way had its place in a polite and civilized society, where everybody respected each others' established boundaries.

But based on the fact that my friend was currently less than an inch from crawling up the wall to get away from this guy … I was guessing she didn't feel her boundaries were being respected at the moment. One sympathized.

"Hey, bub," I said, moving past that last table and grabbing the man without borders by his collar, "'no means no,' all right?" And I started to yank him away from the table.

Kat's eyes widened and she shook her head at me. It was a little late to stop doing whatever she wanted me to not do; I physically dragged the guy away and spun him in the two point five inches between Kat's table and the next, and he caught himself just before he went ass over teakettle across someone's tuna nigiri. "No," Kat whispered, so low I could barely hear her over the din in the room.

Which stopped, almost immediately, as Kat's "friend" caught himself on the edge of the table. Really quickly, actually. Too quickly.

Meta quickly.

Shit.

I could see his face now, and it was not what I expected from a guy I'd just manhandled. There was no fear. He was a smooth one, kind of a prettyboy, and he pushed his long hair out of his face. It was parted in the middle, and the way he pushed it back reminded of Jennifer Aniston's 'do when she first came to prominence on *Friends*. The guy let out a low chuckle that didn't have a lot of joy in it, almost more a quality of relief.

"Uhm ... damn," Kat said, a little louder this time.

"Let me belt this one out for the cheap seats, dickhead," I said, right into Prettyboy's face, "when a girl says 'No,' it doesn't mean 'Maybe,' and it definitely doesn't mean 'Yes.' It means 'no.' Definitive. Full stop. So when this lady asks you to move your ass away from her table, that she is not going to accede to your stated request, you need to be Johnny-on-the-spot with moving your ass away from her. Capische? This is basic manners."

He let out another low laugh, and stood up straight. I watched his hands for a weapon, but he didn't go for anything, nor start generating plasma from them, which—given that he was a meta—was entirely possible. "But ... it turns out not to be a 'no' at all." And now he laughed again, but loudly.

"He wasn't propositioning me," Kat said from behind me. "He was asking me to introduce him to someone. That was what I told him no to."

"Who did he want to meet—oh." I got it. A little too late, but I got it.

"I have been wanting to meet Sienna Nealon for as long as I have known of you," Prettyboy said, his smile wide and genuine, and yet laced with a hint of mournfulness. He bowed deeply to me then stood straight. His posture was relaxed yet somehow threatening, as he loomed only a few feet from me in this too-tight restaurant dining area. "And now ... here you are."

16.

Jamal

We'd only just checked into our hotel near the Walter E. Washington Convention Center when Augustus's phone started ringing. He held it up for me to see, his brow thickly knotted in confusion. "DC area code," he said. I peered at it as it dinged with the standard ringtone.

"Maybe the front desk," I said, knowing he was the one who'd checked us in. I let my suitcase lid fall on my bed and was about to take my toiletry bag out and put it in the beige, faux-granite-lined bathroom. "You should probably answer it."

He shrugged and did, saying, "Hello?" as I disappeared into the bathroom for a second. I was keeping an ear out, just in case it wasn't the front desk, but it didn't seem likely it'd be anything serious—yet.

"Uhhhh ..." my brother said as I laid my toiletry bag on the counter. I paused, listening. "Hold on a sec," he said, and then I heard him put his phone on speaker. "Go on."

"Jamal, are you there?" It was a man's voice. It wasn't *high* high, but it was higher than usual for a man. He wasn't going to be confused for an opera singer anytime soon, but he might have gotten mixed up with a little boy a time or two.

"Who is this?" I asked, stepping out of the bathroom to find my brother with a dark cloud over his features. Whoever it was, it looked they'd surprised him, too.

"Ray Spiegel with the Beltway Blog," came the voice again. "A source told me you guys were in Washington right now. Is that true?"

"Maybe," I said, a little too gobsmacked to refute it flat out.

"Awesome, awesome," he said, with genuine enthusiasm. "Listen, I've been a longtime fan of your guys' work. I really think you have the potential to be the next big thing in the metahuman hero space, now that, uh—well, *you know who* is out of the picture—"

"Tell me he means Voldemort and not Sienna," Augustus whispered, meta-low.

"—so, anyway, I was wondering—are you guys free for a coffee and a talk? I'm downstairs in your hotel's coffee shop." His voice changed a little to reflect a surprising amount of glee.

"Your source told you where we were staying, too, huh?" I cracked.

"That's the way it works, you know," he said with that same amused enthusiasm. "So, what do you say? You up for a chat?"

Augustus looked at me and shrugged. He was clearly lost in the woods on this one. I wasn't much better off; I was used to people coming at me with fists and powers, not reporters with questions wanting to "chat."

"Sure," I said tightly. "We'll be down in a few."

"Great, great. See you guys then." And he hung up.

"What the hell was that?" Augustus asked.

I didn't answer for a second, instead pulling up my phone. I checked two things—the first was a camera feed from the coffee shop downstairs. Sure enough, there was a geeky little guy sitting there at a table for four in a short-sleeved dress shirt, in front of a laptop, just putting his phone down from a call. Ray Spiegel, I guessed. Then I hacked the wi-fi in the coffee shop and discovered that his computer—which had a wickedly hard firewall, not exactly off-the-shelf software—identified itself as "Ray's Laptop." I considered that confirmation.

Second ... I went back to the article that Arche had sent

me about the Custis family. I didn't have to look very far, because all I was searching for was the byline at the top. Suspicion confirmed, I ended my connection with the phone and sat down on the bed a little hard. "That's what I thought," I muttered.

"What did you think?" Augustus asked. He was fully intent on me now, wondering what the hell was going on.

"Ray Spiegel," I said, looking up at my brother, "is the guy who wrote the article that brought us here." I watched as Augustus's face turned into a cloud of suspicion, which pretty much matched my own feelings. "What do you want to bet that his source—the one that led him right to us—is the Custis family? Because it seems that not only do they know we're in town ... but they're already sending out their pet reporter to talk to us."

17.

Sienna

"I guess I have fans everywhere, too," I said as I stared at Prettyboy. His looks were classically good—sharply defined cheekbones; dark, mysterious eyes. He wasn't holding himself in an offensive stance; in fact, he looked completely relaxed as he stood in front of me, back against the next table while mine was up against Kat's.

"I am a great admirer of your work," he said, and now he giggled, his voice hitting a higher pitch.

"And who could blame you," I said. "What's your favorite thing I've done? Shredded Sovereign with my teeth? Beat a handcuffed Eric Simmons like a red-headed stepchild when he sexually harassed that waitress? Annihilated that insubstantial mass killer with fire in LA? I could go on, but go ahead—tell me your fave."

"I like it when you kill anyone," he said, and it was chilling how casual he was about it. Also, how little tension there was in his body as he admitted—with a smile—that he liked to watch me murder fellow human beings. I'd *done* the freaking deeds, and I wasn't that cavalier about it.

"Oh, yeah?" I asked, pushing my voice toward menace. This dude was giving off a bad, bad vibe, and people were picking up on it. Folks were already starting to head for the exits, which I thought was sensible; I wished I could follow them. But no, I was stuck here engaging with some shitbrick who thought killing people was "cool." "You want to see me kill someone up close and personal? Is that your angle? You a voyeur?"

"Yes," he said, and there was waaaaaaay too much unrequited lust in how he said it. "I want to see death. Very close."

"You're certainly heading that way, bucko," I said, trying to buy time for the dining room to clear. Some stubborn holdouts were still watching things unfold, and I cursed both them and the fact that my days as a redhead were now over. I was running out of shades to dye my hair, and at this rate I'd be going fluorescent with my next dye job.

"Good," he said with unmistakably demented joy. "I want it. I want to see it. Feel it. Show me … death. Give it to me."

"That sounds a little closer to what I figured you'd asked her," I chucked a thumb over my shoulder at Kat. "This death thing kind of a fetish for you? Am I going to have to turn you Fifty Shades of Purple?"

He still smiled, and OH MY HEAVENS was there something terribly wrong with it. "Yes. Please."

I raised an eyebrow at him. "To be clear … are you asking me to—"

He stood, smiling, and his breath came out in a way that reminded me of—nothing I terribly wanted to be reminded of. It was way too sensual, way too close to intimate, and in a public place, no less. "Yes. I want you, Sienna Nealon … to kill me."

I just stared at him. "Huh," I said.

For the first time, he evinced a flicker of uncertainty. "… What?"

I blinked. "Well … usually that's the subtext when someone picks a fight with me nowadays, but kudos to you for having the honesty to say out loud that you've got a death wish. 'I'm going to pick a fight with Sienna Nealon because I want her to kill me.' That's bold. And it's also what always seems to happen when someone starts shit with me, but I mean … just, bravo on having that self-awareness. It's so refreshing." I cast a look around the dining room. There were still about twenty or so people scattered around the room and a bunch more clogging the exits as they tried to flee. This was as good as it was going to get unless I got a little more active about it. "Well, what the hell are you idiots just staring for?" I asked, raising my voice to a thunderous volume, "Get the hell out of here so I can kill this idiot like Sean Bean in everything he's ever been in!"

I can't imagine most of the people there actually understood what I was saying, but my tone was enough to get the stragglers moving, bringing the gawkers back to life and making them head for the exits. Within a few moments, the room was clear except for one table at the back with five other guys dressed exactly like my dance partner here. Black suits, white shirts, black ties ...

Oh, and a few of them were missing all or part of fingers on their left hands, starting with their pinkies. When they caught me looking, they rose, unfolding themselves from the booth, and I rolled my eyes and looked back at Prettyboy. "Yakuza? Really?"

He grinned and inclined his head in a subtle of bows. "I am who I am."

"Explains why you haven't lost any fingers," I muttered, figuring it was time to go for the gusto. He wasn't nearly far enough away, his stance was pathetic for defense, wide open and poorly positioned to defend, so I decided to gauge how much trouble this bastard was about to give me. Surging forward, I hit him with a short punch to the throat that would have crushed a human's—or even most metahumans—trachea.

Unfortunately ... the only thing that got crushed were my hopes for a brief fight. My hand bounced off his neck like I'd punched a wall, and Prettyboy didn't even look surprised when I struck him.

"Shit!" I said as I pulled my hand back, shaking it in the universal sign of, "Damn, that hurt." I had a sudden burst of empathy for Harry that I'd maybe been lacking after the hand-breaking thing at Narita. I stared at Prettyboy, he stared at me. "Achilles?"

He just grinned. "We call it ..." And he said something unpronounceable in Japanese.

Then the bastard hit me.

Unfortunately, I did not share his invincible skin. Mine was as pliable as a normal human's, and so I took it pretty hard. I managed to mitigate the blow somewhat by twisting away at the last second, but still, there's only so much you can do when a human wrecking ball winds up and tries to level you when you're inches away from them. It was my own fault, getting caught up in the pain in my hand instead of moving to the next attack in my tactical toolbox—which would probably involve trying to rip this asshole's soul right out of his body like I was a crazed, red-headed Scot and he was some sort of sexy, brilliant American succubus who was clearly the most misunderstood person on the planet.

Except I wouldn't have played around; I would have finished the job on his sorry ass.

I flew through the air but only a couple feet, smashing into the wall above Kat as she let out a shriek beneath me. She caught me as I fell, praise be to Little Miss Persephone's meta-reflexes, and I felt her bare hands on my wrists. There had been a curious shattering sound in my skull as I'd hit the wall and failed to crash through, a sound that told me that a) it was concrete and b) my skull was softer than concrete and my momentum not great enough to overcome the challenges of smashing through.

"Hold still a sec," Kat muttered, still gripping me skin to skin. I could barely understand her because I'd just experienced skull trauma of the sort usually reserved for people who have just been hit with a falling piano. From the top of the Empire State Building. Or something of the sort.

The black blurring around the edges of my vision faded, and I broke contact with Kat with a subtle, "Thanks," as I sprang back up five seconds after landing, shaking off the feeling of getting battered and nearly one-shotted by this douchecanoe.

"Don't mention it," Kat said, sounding woozy herself, "and don't expect a second round anytime soon unless you want a new passenger."

"I like you as a close friend, but not that close, if you know what I mean," I said. "Also, if you think Harry is creepy now, it would be so much worse if you were in my head when we—"

"Okay, thank you, go fight now," Kat said, sounding caught between exhausted and repulsed.

Speaking of Harry, I caught a glimpse of him lingering in the doorway, eyes on the five yakuza standing across the room. They were leering at me, but they weren't moving yet. And Prettyboy was just standing there, doing a little leering of his own as I came up off the mat from my near-first-round knockout.

"I thought you wanted me to kill you," I said, putting my dukes up and watching my foot work. I was going to need to get in close with this guy, and frankly—and this bothered me at least a little because of the consequences—absorb his soul, since otherwise beating an Achilles with their impenetrable skin and near invulnerability required weapons and powers I no longer had.

"I do," he said, still smiling. "But do not think I will simply surrender, lie down, and die. You must defeat me."

"Oh, I'ma defeat you, all right," I muttered, keeping both eyes on him. "You're gonna wish you hadn't asked for that by the time this is done. I've killed harder Achilles types than you in my sleep." Technically true, though Reed had been heavily involved in that, beating the living tar out of Anselmo Serafini and tossing him onto my insensate body, which had been wreathed in superhot flames at the time.

"Tell me more," he said, just standing there, waiting for me to come at him. "Or better still—*show me*."

It was pretty obvious to me he wasn't just going to stand still and let me absorb him. And he was bound to know about that, because everyone on the freaking planet who had even a nodding acquaintance with the name "Sienna Nealon"—and this guy was way past nodding and into Annie Wilkes territory—knew I absorbed souls through skin-to-skin contact. Whatever his death wish was, it didn't look like he was down to just be drained, or at least he wasn't going to simply surrender to it.

Which only left me a few options, none of them great.

I came at him in an obvious jab, something straight out of

a boxing match, and he slapped my hand aside. None of my punches were going to do squat to him. If I landed a true, brutal, grand slam haymaker, it might annoy him slightly, and come at the cost of my knuckles getting broken. Achilles were truly, nearly invulnerable, possessing a bone structure that was hard as diamonds and skin that was resistant to blunt force trauma like it had been hardened into steel. Fire worked on it, but unfortunately I didn't have a blow torch secreted away in my bag. Guns did nothing against these guys. Eyeballs were kind of a weakness, but not much of one; they were slightly more susceptible to a good strike, but I couldn't really pop them like with any other, normal(ish) meta.

But that didn't mean they weren't vulnerable in other ways.

Glancing at the nearest table out of the corner of my eye, I took a mental inventory of the discarded dishes that the patrons had left behind. Rice, ramen, rice, tempura, rice—yakisoba—

Yakisoba noodles in thick brown sauce. Perfect.

I made a feint at Prettyboy and then swept my hand around, grabbing the plate of yakisoba off the table and hurling it into his face from less than two feet away. He must have been expecting to intercept my hand midair, because he slapped at me and knocked it aside—

But not until after I'd loosed the yakisoba right in his face.

There was nothing chemically bad about the dish as far as I knew. It wasn't hot enough to burn him, it didn't possess peppers that would irritate his tear ducts. It was just noodles in a nice, thick sauce that'd make him blink for a second and maybe obscure his vision.

That was all I needed, really.

Another flaw of the Achilles was that they were just as susceptible to laws of physics as anyone else. Once Prettyboy had his hands on his face, trying to clear the yakisoba, he was blind as an old beggar, and nicely distracted. I slipped a couple feet to my left, circling around him and avoiding the chairs in my path with a quick jump that placed me just over his right shoulder. He was grasping at his eyes, trying to restore his sight, even though he probably could have just opened his eyes at any time and stared through the blur of sauce without having any problems at all.

The human instinct to protect the eyes is a powerful thing. Even in a being whose eyes couldn't actually take damage from getting something like yakisoba in them.

I jacked Prettyboy in the back of the head with a haymaker, slamming my fist into the soft-ish tissue at the base of his spine. I got a little hit on the bone, too, which stung me, but also caused him to lurch forward from the force of my donkey punch, and—I suspected, at least—sent his brain hard against his invulnerable skull.

I'd recently proven that an Achilles's brain was not invulnerable, mostly by turning Rose's into pudding with a bullet trapped inside her own invincible skull. That gave me a tactical direction to move in, which was to say that my current plan B (since plan A, drain his soul, was being blocked at present) was to use his own invulnerability of skin and bone to turn his head into a makeshift brain blender. I also had a few suspicions that his spinal cord, while more durable than most, was probably not as invincible as the bones protecting it. That was Plan C, though, because I didn't know if striking him hard in the vertebrae was going to be something I'd get enough time to test, at least not right now. I'd just done it, after all, as hard as I could, and since he wasn't dead or paralyzed, it suggested I'd need to bring a lot more force to bear on his spine in order to dislodge a vertebra and break the cord.

Right now, though, I was focused on Plan B, turning his brain to slurry. Next: take his legs from underneath him. I couldn't just bust out his knee joints, either, which was always the quickest way to take a person to the ground, because his knee joints weren't exactly breakable.

I came around him, circling to behind his left shoulder as he lashed out blindly toward where I'd thrown the punch only a second before. I didn't bother trying to do what I normally would have, peppering his kidneys with painful blows, because he wouldn't have felt the pain anyway. Instead, I kept circling and shot my right hand out over his shoulder like I was going to tap him, but kept going until it hovered over his left collarbone. Then I swept my right foot forward at the back of his knees until I just barely touched them. It wasn't a kick, and it wasn't a traditional sweep, the kind where you try and deprive your opponent of footing and do them a little damage at the same time. Doing damage to him with a kick was the kind of fruitless stupidity I tried to avoid in my life.

Instead, I just placed my leg there as a brace, and then brought my hand down—relatively gently on his chest, palm flat against his collarbone. I was still wearing my gloves, which was a tactical error, but alas, not one I could remedy right this second. Once my hand was placed, I yanked on Prettyboy, jerking him backward with all the force I could bring to bear. I'd manhandled him once, after all, and it wasn't like his strength was ridiculously greater than mine.

He staggered backward against my sudden forceful yank, and the back of his knees stumbled over my right leg, which acted as a perfect tripwire. He grabbed futilely—at the air, at me, at anything he could see through his partially noodle-blinded eyes—

Then I sped him up with a little more force applied to his collarbone. He smashed into a table and bounced (!), his invulnerable skin stopping it from doing harm to him. I took advantage of this sudden change of his momentum and spun him, midair, his feet off the ground, his body free of anything to grab hold of or hang on to—

And I hurled him, face first, into the floor and jumped on his back.

"Yee haw!" I announced as his chin thundered into the tile, shattering it. The table he'd just hit skidded and crashed into the next one. "Ride 'em, cowgirl!" And then I thunderpunched him in the back of the head again.

"Sienna!" Harry shouted, and I realized he was in the middle of a hard squabble with the five yakuza. Two of them were already down, but the other three looked like they were giving him a heckuva a fight. Or at least trying.

I didn't have much time to process Harry's warning before I was lurched skyward, thrown off Prettyboy's back like he was a bucking bronco. I fell way, way short of eight seconds,

I reflected as I smashed into the ceiling, which was—thankfully—not concrete and yielded to my skull's impact.

As I crashed back to the ground, landing on my knees (yes, it hurt as much as you'd expect), I saw Prettyboy roll sideways and out of my crash zone. It stung, not gonna lie, but it could have been a lot worse if I hadn't caught myself before my face smashed into the ground like a meteor.

"Owww," I muttered, on all fours. I threw a kick blindly with my right leg and struck Prettyboy. He let out a mild grunt at the impact, and an even milder one as I shoved him, hard, away from me so I could have another second or two of recovery, then snaked my leg back before he could get his hand on it and do more damage to me.

"You ..." Prettyboy mumbled, looking a little hazy. Maybe I'd rung his bell a little. I could hope, anyway. He was a few feet away, and on all fours himself. My shove had moved him far enough out that he'd have had to come at me pretty awkwardly in order to get hold of me, but I wasn't discounting the idea that he might.

"Yeah, me," I muttered, and grabbed a nearby chair and threw it at his face. You couldn't exactly block that sort of thing, and he didn't, though he did throw up a hand and catch it across the back of his wrist without so much as a grimace. Instinct, again; he had nothing to fear from a chair right across the bridge of his nose, yet he took pains to avoid it. "Your fondest dream. I'm not done with you yet, spanky." I paused. "Also, I'm not usually in the business of fulfilling fantasies for strange men who accost me, but yours—I'm seriously going to fulfill. This kink of yours is right up my alley, pal, but I don't think you're going to enjoy it nearly as much as you seem to think you will."

He shook his head, like he was trying to shrug off what I'd done to him, and for the first time, a look of fury cracked his smiling visage. "You ..."

I threw another chair at him, and he tried to block it but the leg cracked him just above the eye, doing exactly nothing. "Stop saying '*You*' all dramatically. Your dumb ass already has my full attention. Compose yourself and start speaking like a proper villain, not a drooling moron." I threw another chair at him and this one got him right in the middle of the forehead because he didn't bother to block. Now he was learning. "I expect a certain level of banter with my prey, and you are failing on all fronts. What's the matter? Did all your wit points go into buying you that invulnerability?" I chucked another chair, but to my rising alarm, he shrugged it off, getting madder and madder as he started to rise to his feet. I matched him, not wanting to be left on the ground.

"Uh, Sienna?" Harry asked, standing amid a field of five downed yakuza thugs, like he was just another American tourist here to deliver ass-kickings and rudeness. "We gotta skedaddle." He raised a finger and pointed to the ceiling, and it took me a second to realize what he was getting at.

Sirens. Distant sirens.

"Shit," I said, and thrust a finger at my opponent. "Look, I only have a limited time here—"

He lurched at me, fury cracking his face into a terrible grimace. He came at me full bore, and the only thing that stopped him from jumping all over me and going right through my (ineffectual against invincible people) defenses was a sudden table that hit him from the side, altering his course and flinging him across the restaurant.

At that, I made another mental note: Achilles types were extremely weak when separated from the ground and susceptible to all sorts of mayhem that probably wouldn't kill them but could at least get them off my back for a little bit.

Prettyboy went smashing through a plate glass window that separated the dining room from the room where the ordering line had snaked. He disappeared behind a waist-height wall while the table stopped, unable to pass through the window. It came crashing down on top of another table, destroying the dishes left behind by fleeing patrons mid-meal.

"Thanks," I said to Kat as she joined me in staring across the restaurant at the place where Prettyboy had just vanished. "Nice toss. A-plus Frisbee form."

"Sorry I couldn't help out sooner," Kat said. She was looking a little pale. "Your succubus powers leave me twice as drained as a normal heal."

"Sorry you needed to use them," I said. "Bastard caught me flatfooted. Won't happen again."

"Don't make promises you can't keep," Kat said, a little lethargically, as she started toward the door.

"We gotta hurry," Harry said, suddenly right there and ushering us toward the door. "This place is going to be swarming with cops in minutes, and also? Our train's leaving in like ten."

"Okie dokie," I said, grabbing my bag and Kat's and boogieing for the exit a few steps behind Harry and my blond-haired savior. "Let's vamoose."

"Ugh, 'vamoose'? I'm partying with old people," Kat said under her breath, still white as a sheet as we stepped out into the Tokyo twilight. Neon lights were beginning to spring to life on the buildings around us, and she let Harry lead as we hustled her toward the train station. "Next, you'll be wanting to eat at four for the early bird discount, and crash at seven p.m."

"Whatever, man, I'm younger than you," I said, trying not to communicate too much umbrage, since Kat had been pretty clinch in not letting me get my ass handed to me back there.

"Yeah, but you're like … an old soul or something," Kat said, throwing a look behind her as we tried to disappear into the crowd flowing along the sidewalk. The train station was just ahead, and the sirens were growing louder and louder. People were clearing out of the way for us, leaping aside with surprising alacrity at the sight of three tall westerners pushing through. We must have looked like hell.

"Thanks … I think," I said as we entered the train station and the cry of the sirens seemed to fade behind us. I let Harry lead us on, but I didn't take a breath until we were safely in our seats and the train was pulling out of the station.

18.

"What the hell was that all about?" I asked from my place on the aisle. The seats were three across, like coach on an airplane, and Harry was at the window. The train was running so smoothly that I was barely aware of it moving at all.

Kat, sandwiched between the two of us, was looking a little disoriented, still waxy pale from draining her life to heal my wounds. But she was coming back herself quickly. After a quick look from side to side, she asked, "Why am I stuck in the middle?"

"Because you're the youngest, clearly," I said with a certain smugness.

"Ugh, bad deal," Kat said, sagging back in her seat. Harry, for his part, seemed to twitch slightly at that.

"Privileges of soul age," I said, and turned to look out the window. I had never been on a Japanese train before, but it was moving FAST. The terrain outside was sliding by at extreme speed, which begged the question—how fast were we going?

"200 miles an hour is the max speed," Harry said absentmindedly. His precognitive reply suggested he was getting back on his usual footing. He turned his head to look at me. "Klementina's going to do an internet search in a second."

"What?" Kat asked, looking offended all over again. "I told you to stop calling me—whatever, it doesn't matter." She looked back down at her phone. "Creepo is right. They go 150-200 miles an hour." She put her phone down and stared at me. "What do we do when we get to Nagasaki?"

"This is gonna be good," Harry said, folding his arms and settling back in his seat, slightly amused.

I didn't have to ask him what he meant; my reply supplied its own answer. "I ... don't know exactly."

Kat's eyes didn't quite leap forth from her head, but close. "We crossed an entire ocean to get here ... and you don't know where we're going other than the city?"

I shrugged. "We'll figure it out."

"How?" Kat asked, a little more juiced than usual. "You want to ask at the visitor's kiosk, 'Hey, you guys seen any weird time breaks around here'?"

"Akiyama's on his own island," I said. "I'm sure we can figure out which island he's on, assuming there's more than one."

"Do you know how many islands there are in the Japanese archipelago?" Kat asked.

"At least five," I said, a little smartassedly. "Kyushu, Honshu ... uhm ... another shoe ... maybe Jimmy Choo ..."

Kat let out a breathy sigh. "The other two main islands are Hokkaido and Shikoku. Oh, and by the way—we have to change trains at Hakata in Fukuoka." She sat back in her seat, a little surly and still pale.

"Okay," I said. Were those cities? Stations? What the hell was I supposed to do with that information? She'd kinda tossed it at me all pissed. "How long is the trip?"

"About five hours to Fukuoka," she said, staring straight ahead, "and then about two to Nagasaki."

"That's not bad," I said quietly, as Kat frowned at me, looking at me like I was weird. "What? It beats the hell out of waiting for crew rest to end back in Tokyo."

"Yeah, okay," Kat said, and stared forward again, still surly.

"Thank you, Kat," I said, and she looked at me again like I was out of my mind. "For all of this."

"You got stuck in time in the airplane," Kat said, in disbelief, "we ended up in the wrong city, and so far you've gotten in a fight in a public place and had the cops called on us. What the hell are you thanking me for?"

"Because," I said, keeping my own expression utterly straitlaced, "this still beats the ever-loving hell out of the last international trip I took."

Kat kept a straight face for about two seconds before she dissolved into laughter, the kind of deep, belly laughs that rang through the train compartment and had everyone looking at us. She looked right at Harry as she was laughing and then stopped, abruptly, all the joy sucked out of her. Composed once more, she looked back to me. "Well ... for whatever it's worth, you're welcome. But I think we would have been better off without Mr. Invincible back there deciding to test his courage and power against 'the great Sienna Nealon.'"

Something about what she said bothered me. I couldn't quite put my finger on it, though. "Yeah," I said instead, "it'd sure be nice if I could go somewhere and not get into a fight with random troublemaking strangers." Actually, that wasn't true. It'd be really boring if that happened. It'd be like the Oregon Coast, in fact, over the past two months. And Florida before that. My life had become a series of battles broken by intervals of peace.

And the sad thing was ... it was the peaceful times I dreaded, not the fights.

"What do you think that guy wanted?" Kat asked. "Other than the obviously stated, 'I want you to kill me'? Which was clearly just bravado."

"I'm not so sure it was," Harry said, leaning into our conversation. We'd switched to meta-low a while ago, as tended to happen when there were people about.

"What are you talking about?" Kat asked, frowning at him. Her feelings about him were not ambiguous in the slightest, and boy did she let it show. "Nobody wants to die."

"People want to die every day," Harry said quietly. "Suicide isn't uncommon, especially in Japan. Imagine being an Achilles and wanting to kill yourself. What the hell do you do? Pills won't work. Knives are pointless. Jump off a building? You'd break the pavement, not yourself. Drowning would fail, even a gun—assuming you could get one—wouldn't do a damned thing." He shook his head. "I think this guy was sincere, albeit a little crazy. I think he genuinely wants you to kill him, Sienna."

"Then he shouldn't put up a fight," I said. "If you're going to ask me to end your life, you could at least not start swinging on me as I try to oblige."

"I'm not so sure that's true," Harry said, looking a little pensive. "Think about it—you don't just kill random people who pose no threat, despite what the American press might say. If he's studied you, he probably knows this, which means in order to get what he wants, he knows he has to present an actual, credible threat, otherwise you're just going to knock him out and let the cops handle him afterward." He shrugged. "Or so it seems from my seat. Maybe you see things differently."

Harry had a point. "Hm," was all I said, though. For all I knew, he'd read forward into the future and learned exactly why this guy was acting the way he was. I doubted it, but I didn't want to ask in front of Kat, because things between the two of them ... man, they were just weird.

We lapsed into a little silence, which gave me a chance to assess the Kat/Harry dynamic. They were sitting next to each other and yet Kat was treating Harry like he was a black hole in the seat. Harry, though, would glance over at Kat every once in a while, pretty much always when she wasn't looking. If I had been the overtly jealous type instead of the sort who just quietly buried it and died inside, this would have been the sort of shit that would have definitely set me off.

I didn't go off, though, because I was super mature and burying my feelings under mountains of internal turmoil. And also, I was pretty sure the Japanese police were probably wise to the fact that Sienna Nealon was now on their shores, and having a freakout in a bullet train seemed like a good way to pull more heat down on me.

Catching Harry looking at Kat again out of the corner of my eye, I tried to analyze the way he was glancing at her. There wasn't anything overtly obnoxious about it; he didn't have a twinkle of lust in his eye or anything. I tried to think back to what he'd said about the two of them, and it all came down to a couple conversations in Chicago almost two years earlier. In the first, he'd sort of inferred that they'd spent a romantic winter in Smolensk. In the second, he suggested it had lasted a lot longer than just a season.

It could have been a hundred years ago, for all I knew, when Kat was just coming into adulthood, but the fact that I didn't know was the part that was making me just a tiny bit queasy, and the fact that Kat didn't know was the ipecac icing on the thing. Of course, it wasn't like I'd lived my life before Harry came along as a nun, and Harry, when I'd met him before, had been a heavy gambling, hard-drinking hedonist. The fact I hadn't seen him drink a drop or play a game in the last few months ... well, it was a little strange, I supposed.

But the idea he'd been chaste for however long he'd lived before I came along? Ridiculous. After all, however I felt about him, he'd surely had much longer relationships than our little two-month association. Right?

Clearly. And it just so happened I was sitting next to one of his exes right now.

I decided not to say a word of this aloud, not even a little bit, which I hoped meant that my thoughts would go completely unheard by Harry, who snuck another corner-of-his-eye look at Kat. And not at me.

Gag. Frustrating. That was how I found the whole thing. It wasn't as though I wanted to make a notebook of my romantic history for Harry, and, hell, I didn't even really want to know how long his was.

But ... I was curious about his relationship with Kat, especially since it didn't seem like he was totally ... over her.

Kat was staring straight ahead, and I noticed a certain amount of storm clouds building under her usually sunny facade. "Stop looking at me," she said, at normal volume, which was a lot louder than our conversations had been thus far.

"I haven't looked at you for a couple minutes," Harry said. Which was true. Clearly Kat had let it build for a short while before blowing her stack at him, which was probably why he hadn't seen this coming and avoided it by looking elsewhere sooner.

"But you were looking before that," Kat said, sound of ratcheting tension in her voice, which she made no attempt to lower to meta volume. "Constantly. Look, guy—you don't know me—"

"All evidence to the contrary," I said under my breath.

"You can deny it all you want," Harry said calmly, "but I actually do."

"No," Kat said, so firmly it was like she was slamming a vault door in Harry's face. "Maybe you knew a previous iteration of me. Maybe you even knew her well—"

"Same body, same skin, mostly same persona—yeah, I think I did," Harry said.

"—but you don't know *me*," Kat said, steel shining through every word. "*Actual* me. Not the lady I show on TV—"

"Whuuuut?" I asked, getting my sarcasm in. "Surely you don't project a different persona on an unsuspecting television audience than you have in real life, Kat?"

"—or on the tours, or whatever," Kat ignored me, probably strategically, "but the actual me. See, people *think* they know me all the time from watching me, but they don't. You see what I want you to see. You only know what I want you to know."

"I feel like the opposite happens with me," I mumbled, "like people only see the bad things, like when I burn someone alive and it goes viral on the internet."

"But you don't know me, Harry," Kat said, very forcefully. "Not who I am now. Maybe you *wish* you did," and here she trotted out the starlet eyes, which made me cringe, because it was kind of an asshole move and she was fluttering them at my putative boyfriend, "you just don't. So stop acting like you do. There's literally nothing between us—"

"Except an armrest and about twelve inches of empty space," Harry said, rolling his eyes and looking straight ahead.

"—so stop acting like there is," she finished. In another circumstance, I probably would have applauded Kat for putting her foot down with someone so firmly, especially after she'd acted like a human carpet with at least one producer back in the day as he walked all over her for a year or better.

But in this case ... it grated on me that first of all, she'd targeted Harry, whom I was fond of, and second, that she was really denying reality hard in favor of staying in her own, make-believe bubble that revolved around her not having any sort of past that she couldn't remember. Reinventing yourself was all well and good—hell, I was due for one now that my redhead look had been exposed—but given the nature of Kat's powers and their ability to drain her memory from overuse ...

Didn't it seem a little delusional to just pretend anything you didn't remember ... didn't happen at all? That'd be like me denying that the invasion of Normandy occurred, simply because I wasn't alive or there at the time, and yelling that ignorance in the face of a survivor of the battle.

"Uh, Kat ...?" I started to say.

"Yes?" she turned to me, asking ever so sweetly. Her demeanor with Harry versus how she was speaking to me was like night and day. Harry was still silently fuming, looking straight ahead on the other side of her, seemingly unwilling to so much as glance in her direction now.

"Something I'm confused about," I said. "Well, a couple things, actually—what does 'bozshe moi' mean?"

She blinked. "It means 'my God' in Russian. Why?"

"How do you know Russian?" I asked. "Have you ever been there?"

She frowned, creases appearing in her face. "I—what, no, I mean, I went through Moscow once, but—I don't know." She shook the question off like it was no more than an annoyance.

"How do you know Japanese?" I asked.

She let out a little rankled sigh. "I don't know, Sienna. I just do. Because I'm awesome, that's why."

"I'm not disputing your awesomeness," I said, genuinely. "I believe in your awesomeness. You're a person who's gone to great pains to save my life at times when no one else could have. You've got guts beyond belief, you're the object of admiration of countless men and women around the world—that's you, Kat. No one's denying or taking that away from you, but ..." I cleared my throat, trying to remain as far away from nettled and pissed off—basically as *not* Sienna—as I could as I asked this question: "Don't you think ... it's kinda cool that you have all this ... additional experience and skills to draw on? Even if you don't remember how you got them?"

"What the hell is that supposed to mean?" she asked, her patience obviously fraying.

"Like ... I don't remember my childhood," I said. "At all. From before the age of ... I dunno, five or so? Before I got locked in my house. But that doesn't mean I sprang, fully-formed, out of a test tube or something at age five. It just means that those memories were probably traumatic or something, and my child brain didn't want to remember them." Which seemed an eminently reasonable explanation given the horror that followed that period.

"Yeah, so?" She didn't completely dismiss me, but she was plainly on the edge of severe irritation, which was ... not very Kat-like.

I lowered my voice, which was already as close to soothing as I was capable of producing. "You forgot your relationship with Scott. Completely. I saw it all—or a lot of the parts that weren't X-rated, anyway—and I know it happened. But you don't remember it."

"I think that's probably for the better," she said, her restraint fading, "especially given what you two did like a year later. I bet you remember those X-rated parts."

I ignored her swipes with a cringe. "Isn't it possible that some of the things Harry knows about you ... might be true? In the same way that the things I remember about you and Scott were true?"

She stared at me dully. "I just realized something." And she looked back at Harry, then to me, and thin amusement draped itself over her features. "You think he's telling the truth? That Harry and I were an item at some point?" I caught a grimace from Harry behind her, like he could read what was coming. "I gotta ask—why do you keep dating my cast-offs, Sienna?"

Oof. She stabbed right to the heart of me on that one. I hadn't thought of it that way. "Argh," I said, cringing, my eyes closing almost of their own accord. "I have no answer for this, but know that it hurts me."

"The truth often does," Kat said, a little more peppy. "I don't see why it matters, though, anyway. Even if I admitted you were right—which I totes don't, by the way—who gives a fig about what happened in the distant past? If I don't remember something—like my boyfriends before they rebound into you—then like a tree falling in the forest, it kinda didn't happen."

"I don't think that's quite how the saying goes," I said, my eyes still squeezed mostly closed. "Listen—"

"No, you listen," Kat said, and here she leaned over in my face, and I don't think I'd seen her more serious, ever. "This is something you taught me, Sienna, about power and identity. You're the biggest badass, and it's not because you're never vulnerable. You're the biggest badass because you don't let other people *see* you vulnerable. You define you, at least where everybody's perception is concerned. You don't let your weakness be seen outside your inner circle. And that's awesome. I like that. For me, it's a little different."

She leaned back in her seat, confident self-assurance just flowing off her, skin back to her normal glow, paleness faded away. "For me ... it's about defining myself to everyone by showing them the best parts of me, and that means not even acknowledging the past stuff, because—again, let's just say it was me, which it totally wasn't—it's not part of who I am now. None of it. It's of the past. I'm of the present. Anything that happened before about—" And here she lowered her voice, "—1954 ... I don't remember. So it didn't happen to me, it happened to someone else who's not me. That's all."

I frowned. "Wait ... you remember back to 1954?"

She let out a little sigh. "Yeah ... Janus had Omega administer a serum to me before I lost my memory and became Kat, and what it does is ... it kinda brings back memories that I lost on previous brain drains. So, after the Des Moines thing where I forgot Scott, I remembered ... lots of stuff from before I became Kat." She looked pretty cagey about that, and gave Harry a fiery glance. "But I don't remember him, I don't remember being Klementina, and I damned sure don't remember coming to Japan before."

"Huh," I said, deciding to keep my response on this side of anything that might offend Kat. Harry might as well have been a stone statue for all his response to this revelation. He was as surly as I'd ever seen him, arms still folded in front of him like they were a brick wall that could keep out anything but the stuff that Kat was saying that annoyed him.

"Yeah," Kat said, and she pulled a pair of wireless earphones out of her bag and put them in her ears. "And on that note ..." And she winked at me, then adjusted her phone. The music coming out of them was loud enough to be distracting to me, even though I wasn't wearing them. She put her head back on the seat rest and closed her eyes.

I thought about trying to talk to Harry over her, but he was just staring straight ahead, still as death. I decided against rocking the boat—or the train, in this case—and just settled back in my own seat, staring at the Japanese countryside flashing by—or at least what little of it I could see in the fading light of day—and rode on into night as the darkness fell outside our carriage and the silence stayed unbroken within it.

19.

We changed trains at Hakata Station in Fukuoka and took a short, two-hour jaunt to Nagasaki that arrived in the early morning hours. We pulled into the city of Nagasaki just before dawn, and the quiet was ... almost disconcerting. I counted my blessings that I hadn't had to deal with any time freezes while trapped in my window seats, because if I'd had to get up to use the bathroom, I might have broken Harry or Kat's kneecaps while trying to climb over them to go pee.

Now that we were free, I debated our course—head straight for the exit and get out onto the streets of Nagasaki, or try and figure out what do first? As fun as blindly striking out into a completely unfamiliar city sounded, I meandered up to a tourist kiosk instead, Kat rolling her bag along beside me.

"Hi," I said to the woman manning the counter. She was young, probably in her twenties, and looked at me very attentively. "Speak English?" I asked hopefully. She nodded. "Uhm ... I'm looking for an island around here ..."

She frowned at me. "There are ... many islands around here," she said in slightly accented English. "Are you looking for a special one?"

"Yeah," I said, trying to decide how best to phrase my request. "I'm looking for ... kind of a haunted island. One that people try and avoid." I felt incredibly stupid just saying this aloud.

She stared at me a little blankly for a second. "You ... want to visit a haunted island?"

"Yes," I said.

She cocked her head at me, as though she was trying to decide whether this funny westerner was attempting to pull her leg. "There are several island tours from nearby ... you could visit historic Hashima Island—"

"If lots of people visit, it's probably not the island I'm looking for," I said, trying to be helpful and not snarky. She seemed very sincere. "Again, I'm looking for one people would tend to avoid."

She looked uncomfortable for a moment, then moved to the series of brochures in a display behind her, pulling out a map and bringing it over to the counter. She unfolded it and placed it between us, a nice, full-color picture of the nearby Japanese coastline, with names in Japanese characters with English subtitles beneath. "Many of the boats leave from the docks, here," she said, pointing at a place right on the water. "We are here," and she circled what I presumed was the train station with her pen. "I do not believe I can help you with finding a haunted island tour. This not something I have heard of, but ... there are many boats available for chartered tours at the docks." She bowed her head at me and pushed the map gently toward me. "Perhaps you will find what you seek there."

"*Wakarimashita*," Kat said, sliding the map further toward me, and bowing her own head toward the girl. "*Domo arigato.*" She said something else that I didn't understand, then turned away from the counter. I picked up the map and followed her away, back to where Harry was standing with his arms folded—still—waiting for us.

"I think we're better off going to the docks and asking a local fisherman about haunted islands," Kat said once we were back within earshot of Harry. "Asking the local tourist guides isn't going to be super fruitful. Their job is emphasizing the good parts of Nagasaki. They're not going to be keen to discuss a real haunted island in most cases, it'd be kind of a smudge on their reputation."

"That's ... so very different than it would be in America," I said.

"Because this is Japan," Kat said, way too seriously, and then she turned and started pulling her rollerbag toward the exit.

"She's gotta be a way different person than you knew," I said to Harry, meta-low, before I started after her.

Harry grunted at first, but then, almost so quiet I couldn't hear it, said, "Nope." And trailed along in her wake, his own bag slung over his shoulder.

Nagasaki's train station was a sprawling thing, and the exit was like an entry to a mall or stadium, a kind of courtyard with shops on either side covered over by a cantilevered arch. It was a pretty cool piece of architecture, and it led right out to where cabs waited to pick up passengers, even in these early morning hours.

My view of the city was somewhat limited; I was looking for signs of the destruction that had fallen upon this place on an August day in 1945, but I couldn't see much of the city from where I stood, and it all looked pretty normal and citylike from here, nothing like the wastelands from those post-nuclear games Reed played. Not that I'd expected that, exactly, but I figured there must be some sign here somewhere of what had happened.

Before we even made it halfway down the forecourt mall, Harry's hand fell on my shoulder, an iron grip that almost yanked me around in place. I started to look back at him to call out my aggravation at his sudden arresting of my momentum, but Kat had stopped in front of me, and her suitcase fell from her grasp, landing with a thunk on the pavement.

"Uh, Sienna?" she asked, not looking back at me. "You have a problem."

And I damned sure did, I realized a moment later.

Because standing there, blocking our exit to the cabs, that same hollow, wide smile on his face and backed by a half dozen yakuza accomplices ... was Prettyboy.

20.

Jamal

We found Ray Spiegel sitting at a café table with his MacBook in front of him, the glowing white Apple logo matching his shiny smile and his lack of tan as he saw us come in. He stood and thrust his hand out to us. I put him at late twenties, longish hair down to the back of his neck that almost looked like a postmodern mullet, the kind of style a hipster might wear ironically. He also had a pitiful little pornstache on his upper lip while the rest of his babyface was totally clean shaven. "Hey, guys," he enthused, shaking my hand as I came up to him. He sat down and gestured to the seats across from him. My brother and I each took one. He didn't offer to get us coffee.

"This is a pretty good place," he said, nudging the cup in front of him. "Not as good as Dolcezza, but not bad." He wore a wide grin, the kind that said he knew stuff, or maybe was in on a particularly good joke. "So ... you've only been in town a few hours. This your first trip to DC? What do you think?"

I shared a look with Augustus. It wasn't our first trip to DC, but he didn't need to know that. "It's all right," I said, skipping past that first question. It didn't escape my notice that he knew we'd only been here a few hours. "Who told you we were in town?"

"Gotta protect your sources, y'know," he said, a twinkle in

his eye. He was playing hard on the boyish attitude. "I can give you guys some recommendations for great dinner spots and some bars that might be good. What are you into?"

Augustus looked at me and I could read his thoughts: *This mofo's trying to charm us,* he seemed to say. My brother remained unimpressed.

"I'm into people who know stuff," I said, trying to be a little nonchalant about it. "Where are the movers and shakers in this town?"

"Up by the hill, mostly," he said, eyes still twinkling. "Try Le Diplomate. Very 'in' spot nowadays. You might even see your congressperson or senator there."

"And wouldn't that just be the highlight of a lifetime," Augustus said with all due sarcasm.

"Heh," Ray said, clearly picking up on it. "So ... what brings you guys to town?"

"Sightseeing," I said, and by Ray's reaction I could tell he didn't buy it.

"Listen, guys," he said, still smiling smugly, "let me kinda lay it out for you, since you're new in town and I'm sure things work differently in *Minneapolis*." He made a funny voice as he said the city's name, like it was some bizarre hinterland that lacked civilization or wi-fi. "DC is its own thing. Politics rules the roost here. It's junkies for that kind of wheeling and dealing all the way down. Everyone here either works for the government or else works on the people who work for the government in some way—lobbyists, baristas, masseuses—whatever. This town thrives on two things—politics and the occasional sporting event."

"So much for the Kennedy Center Honors," I said under my breath. Augustus snickered.

"Because of that," he went on, "the people who spin the wheels of politics—they have a lot of power. You probably know that, of course, but I doubt you know exactly how deep that power goes." He smiled and leaned in. "See, I'm telling you this because you seem like nice guys, up and comers ... and I wouldn't want you to stumble into town and make a big mistake right off the bat, stick your dicks into the hornet's nest instead of the honey pot, y'know?"

I blinked at him. The way he'd said it was a little surprising. "That'd be regrettable."

"Exactly," Ray said, snapping his finger and pointing at me. "And especially since it's your first time here—we want no regrets, no mistakes—just a good experience, am I right?" He was grinning again. "So ... what brings you guys to town? Work? Pleasure?"

"A little bit of both," I said. If he didn't have a pretty good inkling of why we were here, I'd have been prepared to chow down on his coffee cup.

"Mmmhmm," he said, and jotted something illegible down on a yellow pad in front of him. "So the reason you're here has nothing to do with a certain world-famous lady superhero-turned-villain who's recently lost her powers." He rested the pen against the corner of his mouth and waited for us to answer, eyes still twinkling.

I looked at Augustus, he looked at me. We were both cool, and I turned back to Ray and shrugged. "I haven't seen her in years. Why would I come to town for her?"

"Because there's this rumor going around, see," Ray said, still wearing his smug demeanor like a jacket, "that there's some kind of secret evidence that proves Sienna Nealon isn't actually guilty of that stuff out in *Minnesota*." He said *Minnesota* with the same goofball accent he'd said *Minneapolis* earlier. "Or that nuclear explosion thing in LA," he said normally.

"Where are you from, dawg?" Augustus asked.

"I'm a Long Island boy," Ray said proudly. "Born and raised. Got my journalism degree from Columbia."

"Ooh, top marks," Augustus said. "You must be a big brain, coming up that route and getting on this blogging thing like you have."

"I have the most-read politics blog in DC." Spiegel said proudly, oblivious to Augustus's snarkiness. "Everybody reads me—staffers, reps, senators—I hear some of my work even makes it up to the Oval." He winked. "I've met him, you know. President Gondry. A couple times. He's not like what everybody thinks."

I held my tongue on that one, because I didn't know much

about Gondry. I knew all about his predecessor, though. "That's cool," I said, not starting an argument I didn't care about. "So, if you've heard rumors about this supposed evidence that clears Sienna Nealon ..." Spiegel perked up when I said her name. "... what all have you heard about it?"

He shrugged. "It feels like kind of a MacGuffin, Rey's parents, Clean Slate, wish-it-were-true sort of thing perpetrated by people ... *not in the know*," and this last bit he said with delicious malevolence, like they were some disfavored caste. "Go with the conventional, reported wisdom on this one—it doesn't exist. Cuz she did it all."

"Interesting," I said. "Hm."

"But what if she didn't?" Augustus asked, and I realized for the first time my brother had been on a slow boil this entire conversation. His temper was starting to come to a head, which was ... worrying, given the company.

"She did," Spiegel said, shrugging again. "Everybody who's anybody knows it."

"Then everybody who's anybody is wrong," Augustus said, as firmly as if it were one of his rock walls he'd just put up.

Ray snorted. "Look, maybe you feel that way because she was your friend or whatever—"

"She *is* my friend," Augustus said, "no 'whatever.' And y'all are all wrong about her."

He gave my brother a pitying look. "What makes you say that? Because if you've got evidence of it ..." And he clicked his pen and set it to his notepad to write. "I'm all ears. Always on the lookout for a scoop."

"Oh, I have all kinds of evidence," Augustus said, and I was having a hard time figuring out if he was blustering or he had something particular in mind. "And you'll see it—in one of the major newspapers, when the time comes." He sneered, and I realized my brother had the measure of this guy maybe even more than I did. "I ain't wasting the story of the year on some fringe politics blog read by a bunch of circle-jerking DC bureaucrats."

Ray flushed, moving slightly more upright in his seat. "Sorry you feel that way," he said, lips tightly puckered.

"I'm sorry you felt the need to come out here and waste

my time," Augustus said, pouring on the heat while I sat back, a little open-mouthed at all this, "Washington-splaining to me how things work in this town. Punkass, I know who your sources are, and I know the Custis family is rotten to the core and up over their heads in a cover up." If I could have fainted dead away right now, I would have, because now he was giving away the whole game, and I lacked the presence of mind or ability to stop him because I was too busy sitting there slack-jawed in the face of it. "When this thing blows up, you're going watch lots of the people you worshipfully report on and use for sources get dragged into the local jailhouse in handcuffs. Try and imagine how that shit's going to feel, especially if some of your friends get found out for holding onto evidence, too."

Spiegel broke into a smile again. "Wow. That's, uh ..." He laughed. "You've got a powerful delusion thing going on there. You think we're sitting on a story like that?" He shook his head. "You're crazy. Any blogger or reporter would kill to get an exclusive with evidence that Sienna Nealon is somehow innocent." He almost snorted. "But you'd have to fight about fifty or so national reporters' stories, since they were on the scene when it happened—"

"Bullshit," Augustus said. "They were fleeing their asses away from the scene when it happened because they'd just been mind-controlled by one of the prisoners they'd been lovingly reporting on for days before. He turned them into nothing better than dogs and sicced 'em on Sienna. I don't know what it is they 'recollect,' but it ain't what happened, because they were busy being chickenshits while it went down, running away so they didn't get burned. And I find it funny that she somehow turned on everybody and killed all these criminals, but not a single reporter died in the incident, especially considering they were reporting right there live from the scene only minutes before, exactly where the explosion took place. Funny how that happened if they were all 'on the scene.'" He sat back. "Almost like they weren't there—or at least not close enough to get burned to death by a several hundred-foot blast of fire that leveled buildings around them."

TIME

Ray just sat there, his face a little red as he considered his reply. "You'll never make the case," he said quietly, looking withdrawn. "Even if you had something. Never happen."

"Oh, are you finally being honest with us now?" Augustus asked. I was still blinking through the horror of what I'd just heard, some seriously bad feelings stirring inside me about what my brother had just done—through impatience—yet again. "Is this part of your philanthropic 'tour of Washington'? 'Try the crepes at over here, and don't go exposing the bullshit we pumped out to smear Sienna Nealon'?"

Ray gave another snort, but it was a weak one, and his eyes were fixed on his laptop closed in front of him, as well as the pen and pad that rested atop it. He adjusted them, then touched his phone—I realized at last—turning off the record function he'd had running during our entire conversation. Then he looked up, meeting my brother's gaze with a much calmer one of his own. "Sienna Nealon is a cautionary tale. You might want to take a lesson from her."

"Oh, yeah?" Augustus leaned in, too. "What's the lesson I should take away?"

"She thought she was the most powerful person in the world," Ray said. All his smugness had evaporated, and he sounded ... almost dead inside. "But she wasn't, and now she's less powerful than ever." His lips drew tight and anger creased his brow. "I tried to tell you about the way things work in this town. You do whatever you want, but you should really watch yourselves."

Augustus stood abruptly, looming over the table and causing Ray's eyes to widen. "You want to throw down with me?" he asked Ray, throwing his arms wide. "You want to threaten me?"

"Whoa, whoa, bro," Ray said, putting his hands in front of him and smiling, though a lot more limply than he had at the outset of this conversation. "This isn't the way this town works. It's not fights, man. Having to throw a punch? That's not power. And it's definitely not the kind they deal in around here."

He picked up his laptop and slid it into a manbag, along

with his pad, and then picked up his phone. He slung the bag over his shoulder and it creased his short-sleeve dress shirt, his slightly chubby upper body weighed down by the contents. "I just came here to talk, to give you the info, gents. The Custis family that you're thinking you want to get into a scratch fight with? Don't do it. They've got nothing to do with whatever's in your heads."

"I just told you what's in my head," Augustus said. "If you think your friends aren't connected, why are you trying so hard to protect them? Don't you think we'll just figure out the truth if they weren't involved? That's what we do, see—get to the truth."

"No," Ray said, almost laughing. "You guys fight. Brawl. With metas—you know, like the Custis family. But you don't want to do that here." He leaned forward seriously. "They're not your enemy. But if you mess with them ... they're nice people, they probably wouldn't rise to the bait. But they've got friends. Powerful friends." Picking up his coffee cup, he nodded at Augustus, then at me. "Friends you don't want as enemies. Because you guys seem ... nice." He might have been struggling a little to get that out. "I'd hate to see you end up like ... well, your old friend." He smiled tightly. "Take it easy, fellas. Maybe I'll see you around." And then he walked off.

I watched him go, kicking myself for being cowed into silence during the last half of the conversation, and I wondered as I watched him walk away exactly where—or who—his next stop was.

21.

Sienna

Prettyboy was leering at me over Kat's shoulder, waiting at the mouth of the forecourt's mall exit for me to come to him, only a couple dozen paces away. The fact that he'd gotten this close was disquieting. The fact that he'd beaten us here from Tokyo?

Less than surprising. The fact that there were no cops waiting here for him said a few things about how effectively the police were investigating me, or how possibly how corrupt they were. I didn't want to speculate on which it might be, but the fact that the yakuza had tracked me down before the cops said something.

"Look, dude," I said, stepping out in front of Kat, "it's kinda been a long night, and we're heading into the time when I'd normally be sleeping, so can we put a pin in this 'me killing you business' for now? I'm not in the mood." All true. I wasn't a psycho, and I didn't enjoy killing people, even those with a death wish.

"Our fates are tied together by the inescapable cords of destiny," Prettyboy said with a smile. "You can no more untether them than I can separate myself from life without your help."

I sighed. Full marks to Harry for diagnosing this guy's desire for assisted suicide. "Have you tried just drowning yourself in hemlock or something?"

Prettyboy bowed his head to me, just slightly. "There is nothing I have not tried."

"Oh, man," I muttered, trying to decide how best to approach this. Admitting I didn't want to kill him probably wasn't going to make him happy, since he truly did want me to. Taking it easy on him wasn't going to do me any favors, either, because he'd just keep coming at me harder and more threatening until I gave him what he wanted and actually did kill him—which I wasn't entirely sure how to do, save for by draining his soul, which was probably not cool with him, since it didn't result in actual death. Short of putting him in a different succubus and then somehow blowing that succubus's brains out, I was at a bit of a loss. "This is a pretty unkind thing you're asking of me. I mean, it's a lot."

"It is the simplest thing in the world," he said, moving to a fighting stance and extending his hand to me. "You will kill me, or I will kill your friends." I blanched, and he smiled wider, because he'd gone and stumbled on the magic formula for getting me to be a lot more serious about this.

"Now we're getting down to the crux of things," I said, glancing around. We were pretty close to the road where taxis were passing in front of us. They were moving slowly, in a very controlled manner, which didn't do me any favors. I gave another quick glance at the arched covering above us. It was pretty high up there, and tossing my foe through it would probably just piss him off, given his power set.

No, I was going to have to do this the old-fashioned way: deliver an ass beating. But first …

"HOLY SHIT!" I shouted at the top of my lungs, letting my jaw drop and pointing a finger over Prettyboy's shoulder, trying to emulate perfect disbelief out of absolutely nowhere. "WHAT THE HELL IS THAT?!"

The dumb sonofabitch actually looked. In fairness to him, I'd been as loud and shocked-sounding as possible, and after a nice lull from a conversation like we were having, you start to feel … complacent, maybe? Then your conversational partner goes and shouts about something behind you … Well, you'd just have to look, right?

And look he did. He said something in Japanese to the

yakuza backing him, but I have no idea what it was and I don't really care.

As soon as his back was turned, I was on him, grabbing him by the hair in a manner reminiscent of what I'd done to one of the Wolfe brothers once upon a time. I kicked him in the groin to get him off the ground and then slung him in a circle like an Olympic hammer thrower. His face was pure panic as I made the second loop, slinging him like I was a centrifuge.

"Nothing personal," I said as we made the second orbit. His yakuza buddies were coming at me now, but Harry was on the case, jumping in front of me and dealing some serious beatdown, one-hit knocking guys out. "And I don't mean to contribute to your depression, but I just don't have time for your bullshit right now."

Reaching the apogee of my next swing, I started to send Prettyboy flying. I had it all planned out. I was going to release him and let nature—and physics—take their sweet course. He'd come to rest in the middle of a street a few blocks away, and I'd have enough time to grab a cab to the docks without his invincible ass dogging my steps. I'd solve this time problem with Akiyama, and then I'd leave Japan and never see Prettyboy again, if the fates be kind.

The fates were not kind, though.

Time stuttered just as I started to release him. Not a full freeze like I'd grown used to, this one was a stop-start within a second, just long enough to throw me off my game, make me wonder why his hair was still touching my hand after I released him. I blinked, and accidentally hit him with my elbow on the inadvertent spin-around I did after release. It wasn't intentional; I'd been spinning so fast to chuck him that I couldn't just stop immediately, and he should have been clear of my elbow if not for the damned time stoppage.

My hit knocked his head aside, and time shot back into motion. Prettyboy's momentum changed abruptly, his head snapping back like he was a baseball and I'd just knocked him out of the park, but instead of shooting out the front of the forecourt, he suddenly shot sideways as the strength of my elbow dinging him was magnified many times over by the time stoppage.

It took me a second to put all that together, much longer than it took him to crash into a shopfront to my left and then rise, fresh as a daisy, as though I hadn't just tossed him like a garbage bag. His face was suffused with rage, though, and he wasn't nearly as far away as I'd hoped he would be right now.

Damned time. Talk about inconvenient to my plans.

On the other hand, I'd just learned something interesting. Next time stoppage, all I needed to do was pound on him as hard as I could from the opposite direction to the way I wanted him to go, and I suspected he'd launch on his own accord. It all came back to physics; with time stopped, I could act on him with incredible force, stacking physical punishment upon him to the point where it functioned like a magnifying effect, the force of ten or a hundred blows being directed so tightly in time upon him it was like they were all landing within a millisecond of each other. If I'd just hit him with my elbow accidentally while time had been moving, it'd maybe have snapped his head back.

But hit him with a simple elbow motion while time was stopped, and it had whole different effect. It was as though I was hitting him at several thousand miles per hour due to our relative velocities. The math made my head hurt, but probably not as badly as his right now.

He screamed something unintelligible at me in Japanese and came charging out of the wrecked shop front, covered in shards of glass and little bits of drywall powder. I thought about hightailing it, but running wasn't really my style, and Harry was still firmly ensconced in dealing with yakuza thugs. Two were down, four were still working on trying to land even a single blow on him, and meanwhile one had come around at Kat, which I suspected was about to be to be a major mistake. I had to focus on Prettyboy, but it would have been impossible to miss the hard crack of fist on bone from approximately where Kat was clashing with the guy. I had a feeling it wasn't him that had scored the hit, either.

Dumbasses. Always underestimating the pretty blond girl to their eternal regret. Or at least as long as it'd take for an orthopedic surgeon to put their jaw together correctly again.

Prettyboy ranted at me in his native language as he tore up the ground between us in a flat-out bull run. He wasn't a big guy, but he didn't need to be with meta strength and invincible skin. He could just about run me over and it'd kill me plenty. As he got closer, I tensed slightly, readying my stance as well as I could.

He reached out as he got to within a few feet, plainly intending to make his attack so much worse by yanking me into it. It would have hurt me badly, no doubt, had he landed what he intended. We're talking broken bones, pain, all that jazz. I'm not sure how it would have helped him get to his professed goal of me killing him, but, hey, when you're pissed, logic kinda goes out the window.

Unfortunately for him, he was hardly the worst person I'd been bull-charged by, and even more unfortunate for him, acting stupidly in a fight not only doesn't grant you any advantage, it usually nullifies any you might have. Like, say invincible skin and near invulnerability.

It was always the same with these assholes; give a man enough power and he neglected to upgrade his fighting skills, thinking he had it covered by strength alone.

But when it came to using someone's strength against them, I had been trained by the best.

"Ever heard of aikido?" I asked as I swept a hand around Prettyboy's arm and dropped, turning his momentum against him. His eyes went wide as I went into a roll. His forward momentum went sideways, and, using techniques my mother had taught me back when she had superpowers and I had none, I sent his ass sailing again, right into the shop on the opposite wall.

It was hardly world-ending for him, being about half as hurtful as the last impact he'd made, but it kept him from running me over. As he rose from the debris of his hard landing, though, his face showed that he'd upped his game to double-pissed, or maybe triple-pissed now. It wasn't a great look, but hey, I was happier that he was all bellicose rather than coolly calculating how best to use his superpowers to my immediate detriment.

He came at me again, even less cautiously if that was possible, and this time he caught a face full of concrete as I tossed him even higher into the air, and he came crashing down on the concrete a dozen feet away.

I had my doubts about how long even pissed-off Prettyboy could continue to enjoy the insanity loop—doing the same thing and expecting different results—and sure enough, as he peeled himself off the broken pavement where he'd come to rest after landing, he did so a little more cautiously than the last two rounds.

"You ..." he said, grunting, unsteady on his feet. I wasn't sure if that was because I'd rung his bell or if he was feeling some other form of bodily discomfort. I suspected the former.

"Why does everybody always say, 'You ... '? when they're looking at me and wondering how they got to be in such a state?" I asked, genuinely curious. "It's like an insult no one can ever quite finish. Like 'You bitch, I can't believe you're beating my dumb ass senseless'? Or 'You heinous individual, how dare you violate my person in such a way, you've hurt my feelings!' Hm? Whaddya think, Prettyboy?" I needed to goad him back into stupid action, if possible. I figured if he had any other easily exploitable flaws, one of them was probably failure to do cardio. Not that that'd be an immediate boon to me, because metas tended to be able to go longer than normal humans in almost every circumstance, but maybe over the long haul I could wear his ass out.

He rose back to his feet, breathing heavily but not nearly heavily enough. "You ... will kill me ... or I will kill your friends ... and your family ... and every one you love ... until you give me ... peace ..."

"Man," I said, staring at him as he started to walk, way too calmly, toward me, "seriously. This is way new for me. That last part makes a huge difference. No one's ever really asked me for—well, okay, one guy kinda did, but—"

Prettyboy was just walking toward me, and then suddenly everything seemed to ... blur.

Harry and Kat were fighting off to my right, doing their thing, taking out the other guys, and suddenly Harry and his nearest opponent launched into fast-motion speed. The guy came at Harry with a baton that blurred with speed and Harry dodged it perfectly. I caught the movement out of the corner of my eye and turned my head to look—

And suddenly Prettyboy was *right there* in front of me, and then I felt something unbelievably hard hit me in the midsection—then another something—then another, as though someone had positioned a construction piston of the sort they used to utterly destroy concrete right over my abdomen and switched it on hyperspeed.

Now it was my turn to fly through the air and catch a shopfront, shattering glass and smashing through shelving. I didn't know how it had happened, but time had just turned on me, hard, snapping into high speed around me while I remained nearly still. Prettyboy had walked right up and beat the living snot out of me, and when time had resumed—

I'd gone flying. I lay in busted shelves, glass shards sticking out of my bleeding arms and back, and I stared up at the ceiling. Unlike Prettyboy, I didn't have the advantage of invincible skin when I sailed through the plate glass window. I could feel pieces of it embedded in a few places along my back, and they all hurt, my life's blood draining out into cardboard boxes that surrounded me.

Prettyboy loomed into my view and stared down at me, his rage replaced by a near-disgust, lower jaw jutting out. He made no threatening move toward me, but looked down at me as though I were unworthy of anything. Then he spit, right in my face.

"*Baka*," he said, his contempt obvious. "Now ... I will kill your friends. And when next we meet ... when you are healed ... it will be upon the terms I dictate. You will give me what I want."

And he started to walk away, back toward where Kat and Harry waited ... and I knew, in my heart ...

They didn't stand a chance against him.

22.

"No," I moaned, trying to get to my feet. I was bleeding, sick to my stomach, the trauma of what my body had just been through coming out in the physical reactions of shock. I was blinking, hyper-fast, trying to stimulate my body back into motion when it didn't want to do anything but lie down and die right there ... or at least try to be still and heal so I wouldn't die.

I pulled a long shard of bloody glass out of my shoulder and hurled it at Prettyboy's fading back. It shattered across his left shoulder like one of those beer bottles that you see in the movies, smashing to tiny pieces. I had enough strength to do that, even wounded and weak, and Prettyboy turned around to look at me as I pushed to my knees.

"Don't ... even ... think about walking away from ... me ..." I said, barely able to remain upright even on my knees. I pulled another shard out of my left trapezius, this one larger than my hand, and beckoned to him with the bloody glass. "Come on, asswipe. You wanna die? I'm working up to granting your fondest wish."

His lips split into a feral smile, and he looked at me just a second longer than he really should have. Harry blindsided him with a chunk of concrete, and while it shattered over his head into dust, it also staggered him for a second, letting Harry slip past and give him a forceful shove that launched him back, head over heels.

Harry slipped in between us, interposing his own body

between Prettyboy and myself. I tried to get to my feet and failed, but Harry motioned to me with a hand behind his back, urging me to stay down. "Hey," he said, and added some unintelligible Japanese that felt like it held the aura of an insult, "… your fly is down."

Prettyboy stared at him for just a second, and then bent over to look at the front of his pants. I couldn't believe he'd fallen for that, but then, Harry did presumably know before he tried it that it'd work. Or maybe not, since he couldn't read his own future.

It didn't last long. A second later, Prettyboy was looking up again, a tired smile draped across his lips. "You think this will stop me?" He threw his head back and gave the appearance of a deep laugh. "This will not make quit my pursuit of—"

Squealing tires heralded the arrival of something else, and a small Japanese car slammed into Prettyboy, destroying the front end but also launching him into the air. It arrested its own momentum in a heartbeat, bouncing off him and going back about ten feet, coming to rest just outside the shop door as Prettyboy was ejected from my field of view with all the violence of a football being punted.

"Come on," Harry said, grabbing me by the elbow. "We don't have much time."

"Wha …?" I managed to get out before he jerked me along, practically carrying me out of the wreckage. Kat was just extracting herself from the ruined car, a little blood running down her forehead as she joined up with us. She scooped up her suitcase as well as my bag and Harry's as he pulled me over the fallen yakuza, some of whom didn't seem like they'd be waking up anytime soon.

Kat ran ahead and flagged down a taxi extremely-mini-van, yelling at them in excited Japanese and then opening the side door as Harry tossed me in and followed. Our bags landed in the seat behind me, thrown by Kat, and she yelled at Harry to get in the front seat while she slipped in next to me. Harry was already moving, though, and they were in the car seconds later. Kat shouted something else at the driver and he floored it, taking the corner at high speed as we left the station forecourt behind. We were on the main road a second later, and suddenly my world started to clear up.

"Just chill," Kat said from beside me, hand on mine. She had a waxy look on her face already, and the blood was still seeping from the injury on her forehead. She was looking pretty drawn by the time she withdrew her hand from mine, and my skin was tingling at her touch in the most pleasant way. I'd heard a faint voice in my head, reminiscent of the souls I'd so recently—and dreadfully—lost, but this one was higher, more pleasant.

I could hear Kat in my head. Faintly, like she was whispering outside a room I was in, but still ... it was a pleasant, if somewhat painful, reminder of what I'd lost.

"Thank you," I croaked, dragging myself upright again.

Kat plucked another shard of glass out of my arm and opened the window, tossing it out. "You're welcome," she said, looking white as a glass of milk. She pulled a few more shards out, whatever hadn't fallen out on their own as Harry had pulled me through the promenade. I removed one on my left side myself, and handed it to her for disposal. Points to skinny, pale, delicate-looking Kat—she didn't blanch at all as she tossed the blood-soaked glass shard out the window.

The cab driver was stiff, eyes pointed straight ahead, not daring to look back at us and shaking in his seat. Kat said something to him quietly, and he nodded, shoulders quivering as he moved.

Harry looked back at us, tense. "He's going straight to the cops as soon as we're out," he whispered, meta-low. "We're going to need to change vehicles and get to the docks at uber-speed."

"I can't imagine why he'd be terrified to the point of wanting to run to the lawful authorities," I murmured, low enough he couldn't hear it. "I mean, his cab was only just hijacked by three people fleeing a metahuman brawl at the train station, one of whom is bleeding liters all over the back of his livelihood."

"There's no path to dissuading him, either," Harry murmured. "Unless either of you is in favor of taking stronger measures?"

"I'd be okay with knocking him out," I said, "or I could

steal his memories. That's about as far as I'm willing to go."

Harry concentrated for a moment, staring into empty air. "That'd be enough. Take his memories, it buys us a lot of time. Hours, actually. Just wait until we get out."

"Okay," I said, settling back in my seat and closing my eyes.

"Sienna," Kat said, suddenly an ominous and hovering presence right next to me, "what the hell happened back there?"

"Ugh," I moaned, still keeping it low, like the others. "Time snapped into superspeed for me. Prettyboy pummeled me while I was basically standing still, unable to do a damned thing about it. Hence my sudden flight into the glass." I plucked a small shard out of my left forearm and presented it to Kat, who palmed it and tossed it out the window without comment.

"How does that even happen?" Harry asked.

"I dunno, Harry," I said. "How does time stop for everyone else but remain constant for me? It's all kind of a mystery until we can talk to Akiyama and get the straight dope from the horse's mouth ... or whatever, in an unmixed metaphor way. The truth, I guess." I felt exhausted, probably more from travel and blood loss than the brawl I'd just been in on its own. Nothing felt broken anymore, thanks to Kat, but I definitely had bruises aplenty to show for our most recent squabble with Prettyboy. "All I know is this—if time does that again during a clash with Prettyboy, my goose is probably well and truly cooked, because I was barely holding my own, and I don't think he was even using all his strength."

"I don't envision any more clashes with him soon," Harry said, eyes darting. "Things are ... well, fragile in terms of probabilities, but that one's relatively clear, at least for the next few hours." His lips settled into a thin line.

"And are we still on track for the end of time in the next couple days?" I asked.

With a grudging, almost pained nod, Harry grunted. "Yeah."

"Awesome," Kat said, slumping back in her seat. "I hope I

don't feel this crappy at the end of time, because it'd suck to feel this way into perpetuity." She seemed to give that a thought. "How does that even work? Like a permanent time stop?"

"Looks that way to me," Harry said as we took a turn onto a side road. Like in Britain, everyone was driving on the wrong side of the road, but I didn't have the mental energy to give as much of a damn about it as usual. Or maybe Scotland had simply drained all the relative dread out of it for me. "It's like all probabilities, branching paths, everything that happens normally with my power—it just stops. Everything ends beyond that moment."

"What fun—" Kat started to say, but her words stopped as a flash of light blasted through the cab and I felt like someone had jerked me out of my seat.

I opened my eyes into bright light, blinding almost, and then it faded as a blurry world seemed to coalesce around me.

The back of the cab was gone, the Nagasaki streets were gone, everything I'd experienced a moment ago was gone. In its place was a sterile white room, with a single bed in the hospital style, white sheets covering it. They were clumped and wrinkled, wrapped around a petite figure who lay in the middle of it, a lump on her chest.

Kat. Her blond hair was tangled and matted, and there was a thin veil of relief shining through the weariness on her face, a glow that shone, almost lighting up the small room.

A Japanese nurse stood off to one side, her delicate features showing a faint smile, her hands on the bundle that rested on Kat's chest. "Do you have a name?"

I stared at the lump in Kat's arms, the little bundle wrapped in a blanket, the object of all her attention and—more than I'd ever seen from Kat in all the years I'd known her—her happiness.

"Yes," she said, not taking her eyes off the baby in her arms.

Someone stepped out of the blurring at the edge of my field of vision. Dark hair, taller than me, he stepped over to the bed and leaned over, kissing the baby on the cheek. His back was to me, but his figure oh so familiar.

Harry.

He was looking down at the baby in Kat's arms. I could see over his shoulder, but just the start of his profile, because of the way he was facing. "What should we name him?"

Light flashed again, and the scene in the hospital was gone, the cab returning and the chaotic Nagasaki streets appearing again, Harry in the seat in front of me and Kat to my side. Her face lacked the peace it had held in my vision, and instead her eyes were wide, saucer-wide, moon-wide, and her mouth was slightly open. "What ... the hell was *that*?" she asked, and I had a suspicion—maybe more than a suspicion—that I hadn't been the only one to see the hospital room and what happened there.

"It kinda looked like you and Harry having a baby together," I said, jealousy marring every syllable of my trademark sarcasm. "But that couldn't happen, because of course you were two were never together before, especially in that way, amirite, Kat?"

"Dude," she said, "I told you, if I don't remember it, it didn't happen to me." And at this, she crossed her arms in front of her. Behind that facade, though, her eyes moved around a little more than usual, making me think that maybe—just maybe—this vision had rattled her a little.

"Harry?" I asked, turning my attention to him and probably lashing at him with a tone that demanded explanation.

But Harry had his fingers massaging his forehead with both hands. "What?" he asked, eyes closed.

"Would you care to explain this?" I asked, trying to keep from sounding like the crazy, jealous girlfriend I was heading toward being.

"I don't really have much to say." He kneaded his fingers into his forehead. "I have a headache."

"Isn't that convenient," I grumbled, looking at Kat, who just shrugged at me. I could almost feel her mentally disengaging from what we'd just seen, as though backing away from thinking about it would make it not have happened.

"Having an excruciating headache is not really that convenient, no," Harry said, head still in hand, and his voice sounded ragged enough that I believed it. "I think all this shifting around of events is physically hurting me now. The probabilities change so dramatically after most of these stoppages—thanks mostly to you—but this ... vision thing just now ... man, it really put a mule in my brain and let it double-kick me."

I wanted to be sympathetic, so I bit my tongue and let us ride in silence until Harry waved for the cab driver to pull over. He did so, shaking all the while, and Harry looked at me, eyes still squinting in pain. "It's time," he said.

"Hilarious pun," Kat said, throwing her door open. We'd pulled off in an alley, and the cab driver was muttering low under his breath in what sounded an awful lot like a prayer.

"Hey," I said, trying to be soothing, and putting my hands on the back of his neck. "It's all right. We're not going to hurt you. We were just trying to get away from some yakuza." All true. He didn't exactly loosen up under my grip, though, just kept saying the same things, under his breath.

"I don't think he believes you for some reason," Kat said, a half smile twisting her lips, which lacked their usual red glow and looked faded.

"Which is weird, because I'm such a sincere and warm person," I said, letting my fingers hang on the back of his neck gently. He felt the first strains of my power and tried to jerk away, and here I had to be a little firmer with him. "Just for the record—absorbing peoples' memories sucks and is not nice."

"Kinda like you," Kat said lightly as she pulled my bag and her suitcase out of the back. I found it amusing my 10,000 megawatt reality TV star friend had quietly become my pack mule instead of vice versa. "Because of the soul draining, y'know, and your constant talk about being the Queen of Mean or whatever."

"I think that was Leona Helmsley," I said, neatly dragging the memories of the cab driver's last half hour of absolute terror out of his mind. Not for the first time, I regretted being unable to plant something more pleasant in their place, because if you're going to jack the memories of a person anyway, it doesn't feel like it'd be any worse—and maybe even, ethically, a little better—if you could put some peace back in for them.

Alas, the limitations of being a soul-stealer.

"Well, she's dead, so the crown is probably up for grabs if you want to claim it," Kat said with a shrug, my bag over her shoulder and the telescoping suitcase handle in her hand. "I don't know anyone who's going to fight you for it."

"Remember June Randall, that toxin-cloud spreading meta who shot me in the head in Florida last year? She could have made a run at it before she surrendered," I said, taking the last of the cabbie's memories of us and sliding across the bench and out the door. Harry was already out, leaning against the alley wall behind Kat, bag on his back, studiously ignoring the blond bombshell next to him who'd he'd apparently sired a child with. They might have made a cute couple if not for Kat's pallor, her look reminiscent of someone who'd had recent run-in with a vampire—which she sorta had, of the White Court, soul-stealing variety—and Harry holding his head gingerly, looking like a strong breeze might topple him. We probably looked like a beat-down combo platter from hell.

Stepping out into the alley, I didn't feel so hot, either. A little weak, actually, from all the blood loss. Kat's healing powers were amazing, but they were no panacea, and it wasn't like they could do anything to heal the emotional venom that seemed to be running through my soul right now. I looked to Harry, but he wouldn't look at me, and a part of me questioned whether he really had a headache or whether he just wanted to avoid answering questions.

"Where to?" Kat asked, leading us behind the cab and away from the cabbie, who was starting to come out of the soul-burned stun that my touch tended to leave people in. She was laboring a little under the weight of our bags, and thrust mine out at me.

I took it up on a bloodied shoulder. "I think I need to change before we do anything else." I ran a hand down my front. My shirt was shredded, my pants were shredded, and I was drenched in scarlet as surely as if some anti-fur demonstrators had taken umbrage at my attire. "You know—so we don't attract more attention of the troublesome variety to ourselves."

"Good point," Kat said. With an impish smile she added, "I'm so used to seeing you covered in blood that I don't really notice anymore."

"Ow," I said. "That's harsh. True. But still ... harsh."

She was still smiling, but looked at me sidelong. "Here, this'll make you feel better—red really is your color. Shame about the hair having to change now."

"I know, right?" I nodded. "I may have to make the leap into bright blue or something, cuz my blond disguise got totally yanked when I appeared on national television in Minneapolis to face off with the Predator."

"I'd say auburn, but it's probably too much of a middle ground between your current shade and your natural one," Kat said. "Which is a shame, because it'd totally look great on you. Maybe after this is all over—"

"Ladies?" Harry asked from behind us, and I turned to find him nearly bent double, his eyes hardly open. The cab driver was driving off now, making the turn out onto a main road ahead, whereas we were descending deeper into the alley. There was a slight curve ahead, and I thought it might be a nice place to duck in and change, a few darkly lit doors providing some shelter for a quick clean up. I hoped.

"What's the matter, Harry?" I asked.

"Oh, nothing much," he said, sounding a little strained. "Just—"

And his eyes rolled up, and he keeled over right in the alley, thumping down heavily onto the concrete, where he lay, passed out.

"Damn," Kat said, sounding mildly vexed, "I thought he was faking that headache thing."

"Me too," I said, a little more concerned now. "And also ... damn."

23.

Harry didn't wake up, and there wasn't much we could do to make him. "I think we need to move him," I muttered.

"Yep," Kat said. We were both leaning over him, me trying to avoid even brushing against his skin anywhere he didn't have clothing to protect him. "Especially without anyone to act as lookout, a cop could come wandering into the alley any minute now, and we'd have to explain half-dead Harry, assuming the guy even understood English."

"You speak Japanese, Kat," I said, a brief flash of annoyance welling back up. It brought up the very shallowly buried memory of our recent flashback in time to her and Harry having a baby together. Talk about excavating some confusing-ass feelings in me, especially given that it looked like that had happened decades before I was born.

Strangely ... this did not spur my jealousy any less. Who ever said emotions had to be logical? Because that person was a liar.

"Oh, that's right," Kat said. "I keep forgetting. It's not like I even knew that until today!"

"Feels like you should have realized that before now," I said, grabbing Harry by an arm as she did the same. Thank goodness he was still wearing the same long-sleeved shirt he'd started with in Oregon. It was a little less necessary here in Nagasaki, but not much. More probably, though, he had kept it on because his current girlfriend was a succubus. "Like ... you never heard people speaking Japanese and realized, 'Hey, I know what they're saying'?"

"Maybe I did," she said, taking up position under his other arm as we lifted Harry up, shoulder bag still on his back. He was an easy lift between the two of us and our meta strength, but a little awkward if it was just one of us trying to drag him along. Kat was taller than me, but she wasn't exactly WNBA huge. Her main advantage in the body department over me was those willowy limbs and her very natural curves. Albeit lacking much of an ass, she still seemed to have that hourglass shape most men desired. "Maybe I heard them speaking Japanese and automatically translated it without realizing it."

I tried to shake this bit of nonsense out of my head. "This sucks without Harry to help tell us what to do next."

Kat snickered. "Oh, now you need a man to tell you what to do? What the hell happened to Sienna Nealon?"

"She got her ass kicked by a bunch of prisoners, framed for a crime she committed that was actually self-defense, chased by—"

"Yeah, I know literally what happened to you," Kat said, "because I've been there for most of it and watched the rest from a distance. I was just making a joke."

"Sorry," I said after a moment, as we dragged Harry around a bend in the alley. I could see another road ahead, but this one was less trafficked than the one the cabbie had taken us on before turning down this way. There was another of those alcoves ahead, too, a little carve-out for the back door of a shop or something that'd shelter us from view of the main road while I changed and Kat—I dunno, stood around and looked useful.

"I'm not stepping on your Kool-Aid, by the way," Kat said, and it took a second to realize what she meant by that. "Harry, I mean. I have no interest, okay? If something happened between Klementina," and she said her old name with a little distaste, "and him, it is totally of the past. Harry is not my type."

"I know," I said, a little stiffly. "And I was mostly fine with everything until—" And here she stiffened. "Whatever. This last thing."

"Yeah," Kat said at a near-whisper, and I wondered if she'd still be looking pale even without her most recent draining. She certainly didn't want to look at me just now.

We managed to muscle Harry into the alcove and sat him down. His breathing was still steady, though I wished I could test his pulse myself without touching him bare-skinned. Through the cloth of my sleeve didn't exactly give me a strong reading, though I could tell his heart was obviously beating.

"Here," Kat said, taking up my shoulder bag as I shed it. She unzipped it and pulled it wide open so I could see inside. "I'll hand you what you need so you don't get blood on everything."

"Thanks," I said tightly, "but unless I can clean this off," and I held up my crimson-slicked arms and shoulders, "I dunno that you handing me clean clothes is going to do the trick. It's kinda like throwing good clothes after bad, actually." Which was true; I was coated in blood and unless I washed off, anything I put on was going to be just as soiled and gross as what I was currently wearing, and just as bled through in moments.

"Go ... inside," Harry mumbled under his breath. He let out a little moan and brushed his head with his hand.

I looked at him, then at the door just down the little hallway in our alcove. It was solid but not ridiculously so. I could kick it in pretty easily, or maybe even just break the handle and walk in. Kat looked at me and shrugged, so I strode over and tried the knob. It clicked as I broke the guts of the lock, and I opened the door.

Freezing in the frame, I listened, but didn't hear anything inside. Creeping in, I found myself in a shop that had yet to open for the day. Rugs and such were draped everywhere, and I decided we could take a moment here as I passed a bathroom.

"Okay, let's get off the street," I said to Kat, beckoning her in from the alley. She grabbed Harry under the arms and dragged him in, dumping him unceremoniously in the dark, rear hall where we entered.

"Let's hurry," Kat whispered as she closed the door to the

alley. "I don't want to B and E here any longer than we have to."

"Heh," I said, stepping into the bathroom and clicking on the light. It cast a soft glow, and I looked at myself in the mirror. "'B and E' spells 'be', but also stands for breaking and entering. You are occasionally quite clever, Kat."

"Huh, what?" Kat asked. "Oh. I didn't even get that second meaning."

I worked the sink, cleaning myself off as quickly and carefully as I could. Fully aware that this was going to be a crime scene at some point in the near future, I didn't concern myself with anything but getting done as quickly as possible. I used paper towels to sponge the blood off myself as Kat stood out in the hall, watching me with barely veiled nervousness. "Here," she said after a couple minutes, "let me help," and she started tugging my shirt off.

"I can dress myself, you know!"

"You've got blood all over your back," she said, winning the tug of war and shredding my shirt in the process. Just as well, when was I going to wear it again, given its current state? She took a step back, surveying me. "You're going to have to lose that bra, too. How is it that you look like you're lactating blood?"

I looked down at myself. She wasn't wrong, but it still annoyed me enough to slash back. "I don't know. How is it that you eat like a wolverine and I can still see your ribs with your shirt off?"

"I could totally eat like a wolverine right now," she said, grabbing a paper towel and starting on my shoulders, dabbing and rubbing.

She hit a rough patch of tender flesh. "Ow. Owww. OW! OWWWW!" I said, retreating from her.

"And how is it that you can get almost thrown through a wall and not whine, but here I am trying to clean you off and you get all whingey," she said, not letting up.

"Dude," I said, imitating her, "when I get thrown through a wall, it happens fast, like 'blink and you miss it.' This is happening the opposite of fast. This is happening like Akiyama has stopped time in a moment of high pain for me." I cringed. "Geez."

Kat got a little quiet. "So this is the guy from back in the war? The one you went to meet in St. Paul the night …" Her voice trailed off.

"Yeah," I said, finishing it for her. "The night my mom died." The night I figured out how to unleash my succubus powers and survive a fall from a plane. The night I killed the Wolfe brothers, Grihm and Frederick.

The night I figured out how to win the war.

But mostly … the night my mom died.

"Does it feel like it's been a million years since then?" Kat asked, being a little more gentle and a little less steel-wool with her scrubbing. "I mean … that Weissman guy that was hounding us back then. I feel like I haven't seen his dirty, leering face for lifetimes. That I remember things from … back when Omega first scooped me up in the fifties better than I remember those days."

"Well, I imagine your ascent to blinding fame has caused a dilation effect in time," I said dryly. "And thus, everything before you became a superstar seems long ago and painful, like a distant nightmare after you've woken up."

"You such a heinous bitch sometimes," Kat said, smiling at me in the mirror. She was clearly taking my ribbing in the spirit it was (mostly) intended. "I'm glad I never had to actually fight you."

"There was that time I punched you in the face in front of Bastet."

"That was not a fight. One-punching me does not count as a fight."

"You did fold pretty quick on that one."

I could see the trace of a smile on her in the mirror. "Janus told me to take it easy on you."

I felt a little scandalized, holding a bloodied paper towel against what was now a mere angry welt on my abdomen, but which had probably held a sliver of glass a few minutes ago. "You sandbagged me?"

Her smile twisted her lips, like it was trying to escape. "I mean … you hit *hard*, but you didn't exactly throw out your A game at me that time."

"Ohhhh!" I paused in my cleaning. "You are so lucky I like you now or I would show you my A game up close in the face, right now." I let slip a smile of my own. Why hadn't it always been this easy with Kat?

Oh, right. Because I was short, dark-haired, pale, socially awkward, and my touch killed people, while she was tall, blonde, tanned, beloved by all, and her touch healed people and made men shudder with joy and not agony. Why, it was practically written in the stars that we had to be rivals back in our high-school-ish years.

"You know," I said, soberly, working on another bloody patch on my stomach, "you probably shouldn't have helped me back there."

Her forehead creased so hard that dermatologists all over the world would have salivated at the mere sight of it. Relax, boys, in a minute it'll go back to flawless, put the Botox down. "Are you out of your mind? You needed help. You could have died back there."

"Yeah, but," I said, voice a little tight, "you got seen on camera, Kat. It's possible that right now they're building a case against you for aiding and abetting—"

"Pfffft," she said, dismissive. "Who cares? I've got lawyers to deal with that."

I stopped her, turning around to look at her in the tiny bathroom in a shop in Nagasaki that we'd broken into. How many crimes had we committed today? Enough that even super-celeb Kat could be in real trouble if she got caught. "I'm serious, Kat. Just look at us—"

She stared at me, taking me in with one look, and her lip quirked in amusement. "You, half-naked in a Japanese bathroom, and me, washing you off like an actual cat? Yeah, I'm pretty sure meta fanboy loins would be combusting like sticks rubbed together at meta-speed if there was footage of this."

"Not what I meant," I said, "and also—awkward. There are meta fanboys?"

"Totally," she said with a hard nod. "There's slash fic of us out there on the net. My agent told me about it."

"Slash ... what?"

"I think I see what you're getting at," Kat said, and she resumed her cleaning of a blood-gash-turned-red-welt on my shoulder. "But you don't have to worry."

"I think I worry more because you're not worrying at all," I said. "There could be real consequences for you here, Kat. I've dragged you into something serious and dangerous and—"

"Worse than that time I helped you fight the hundred strongest metas in the world, who wanted to kill us all?" A flash of amusement lit her pretty features, but she didn't stop rubbing a crust of blood off my shoulder. "Or more dangerous than the time the president was trying to mind-control the entire planet, and I had to help spearhead the rebellion against him because all our other friends had already gone full Stepford?"

"More personally perilous to you, maybe," I said, wishing she wouldn't just brush this off. "Kat ... you could go to prison for this. Any of this."

"If I do," Kat said, "I'm going to end up queen of that place. I will have so many bitches," she was smirking, "you have no idea. They will not see me coming. Because I totally do know how to throw a punch, an epic one. Not quite Sienna-level devastation, but it will knock those chicas over."

I found myself laughing, the bathroom ringing with it, echoing in the confined space. And it hurt a little, because my ribs weren't entirely mended. "Ohhh," I said once I'd mostly gotten it out, "why can't you take this seriously?"

"For the same reason you keep fighting," Kat said, and she was serious now, save for that trace of a smile. She looked up at me with those bright green eyes, and I could see the soul-deep conviction. "You save the world, Sienna. And you save people. Jail? Pffft. Small price to pay for doing the right thing on the scale you do. I'd take a few years of prison if that's what it means to do the right thing." She put her head down again as she looked at my chest. "Seriously, lactating blood. Did you lose an entire nipple under there? What the hell happened under these straps and—also, we need to introduce you to some actual lingerie type stuff, because this 'softer side of Sears' crap might as well be manufactured by

Craftsman. I know that you have no need of any man, ever, but—come on. You have a boyfriend now, you could be thinking about dressing for him at least a little."

What the hell do you even say to that? "Hey, it hasn't exactly put a damper on my sex life, okay?"

Kat rolled her eyes and tossed a bloody paper towel. "That's because you're in the honeymoon phase. And if you're wearing this during the honeymoon phase, I shudder to think what you'll be wearing if you make it a couple more months. We're talking full-on green goo face mask at night, curlers in the hair—"

"My hair is naturally curly. I use a straightener."

"My point," she said, "is you need to go all Justin Timberlake and 'Bring Sexy Back,' girl. Immediately. We'll find a Victoria's Secret after this is over and get this," she snapped my shoulder strap, causing me to get a very offended look on my face, because it stung, "taken care of." Then she hunched over and started to work on a spot on my side that was coated in red.

"Fanboy pants, exploding all over," I muttered, turning back to the mirror. There really was a lot of blood here, and eventually I was going to have to wash my hair, because I could see the crust all in it. Which would, in turn, require me to spend at least a few minutes putting it up. "And Kat ..."

She did not look up from where she was scrubbing just above my left kidney. "Yeah?"

I paused, feeling a swelling sense of gratitude. "Thank you."

I couldn't see her face, but I could hear the smile in her voice. "You're welcome."

24.

Jamal

Ray Spiegel didn't waste a lot of time getting the hell out of the coffee shop once our little conversation was over. We watched him go, and I was left with that sinking feeling that not only had this not gone our way, but it had gone really, really the wrong way, the really, really not in our favor way—

"Yo," Augustus said, nodding as Spiegel disappeared out the lobby door, "I think that went really well."

I turned my head to look at him over the empty black, shiny tabletop between us. Spiegel had formed the third point of our little triangle, and now that he was gone, I felt like I was drowning in the black table area between my brother and I. "How ... do you figure that?" I asked, sounding a little choked even to my own ears.

"We laid our thangs down with that dude," Augustus said with limitless self-assurance that sprang from ... hell, I had no idea where it sprang from. If I could have struck it with lightning like a tree right then, I would have, because it was the same crazy impatience that had caused me to almost get smushed by a thrown car only this morning. "He knows where we stand."

"Yeah, that's not good," I said.

Augustus's brow puckered as he looked at me. "How is that not good?"

"The dude who reports back to the people we're trying to

extract the truth from," I said, spelling it out for him as my heart thudded in my ears like thunder, "now knows that we're after them, and what for. Our element of surprise is gone."

"Pffft," Augustus dismissed me. "Our element of surprise was gone the moment Whitey McDudebro called us at our hotel and offered to meet us downstairs for a chat two seconds after we blew into town." Augustus sat forward, and my growing horror was centered on the fact that not only did he think he'd done no wrong, but he was stubbornly refusing to consider he'd made even the slightest whoopsie by giving away ... oh, I dunno ... EVERYTHING.

"He had suspicions, then," I said, trying to keep calm but mentally panicking. "Now he *knows*. Big difference."

"Oh, yeah?" Augustus asked, settling back in his seat with a gleam of triumph in his eye. "And who's he going to tell about that? And when do you reckon he'll be talking to them about it?"

"Probably the people responsible, and right freaking now—" I started to say, then, *whump*, a thought occurred.

My brother was grinning. He actually beat me to this one—for once.

I lifted my phone and sparked against the connector. I'd pinged Ray Spiegel's phone before to try and get a feeler for if he was down here, and that latent connection meant I could look for him as he moved from the wi-fi in the coffee shop to the 4G network just outside. It only took me a millisecond to catch up to his digital footprint and find—

Well, shit. Boy had pretty much no network security on his phone, which gave me an open pipeline right in. I caught him just as he was dialing somebody and could hear the digital call in my head, transported there by the little pulses of electricity, digital ones and zeroes that magically transmuted the spoken word through the air.

"Hey, it's Ray," Spiegel said. "I just got out of the meeting with them."

The voice that answered him was calm, kinda old, too. "How did it go?"

Spiegel seemed like he was ready to chuckle. "They're ...

stubborn. Changing their minds is not going to happen. They're convinced you've got some magical evidence that will exonerate—well, you know." A pause. "You, uh ... don't happen to have any magical evidence of that, do you?" He broke into a laugh.

"Surprisingly not," the older man said. I was guessing it was Charles Custis, the patriarch of this little family affair. "Hard to come up with something that doesn't exist." Man, he was a casual liar. Good at it, too, and the smoothness of his voice helped. "What's your gut on this? They're going to hang around town for a while, being a nuisance?"

"Yep," Spiegel said. "I wouldn't be surprised if they came to talk to you next. The younger one, Augustus ... he has all the patience of a bull in a china shop. No subtlety. He'll come right at you, because he thinks you're a *bad guy*," and he made his voice all scare quotey for that one.

"I'm not sorry to disappoint him," Custis said on the other end of the line, a little tense. "But I am sorry that he's not going to just take our word for it."

"What are you going to do?"

"I figure we should talk about that," Custis said. "Face to face. Meet me at the parking lot of that Walmart out in Arlington. One hour?"

"I've got a deadline later today," Spiegel said, and he sounded like he was wheedling. "This is a non-story right now. I need something for publication."

Custis didn't even hesitate. "I have something you could write up. I'll send it over. It's pretty juicy, too—all the right whispers of scandal. It seems a certain freshman congresswoman from Colorado is having an affair with a more senior one from North Dakota. All on deep background, of course, but there are pictures. See you in an hour?"

"But you're going to send this over first?" Spiegel asked.

"It'll be in your inbox in moments," Custis said. "Anything more sensitive—and there's a little more—needs to be talked about face to face."

"I'll be there," Spiegel said, and the hum of a car engine coming to life flared through his end of the speaker. "See you in an hour."

"See you there," Custis said, and hung up.

"... Earth to Jamal Coleman," my brother was saying as I dropped out of the conversation. I was still sitting in the coffee shop, blinking out of the haze from my digital eavesdrop. It was tough to pay attention to what was going on around me while I was decoding that, mentally. "We going to go elsewhere to eat, or do I need to go get some biscotti to take the edge off the rumblings?" He rubbed his stomach.

"Yeah, we can ..." I shook my head, trying to clear the digital fog. "I got a lead on something. We should go."

Augustus stood. "Go? Go where?"

"There's a meet," I said, going meta-low with my voice. "One hour. One of the Custis family—the dad—promised Spiegel a scoop if he'd come meet and talk about us. I'm thinking we should be there for this one."

"Ooh, I like the sound of this," Augustus actually rubbed his palms together in anticipation. "Let's bust some heads."

I shook mine. "No busting heads. Spiegel just told Custis you're going to come at them head on, and he's right. We need to play this cool."

"Pffft, shit," Augustus said, dismissing me in one movement, "who needs subtle when long and strong gets right to the answer?"

I wanted to thud my head against the table until it popped open and my brains spilled out, freeing me of having to think about where he'd gotten that turn of phrase from, and what exactly he was fully suggesting by it. "Why do you always go dumb when you're with me?"

My brother bristled. "Explain yourself."

"You're a college student, Augustus," I said, locking eyes with him. "Your grades are solid. You're not dumb, but anytime we get paired up, all the sudden your brains go out the window, and it's like you're all gonads, man. Wild animal shit. What's up with that?"

"Because you bore the hell out of me," Augustus said, looking just as pissed at me as I was at him. "You overthink everything. I'm all right with thinking, but you just—you don't *do* anything, Jamal. You want to sit back and carefully consider the problem," his voice got effete and mocking, "and poke at it from all angles, and think—think really hard—consider—maybe possibly someday think about doing something other than just *thinking* about it—"

"Don't knock thinking it through," I said snippily, "because it keeps you from getting wiped by a hurled car."

"Man, whatever," Augustus said, and it seemed to be his way of closing the topic of conversation as he stood. "Let's go to this meet. Stop off at a Wawa on the way."

"Fine," I said, getting up. "But when this thing goes down, you got to promise me you're not going to go charging in like a madman. These people aren't stupid. We need to hang back, listen, gather—"

"Yeah, okay," Augustus said, and off he went toward the door, just turning his back on me like I didn't matter. I stared after him for a long second. The days of being together, being partnered? They were wearing on us both, I guess. It was like twenty-odd years of us being brothers was all coming to a head now. A loggerhead, at least. Twenty-plus years of differences, and now was the moment we started to really take that baggage and batter at each other with it.

Damn. Talk about timing.

But what other play did we have but to go on, in spite of it? I just shook my head again at our stupidity, and followed my brother out, on the way to this meeting between the bad guys.

25.

Sienna

Cleaned, scrubbed, shining, hair somewhat straightened in the short bit of time I had, and with some of Kat's cosmetics applied and feeling slightly like a geisha girl because her color wheel was not my color wheel, we made our way down to the Nagasaki docks. It was a slow journey, especially with Harry still unsteady on his feet, but he'd at least regained consciousness enough that he could lean on me and it only looked like he was slightly drunk, no more need to carry him on my shoulders.

"You going to make it there, cowboy?" Kat asked, walking a few paces ahead of us, luggage rolling behind and two bags hung over her shoulders.

"I would like time to resume its normal shape," Harry said, sounding very much like a guy with a hangover, voice scratchy and his entire body carrying the manner of a weary, weary man. "And stop ripping up my brain as everything changes."

"Working on it," I said under my breath, his arm heavy on my shoulders. Not so heavy it was tough to bear the weight, but still—I could feel the added pounds draped across me. "It'd go quicker if you could walk under your own power."

"I wish I could," Harry said, a trace of longing in his words. "But I'm a little worried that I'm going to go tumbling off a dock if I try." And he eyed the water to either side as we walked over the slatted boards, Kat's roller suitcase thumping its wheels at the joints where each met.

The docks smelled of sea and fish, that salty, stinky aroma I'd forever associate with certain ports I'd visited in Alaska. Juneau, Seward—pretty places, at least in summer. This was like that, not so very different save for variations in the style of boats and the utter lack of snow. I sighed, bearing Harry's weight across my shoulders. I tried to make it look natural, like he was just showing me some affection, but it probably looked more like *Weekend at Bernie's* than a date.

There were some rocks and such out in the water, the topography reminding me a lot of Cannon Beach back in Oregon, though the supervillain island rocks were not nearly so foreboding here. Ahead, I could see some of those rising rock formations coming out of the water, way beyond this place where all the fishing boats were moored. "Harry? Any suggestions?" I asked.

"Keep going," he said, voice evincing strain. "Up ahead, there's a guy we should talk to. Or Kat should. You and I should keep our mouths shut, and you should keep your head down."

"Great advice for life," Kat chirped. "Everybody else shut up and keep their heads down, and let Kat do the talking."

"I agree it sounds like a great idea for a shopping strategy if you want to spend tons of money," I snarked back, "but for everything else, I should probably be involved."

"This guy up here," Harry said, nodding at a fisherman just a few boats ahead. He was walking around the dock doing ... I didn't really know what he was doing, not being that familiar with boats or sea-man-guy kind of things. He was raising the topsail, for all I knew. Except his boat didn't actually have sails.

"You want to take a crack at this?" Kat asked, turning to smirk back at me.

"Oh, very funny," I said. "I don't even know what to say."

"Do not talk to him until we're in the boat and offshore," Harry said, looking at me very seriously, "and even then, it'd be better if you didn't say anything or make eye contact, because he will recognize you if you give him enough time."

"Then why are we using this guy?" I asked. "We should go with someone who won't recognize me."

Harry grunted, taking up a little more of his weight as he turned on me, and I saw a flash of impatience in his eyes as he looked down at me. "There's no one on Earth who won't recognize you if given enough time. Your disguises aren't going to work much longer, Sienna. You've been seen in too many of them, and you're famous worldwide."

"Brand recognition," Kat singsonged under her breath.

"Well, that sounds grim," I said, a little taken aback, and—dare I say it?—humbled. "What happens if he recognizes me?"

"He'll inform the Nagasaki police when he gets back to the dock. And since he's the one who'll have dropped us off, he knows exactly where to find us." Harry's strain showed through in his current annoyance, which was unlike I'd seen from him before. "So, I hate to say this, because I know how much you love people telling you what to do, but ... please sit down and shut up once we're on the boat. I'll do likewise, and we'll play like we're totally in love and oblivious to the world, and he'll actively avert his gaze out of discomfort at our PDA and never be the wiser that you were on his boat."

My face was burning. "Fine," I said tightly. "We can do that, and I'll do my level best not to accidentally take your soul in the process."

"Much appreciated," he said with some tightness of his own, as he turned to follow Kat again. She had already hailed the fisherman, speaking to him in Japanese.

I hung back with Harry as she spoke to him and leaned in close to his face as he put his arm over my other shoulder. Now we looked like we were embracing, though I suspected my body language hinted that I'd rather have shoved him off of me and gotten far, far from him right now. "Seriously, this affection thing right now? It's—"

"Going to be a real acting effort," Harry said, taking the words right out of my mouth. "Don't I know it."

"Oh, are you pissed at me right now?" I asked, meeting his gaze sharply. "Because I feel like I've kinda got the high ground here, what with certain recent revelations—"

"I'm not mad at you, no," Harry said, but everything about his manner said this was a lie, "but I can certainly feel the tension in the air from your direction, and it's not making things any easier during what's already the single most stressful time of my life."

I started to snap a response to that, something along the lines of, "Oh, is this a stressful time for you? Must be a walk in the park for me!" but Kat interrupted, coming over from where she'd had a chat with the boat guy.

"Hey, you guys," Kat said nonchalantly, clearly trying to gloss past our little snit. "The uhm ... driver? He says he knows the place, and he's agreed to take us there for a lot of money. Like, hundreds of thousands of yen."

"A hundred thousand yen is only a thousand dollars," Harry said with a frown.

"Oh," Kat said, then shrugged. "I can cover that, then. I guess I'll pay him and we can go. But he said can't come back and get us until late in the day, after he's done his fishing, so ..."

"Got it, it's a one-way trip—for now," I said tightly, tearing my eyes off Harry but keeping close to him, as ordered, his arm draped over my shoulder, and not for support, this time. "Let's get this ship of fools underway."

We loaded up, stepping onto the old fishing boat without further ado. I managed to find a quiet spot with Harry on a worn old cushion, and we sat down, Harry still staring off into the distance and me trying to avoid his gaze without attracting the attention of the fisherman. I didn't even dare look at him too closely, instead paying attention to the busyness of the docks or Harry, when I dared to look at him.

The boat got underway a few minutes later, Kat taking up the responsibility of distracting the fisherman pretty seriously. I heard her laugh at something he said, and I could tell she was turning on the full flirt, vintage Kat. She did well in those situations, and the funny thing was, if I'd been doing what she was trying to do? I couldn't have pulled it off. I'd tried to talk to guys who I wasn't interested in in the past, to distract or keep them busy, and it generally didn't work because people had a knack for figuring out if you ... well, weren't remotely interested in them.

It could have been that Kat was way better at feigning sincerity than I was, but I had a more likely explanation after knowing her for years:

Kat was genuinely interested in people, at least up to a point. She was probably asking the fisherman questions out of genuine curiosity. It was another way we different; once you got past the newly-ish painted Valley Girl persona she'd adopted, she had an actual like for the masses of humanity.

Meanwhile, her polar opposite, over here sitting in my chair? I had a love for humanity, enough to want to protect and save it, but "like," on an individual basis? Meh. I tolerated most people, and by "tolerate," I mean, "didn't murder them all on sight."

I let out a breath I didn't know I was holding as Kat laughed, her soft coos echoing over the outboard motor thrumming as we put out to sea and left the docks behind. Just another massive contrast between Kat and I.

Glancing at Harry, I saw his eyes move, darting toward me just for a second. "Yeah, you guys are different," he said, as though helpfully confirming my own thoughts for me.

"Gee, thanks for that searing insight," I said. "That's a mighty hot take there."

He rolled his eyes a little. "I don't know why you think I'd be interested in Klementina, especially over you."

It kind of stung when he said it as baldly as that. "Gee, Harry, what would give me the idea that you might ever have been interested in Kat?"

He didn't cringe, but one of his eyes fluttered, and his lip curled at the corner. "Incomplete information."

My jaw dropped slightly. "Well, complete it for me, then," I said, more than a little hotly, but fortunately still meta-low. I saw Kat's shoulders tighten in the wheelhouse of the small fishing boat, and I knew she was hearing our conversation, every word of it, even over the engine.

"That's not going to lead anywhere we want to go right now," Harry said, his words thick with stress. He kept his arm around me, but he looked so tense that it seemed like it'd take a jackhammer to get his muscle groups to release.

I clammed up in favor of saying something I'd probably regret later. And not even much later; more like after I heard the words leave my lips. I sat like that for a good while, the sun crawling up overhead and the boat revving up as the fisherman took us what looked to my eyes like south, though the sun was now high enough it was getting harder to tell.

An hour passed without a word exchanged, and still we maintained our close proximity. It was painful being this near to Harry and having him silent, almost resentfully so right now. It felt like he could have said something, anything, to defuse the tension, but he stayed dead quiet.

Part of me wanted to brain him, just to see if that would get him to make a noise, but instead I settled back and listened to the interminable sound of the engine running and Kat making steady conversation with the fisherman in Japanese. I didn't understand a damned word of it, but she had him talking now. Laughing, too, occasionally. Damn, she was a master at this.

No wonder Harry had been interested in her.

The boat slowed as we approached an island. It had kinda crept up on us, and I hadn't realized it was our destination until we turned, making an unmistakable beeline for it. It wasn't what I expected, like an empty island with palm trees or tiki torches or—I dunno, Easter Island heads.

It was like a full-on, developed island, with a crumbling six-story building on the edge immediately facing us like the bow of a ship. The windows were empty, some of them broken by time or maybe rocks thrown by passing vandals. The facade was crumbling, and beyond it I could see other buildings on the island, which stretched maybe a half-mile or so. It was a full-on industrial complex, and it almost looked like a ship rising out of the water and from the horizon, until I realized what it actually was.

"Holy shit," I muttered under my breath, "Akiyama really does have his own island."

Harry just grunted, drawing another fantasy out of me in which I slapped the back of his head and got him to cough up some intelligible and soothing conversation. If he read this as a possible future, however, he did not mention it, which was probably wise on his part.

A small dock, the boards deteriorating, waited before us as we puttered up, the engines making a fraction of their usual rumble as the fisherman steered us expertly up against it. Staring at the dock, I realized this was going to be a little dicey. There were a few boards missing, and those that were still there looked rotted and unstable.

"Okay," Harry said, studying them for a second. "I'll go first. Follow me exactly."

He jumped up on the edge of the boat and landed on the dock a few planks in. It squealed under his weight, but after he steadied himself, he leapt to the next, and I started to follow, bag slung over my shoulder.

Kat was wrapping up with the fisherman, exchanging some kind parting with him in Japanese. I hopped after Harry, taking great care to follow him exactly. "Klementina," he called over his shoulder, not looking back, "fourth board, and mind your suitcase."

"Don't call me that," Kat said, irritation just flooding out. I heard her jump behind me, though, and the board caught her, squeaking.

"Eyes front, Ms. Succubus," Harry called over his shoulder, and it took me a second to realize he was talking to me. He must have avoided using my name to keep the fisherman from hearing it. "Don't look back now."

I followed Harry's lead to the concrete quay, letting loose a breath I'd been holding when my feet touched solid ground and left behind the moldering planks. Harry reached out a hand and caught mine, just briefly, yanking me forward. I didn't look back, and heard the boat's engines rev up as the fisherman started to leave.

"Don't touch me," Kat said, her final hop bringing her down next to me. She waved off Harry's helping hand and set the roller suitcase down, telescoped the handle, then flipped her hair, looking pretty put out. Not by having to come here, but because of Harry, I suspected. "What now?" she asked me, in a considerably nicer voice. Kinda confirmed my suspicions.

"Work our way to the interior of the island until we find

Akiyama, I guess." I looked around now that the boat was pulling away, and since Harry didn't stop me, I figured I was probably safe to do so. I felt a little weird seeing the boat head off, cutting through the mild chop, the fisherman's back turned to us, off to ply his trade while we ... lurked on an abandoned island. "When is he coming back for us?"

"He'll drop by tonight," Kat said, looking a little forlornly at the boat. "If we're here waiting, he'll pick us up. Otherwise, he said he'd pass by tomorrow morning and again tomorrow night. I didn't negotiate any farther than that, but I got the feeling he wasn't going to come looking if we weren't at the dock."

"Smart move on his part," I said, taking a breath and looking up again. From where we stood, the quay rose into a road that led past the edge of the building before us. No entrance to said building waited on this side, though a bunch of windows looked down at us, all of them empty and dark, kinda spooky. "I'm guessing Akiyama is behind the ghost stories. Probably wanted to dissuade people from stopping by. Makes me wonder what he did to dissuade them from—"

A belligerent shout from somewhere ahead caused me to jerk my head around. There was nothing there, just the dying cry echoing through the island's buildings, coming toward us from somewhere ahead, up the winding path that led up the hill into the island's interior.

"I guess we're about to find out," I muttered to Kat, then turned to find her—

Frozen. A quick look confirmed that Harry, too, was trapped in time, face stuck in wide-eyed surprise, looking up for the source of the howl.

And here I was, standing on the edge of a dock on a mystery island in Japan, the howl of someone supremely pissed off the only thing waiting for me ahead ... and time frozen around me.

26.

Akiyama

He heard voices.

Sometimes they reached him on the wind. Fishermen, passing too close to the island, their outboard motors an affront to his ears and peace, to nature itself. He would listen to them, trying to find his inner calm, but … it was seldom to found in the face of such disruption.

Most had gotten the message long ago: stay away from his island. It had taken concerted effort, but he'd managed, creating the illusion through long practice that something unpleasant waited here. Some *o-bakemono*, a ghost or fearsome spirit, unreconciled to the modern era.

But every once in a while … someone needed to learn the lesson afresh. The voices alerted him. His patience had waned long ago, and the outboard motor sounded like grinding metal in his head.

Shin'ichi Akiyama had long striven to be a patient man, but even such men had their limits. He climbed the ruined stairs, as he did every morning and evening for sunrise and sunset, but this time he rose prompted only by the noise of that engine. He needed to see in order to do what needed to be done, to scare the fishermen away from these shores. It should not be difficult; they would be a little distance off, and he could dissuade them with but a display of—

But no. This fisherman was not a distance off at all. He was at the very dock, and three people, Westerners—*gaijin*—were stepping off the boat and onto the dock.

He blinked in disbelief. Could it be …? No. He saw no sign of Weissman, who had been his only visitor in recent memory. Others of his kind had come, too, but … he had turned them all away. Politely, of course. They lacked the power that he and Weissman shared, and thus Weissman had gained an audience and they'd come to their accord. No one else made it past the docks.

The others had been his friends and acquaintances from the days of old. These, though …

They looked like children, Akiyama thought dimly, his patience at its end. The slipping was getting worse, and he could feel it, fraying at his decency. Was there any feeling more terrible than that pitted helplessness that settled like darkness in the belly? These Westerners, these children—they were an inconvenience to be dealt with, he thought darkly as they skipped across the rotted dock boards, showing their metahuman power by their dexterousness.

Akiyama leapt from the height and calmed the flow of time just as he was about to hit the ground. It took the pain out of the landing, slowing his movement to a halt before he could crash upon the pavement, and he stepped as easily down as if he'd descended one last stair. That done, he stalked down the path toward the Westerners, letting out a shout as he came over the hill.

Out of patience, he threw his hand out. They stopped as if he'd covered them in ice, from the blond on one side to the sagging man on the other. He ignored the dark-haired one in their middle and turned from them, his task complete. His mind was on other things—the slipping feeling, after all, was much more concerning.

Akiyama stalked back up the slope, mind whirling. This would need to be dealt with soon. His mind felt sluggish, and he racked his memory—the slipping was recent, was it not? Had it been going on long? The days, they ran together. He passed the courtyard and into the door to the building where he spent his time without even noticing.

He was moving back toward the room when he heard

something behind him. Akiyama froze as surely as if he were one of those Westerners he'd paused in time. He listened, just for a moment, and heard the sound again —

The scuff of a shoe against tile.

Whirling, Akiyama found himself staring into the face of the dark-haired one. She wore a t-shirt and jeans, her hair slightly mussed and her jaw clenched. He said nothing, unsure of what he even could say. There, was, after all, a pale, dark-haired girl in front of him, which was …

Impossible.

He stared at her, and she stared back, until finally, she broke the silence with a simple introduction that seemed to spear his already-whirling mind with further incredulity.

"Hi," the dark-haired girl said. "I'm Sienna. It's nice to see you again, Shin'ichi."

27.

Sienna

Akiyama looked pretty gobsmacked when I walked up and called him by name. My words echoed through the building where we stood. Curiously, the signs of time's wrath weren't as obvious here as they were on the rest of the island. It was almost as though stepping into this building was like stepping back in time. The interior wasn't exactly flawless, but it didn't show nearly the weathering and decay that the exterior did; within these walls, the chairs, furniture, and other stuff were clean and untouched, decorating a functional, albeit slightly foreign (to me) outdated doctor's waiting area.

Fury glowed in Akiyama's eyes now, as the shock passed, and he jutted a hand at me, palm-first, from across the room. It looked violent, like he was lashing out at me, and by instinct alone I made a defensive move, as though trying to block him.

It wasn't necessary; nothing happened. He looked at me, not a hint of recognition in his eyes, then muttered something in Japanese that carried a hint of self-satisfaction as I stood there, staring at him.

"I don't speak Japanese," I said, and he nearly jumped in surprise. "Kat does, but you kinda froze her, so—"

He thrust his hand at me again, barking something unintelligible, his face pinched into a hard scowl. His black hair was cropped short, but a little whorl threatened to cover the middle of his forehead, swaying as he pushed that hand at me again. I got it this time, his hand motion, and nodded. "Ohhh," I said, "you're trying to freeze me in time, like the others. I don't think that's going to work."

His mouth fell slightly open, and he started to speak. It came out a) Japanese, and b) very scratchy, and he seemed to realize this after a second, because he stopped, cleared his throat, covering his mouth to do so (so polite), and then said, "Who are you?"

"I already told you," I said, "I'm Sienna Nealon."

He cocked his head at me. "Who?"

My shoulders sagged. "Famous the world over except for right freaking here, of course, where it would be needed most." I tapped myself in the middle of the breastbone. "Sienna Nealon. Sienna." His eyes were blank, devoid of recognition. "Superhero? Pain in the ass? ... Nothing?" I looked around, searching for a way to break through this introduction business, and a fragment of our first conversation—well, my first, anyway—came back to me. I sighed, looked at the carpet—which was really worn, much older looking than the rest of the room—and raised my head again. "Sienna Nealon. The girl in the box."

That got him to drop some of the hostility and aggressive lack of understanding. "You ... are the girl in the box?"

Yeah. Figures that'd get through. "I have been so-called ... by others," I said. "Long story. Listen ... we need to talk."

"You ... have time powers?" He suddenly seemed a lot more solicitous. Calmer now, as though he were now curious about me rather than enraged.

"Ah, no ..." I said, "... at least not any I can control." I frowned. "Or I didn't, before. But now, suddenly I'm able to stand fast in the middle of these sudden time freezes, and it just sorta flows around me so—I dunno. I guess I have time powers *now*, though I have no idea how I got them—"

"You cannot ... speed things up?" Akiyama asked, staring at me with that suspicion again. "Slow them down?"

"I ... don't think so?" I asked, though now I was not entirely sure of anything. I'd just assumed that these time freezes were happening independent of me and were somehow related to our destined meeting. "I've never controlled time before."

He nodded, once. "This makes sense. I have not felt you make adjustments to the flow of time."

"And you would have, wouldn't you?" I asked. "Because you knew when Weissman did."

His face got stony. "Weissman. That is a name I have not heard in some time. Nor have I felt his touch upon the turning wheel of time."

"You wouldn't," I said, "because he's dead."

Akiyama cocked his head. "You were ... a friend of his?"

"Ugh, God no," I said, almost ready to spit. "I hated that bastard. I would have killed him myself if I could have managed it, but ... my mother did instead."

Akiyama's eyebrow raised. "Your mother ... possessed the power to control the flow of time?"

"No," I said, wondering how lightly I should tapdance around the word "succubus" given how universally reviled we'd been among old-school metas. "She was ... something else."

A cloud settled over his face. "Then how did she defeat Weissman?"

Here's where we were going to hit the first sticky wicket. "Uhm ... you helped her do so. I'm not sure how, but I think you suspended his powers around her."

Akiyama stared at me, and I wondered if he was going to bust out with, "I did not!" or some similar denial that I was going to have to argue through. Credit to him, though, he didn't. "Did I indeed?" he asked, still suspicious, but not flatly arguing against it. "I find this ..."

"Unlikely? Impossible?" I suggested. "Because that's kinda how I felt about it when you came to me in St. Paul seven years ago and said we'd met before—even though I didn't remember it. You said a lot of things I couldn't reconcile at the time—you called me 'the Girl in the Box,' explained the concept of *hakoiri musume*, knew things about me that you shouldn't have, told me about Nagasaki and St. Paul being sister cities—that one's never won me a Trivial Pursuit game yet, but maybe someday—and you helped my mom kill Weissman and save my life." I blinked a few times after spitting all that out. "Oh, and you gave me a bonsai, though it was tragically lost in one of a series of innumerable explosions that seem to follow me around like a dog following someone with bacon in their pocket. Still, nice gesture, and I didn't kill it myself, so …"

I had a feeling that I'd just tried to force-feed Akiyama information through a firehose. I settled back, waiting to see what he might need clarification on—or if I was going to have to repeat the whole thing again—but he just watched me with his dark eyes, thinking it all through.

Finally, he said, "It could be as you say, though I do not see how from here."

"It's pretty simple," I said, folding my arms in front of me. "You told me at the time that I perform some great act of service for you here." I looked around the waiting room, trying to figure out what exactly I could do to help this guy. "And that puts you in my debt. So …" I looked at him. "Whaddya need?"

Akiyama surveyed me with a wary eye, a very peculiar change over his somewhat skeptical curiosity from a moment before. I stood there, trying to be as lacking expression as him, but failing, as I waited for him to process my question and deliver me an answer so we could go on about the business of trading favors and saving the world.

"I … am fine," Akiyama finally said, and then turned away from me, his suit jacket swishing in the wind caused by his abrupt move.

"Uhhhh … all evidence to the contrary there, chief," I said, watching him start to walk away. There were a few potential exits from this retro waiting room, and he seemed to be heading down a long hallway.

"I only wish to be left alone," Akiyama said, turning back to me, standing tall in the hallway, framed by the shadowy dark of this place and its selective lack of electricity. The hallway in front of him was lit, but not until about a hundred yards ahead, and the waiting room we were in was illuminated by a single fixture. Clearly someone had not been performing scheduled maintenance on the space between, cuz the hallway was riddled with holes while the waiting area still looked A-plus, if a bit retro.

"I know the feeling," I said, taking a step closer, intending to follow after him. "Me, I was just chilling on the Oregon Coast, living life to the full, if you know what I mean …" No one knew what I meant because that was a lie. The only way I could be defined as 'living life to the full' would be if you considered long, languid days broken by infrequent sexual activity and occasionally lovey-doveyness with Harry to blunt the monotony as 'living.' I mean, don't get me wrong, those parts were kinda fun, and our conversations were decent, but everything else …

God, I was bored. And emotionally … uneven, due to recent past events.

None of this needed to be said to the solemn Japanese fellow in front of me, though. "The point is," I said, trying to get myself back on track as he frowned at me, lightly, "I don't want to be here, you don't want me here—that's cool. Our desires are closely matched in this case. And I'd love to leave, but—and this is a big but, we're talking pro-wrestler-in-a-way-too-tight-unitard style butt here—time's coming unhinged out there." I delivered this last bit with as little accusation as I could.

Akiyama took it in what appeared to be stride. "That is unfortunate … but not my problem." And he turned to leave again, down the dark hallway toward the light at the end of it.

"I think," I said, turning on the meta speed and cutting in front of him, which caused his eye to twitch at me, "that it's not only your problem, but that whatever's going on out there—time suddenly speeding up and slowing down and stopping, and catching and—anyway, it's a real mess—I think it's the sort of thing that affects the whole world. And that the point of origin is …" And I waved my hands all about like the Hokey Pokey and then pointed one finger at him, like I was narrowing it down for all involved. "Yeah."

He possessed legendary restraint. His face moved maybe a millimeter in response to my accusation, then was still once more. I wouldn't have wanted to put any money into a Texas

Hold 'Em game with him. Way to live up to that stereotype about Asian inscrutability, Akiyama. "I don't know what you are talking about."

"Dude," I said, closing my eyes, "there's literally no one else who can control time at this point. Passing the buck is not going to work."

"I don't know what you just said," Akiyama replied, "but I wish you a good day. I will let your friends go from their current ... position." They were positioned, all right. Like dolls, waiting for someone to come play with them.

Note to self: referring to your boyfriend as a 'doll waiting to be played with' ... sounds really awkward and also reeks of Wolfe-ishness.

Argh. Still hurts to think about.

"That doesn't do me any good if time goes flying off its axle and comes to rest forever, does it?" I asked as Akiyama continued his slow-mo storm-off. Okay, so less a storm-off and more of a calm walk-off. Why couldn't I ever manage one of those?

Oh, right. Emotional restraint. This dude had the brakes on his feelings, big time.

Akiyama did not turn back to me, and I was left with the distinct feeling that he wasn't going to be swayed, at least not now, not even if I managed to run around in front of him—which I totally could have, given his slow, sweeping pace. His suit was ultra-outdated. I began to wonder what it'd take to wake his ass up to the peril, and it occurred to me that maybe I needed to do the unsubtle American thing and just say it.

"Time is ending in two days," I said, and Akiyama slowed his pace of retreat a little. "My boyfriend—er, the guy with me—he's sorta my boyfriend, I guess? Or a guy friend? Guy who's more than a friend—you know what, it doesn't matter right now. The point is, he's a Cassandra. You know what that is?"

Akiyama turned slowly. "He sees the future."

"Normally, yeah," I said. "But right now he just sees the big freeze looming, where everything stops for good. No future beyond that, because we never come out of that last moment. Time ends, the wheel off the axle, laying flat on the road, spinning no more." So poetic ... and stupid. Way to go, Sienna. "It's coming, okay? And given what's happened so far when time stops, I'm going to either starve to death or die of boredom because I'm fresh out of conversation and bad guys to chase and ... everything else." I sagged. "Look, this is fated. You have a problem, I'm the problem solver. So come on, Shin'ichi ... let's get to it already."

He just stared me down, and I could see the gears turning behind his eyes. "I am sorry you have come this far for nothing." And he bowed to me, like that was that, and turned away again.

And even though he didn't actually say the word NO, I heard it in every syllable of what he did say, the politest refusal, as the only guy on the planet who could help stop this cataclysmic shitshow just strode right off like nothing I'd just said mattered one damned bit.

28.

Jamal

"Those sandwiches are pretty good," Augustus said, crunching down the last of a roast beef and fontina panini as we sat in a parking lot, staring out across a few empty rows. Walmart was off to our right, but we were parked a ways out from the store, staring across at the Chuck E. Cheese on the end of the little shopping plaza. I was still slowly working my way through a roasted chicken hoagie, wondering how long it was going to take Spiegel to show up, because I was pretty sure I'd already gotten a read on Charles Custis. He was in a Cadillac Escalade about two hundred feet away, vehicle facing the opposite direction. I'd tagged his plates using the security cameras all around the parking lot, and now was avoiding touching the local network, because I could feel someone else moving around at the edges of it with the same electrical skills I boasted.

"Uh huh." I'd been mostly ignoring my brother the last few hours for the sake of avoiding argument. Also, the sandwiches were pretty good.

"I hate surveillance," Augustus said after a few seconds of silence.

"You don't say," I muttered under my breath, not taking much in the way of pains to hide my irritation. I think I was at my breaking point with him, too, after all this time and effort at being civil and carrying his rash-acting ass through however many near-misses with death.

"Hey, man," he said, a flash of his own irritation showing, "if you like sitting your ass in this car for hours, you could do it by yourself. You don't need me for this part."

"Yeah, maybe you should have stayed back at the hotel," I said. "Chill with wi-fi, catch up on *The Crown* on Netflix."

Augustus bristled. "Hey, that's a good show, all right? It's got real elegance to it."

"Far be it from me to suggest otherwise," I said, concentrating on my phone. Spiegel's Prius came cruising up and stopped next to the Escalade, and a moment later, he got out, nodding at Custis.

Custis dismounted his big SUV a few seconds later, and together he and Spiegel wandered out in front of their cars. He'd picked a row out near where the Walmart shoppers tapered off and the next store over, a CrossFit studio, didn't have quite as much of a crowd, so the place where they'd parked was pretty empty. They were standing in the middle of a field of concrete without a single sound sensor for a long ways, if you didn't count Spiegel's cell phone. Which I did count, because I backdoored it and then projected the sound through my own speakers, while recording it for posterity. Or law enforcement. One of those.

"That going to stand up in court if they say anything incriminating?" Augustus asked, eyeing my phone as Spiegel and Custis exchanged tense pleasantries.

"I doubt they will, but probably not," I said, shrugging. I wasn't a lawyer, but I was more interested in using anything bad they said to light up the press about their misconduct versus actually trying to burn them in court. This was a war for the truth about Sienna, not me building a careful criminal prosecution. After all, these people weren't officers of the court, and if the Custis family did have evidence of Sienna's innocence, I didn't think they were even compelled to share it by force of law. They were total dicks if they were hiding it, but I doubted it would be illegal.

"It creeps me out you can do that," Augustus said, staring at my phone as though it had a visual attached to it.

"Pretty useful, though, right?"

"Pretty invasive," Augustus said. "You ever do that to me?"

"Why would I want to know what you're doing in your off time?" I shot out before I really thought about it. "I don't even want to be spending time with you right now, you think I'm going to waste my off-time digging so I can hear you and Taneshia talk about—I dunno, dumb British royalty shows?"

"I told you, *The Crown* is—"

"I. Don't. Care," I said, trying to spell it out for him.

Augustus's eyes glimmered as he looked at me. "You telling me you've never been curious about what I say about you behind your back?"

I started to issue an angry denial but stopped short. "Why, what do you say about me behind my back?"

"Nothing," Augustus said, suddenly withdrawing.

"No, no, no," I said, "you don't just toss that out there like bait and expect me not to bite on it. You've been talking shit about me?"

"Not shit, no—"

"What the hell—"

"I—"

"You son of a—"

"She's your momma, too, watch it."

"I—"

We both stopped as the conversation between Spiegel and Custis took a strange turn. "What the hell is th—" Custis was asking.

"Oh, shit," Spiegel said. "That's Augustus Coleman. They must have followed me. He's got—"

I blinked. How had they seen us? We were a decent distance away, and I could see them turned, looking in the opposite direction of us. Someone was standing on top of the Walmart awning, and they had a massive piece of rock over their head. While I watched, they threw it, a boulder the size of a mini-fridge, and it shot through the air like it had been launched out of a jumbo slingshot.

"Look out!" Charles Custis said, leaping out of the way and behind the Cadillac.

Ray Spiegel, though …

TIME

He froze.

The boulder came launching through the air, like a car speeding down the freeway, toward him—

"Stop it!" I shouted.

"I can't!" Augustus shouted back, hand extended almost to our rental car window. "It's—"

The rock splattered Ray Spiegel all across the parking lot, tearing him to shreds before our very eyes.

And there was nothing we could about it.

29.

Sienna

Chasing Akiyama was getting me nowhere, and having seen a conversation come to an abrupt, storm-off end a time or two, I figured I'd give the big guy some space. It's what I tended to want when I did a storm-off, though I didn't ever do it as quietly and gracefully as he had.

So I headed back down to the quay, taking him up on his invite to check on Kat and Harry. If he had restarted time around them, they'd probably be wondering where I went. So I picked my way through the debris that covered the island streets and squinted against the daylight as I strode through the wreckage of this abandoned island back toward the dock.

The whole island had a smell, like greenery mixed with decay. Ivy of some species crawled up some of the walls, grass had forced its way through cracks in the pavement. The whole island was slowly going back to nature, save for those parts that Akiyama had apparently instituted some kind of hold over. I thought about that waiting room turned hallway where we'd had our conversation, and how it still glowed with electricity, preserved in its 1950's Japanese glory while just down the hall everything had gone to seed.

Weird. I passed a tree that had grown through shattered pavement, and thought ... yeah. There was definitely something funky going on here with time. Big surprise, right?

1950's waiting room, the rest of the island clearly deteriorated, sixty years of decay having taken its toll.

Walking down the slope toward the docks, I saw that Kat and Harry were still frozen. I frowned, wondering if Akiyama had broken his word. I started to jog down toward them, but when I was about twenty feet or so away, they sprang back to life as though someone had pressed play on a video.

"Yeah, I don't think I'd want to hang around here ... either ...?" Kat's comment turned into a question as she started into motion again and then halted at the sight of me suddenly looking her straight in the face. A moment earlier, by her perception, I'd been walking behind her, going the same way. I'd moved ahead of her and one-eightied in less than a second. Hardly impossible for a meta, but given that she hadn't seen it, it probably didn't look right. A flash of realization lit her eyes. "Time freeze?"

"Kindasorta," I said, looking over at Harry, who stumbled a step, hitting a knee as he came out of it. "Akiyama froze you guys, and I had to go chase him down to have a chat." I caught Harry under one arm, keeping him from keeling over cold. His breathing was suddenly very labored, and his eyes were nearly closed, squinted tight against what I imagined was a tremendous swell to his headache. "You going to be okay?"

"I think I'm going to die of an aneurysm of every single blood vessel in my skull," Harry said. His face was so red that I had little trouble believing he felt that way. "And that's if time doesn't make me and every other person on the earth save my—uh—whatever you are—its permanent bitch." He looked up at me through nearly-closed eyes. "So ... yeah, I'm doing awesome. You?"

"I've had better days," I said. "Or at least ones where I made more progress and spent less time bleeding many pints of my own blood."

"But not many," Kat said, smiling just a little. It released a smidgen of my tension, and we shared a smirk. "What's up Akiyama's ass?"

"That's a really good question," I said, and looked up to the building above us. It was the back side of the one that contained the hospital waiting room, and there, above me, in one of the windows, I saw a shadow.

Akiyama. So he was watching me—us—and that's why he'd unfrozen time when I was almost back to them.

"Do you think you're likely to get an answer anytime soon?" Kat asked. "Because I've got this publicity tour I'm not looking forward to next week—you know, interviews and such—"

"Gonna suggest if it includes one with Gail Roth, you avoid. She's a shark."

"Yeah, they booked me for it, but she's always been a sweetie to me. I think you just kinda got on her bad side."

"She asked me if I enjoyed the taste of human meat. Who does that?"

"That's not quite what she asked," Kat said.

"Well, that's where it ended up."

"And whose fault is that?"

"Excuse me," Harry said, voice strained, face still red like someone had poured tomato soup, or maybe my blood, all over it. "Guy in pain ... here ... world ... time ... ending ... need ..." And Harry passed out. I caught him before he went face down on the concrete quay, but only barely.

I rearranged him and lifted him up in my arms like I was carrying him over the threshold on our honeymoon. "That's adorable," Kat said, taking a quick snap with her phone of me carrying him like that. "And going in the blackmail file, assuming time doesn't end."

"Harry's probably got bigger things to worry about," I said, putting one foot in front of the other as I leaned in, walking back up the hill I'd just descended.

"Don't we all," Kat said. "Seriously—publicity tours suck. Time ending is a bummer, but the upside? Me not answering stupid questions about my hair—"

"Don't pretend you don't like talking about your hair, Kat."

"I did at first, but it kinda loses its luster after, oh, I don't know, a million questions, Sienna. It's tiresome. I'm more than my hairstyle."

"Yeah," I said, feeling the weight of Harry in my arms.

"You're also the dress, the ass, the shapely legs—"

"Ouch, sick burn."

I smiled, something I doubted I would have done with anyone else, given the seriousness of the situation. "Thank you, Kat ... again."

She came alongside, taking care to avoid getting hit by Harry's legs as we made our way up the hill to the hospital. "For what this time?"

"Being you," I said, drawing a slow, steady breath. If there was a hospital, maybe I could find a place to lay Harry down, maybe treat him ... somehow ... with the total lack of medical training I had, and Kat's powers being maxed out. Well, maybe I could find a nice place for him to lie down, anyway. "And for being here with me."

"Like I said," and Kat flashed that quicksilver smile, which I found strangely reassuring as we made our way up the hill, "regardless of how this is going, it still beats the hell out of a publicity tour."

30.

Once we made it through the door into the hospital area, I found things exactly as I'd left them moments before. The waiting area remained lit, and still, as frozen in time as Harry or Kat had been during previous time ruptures. Kat had walked ahead, holding the door for me, and now she looked around with unconcealed awe at the flawless, retro waiting room. "This," she pronounced taking in everything from the chairs, which showed little wear to the propaganda-style health posters warning us of various ailments and such in Japanese, "is really ... really ... beyond weird." She looked at me with a deep frown. "The rest of the island has gone straight down the chutes to hell, time having its frigging way with it, and this place is spotless, like you opened a photo album from the fifties right to this page."

"I know, right?" I asked, because Kat made my linguistic style worse by association. Pretty soon I'd be saying, "Fer sure, right?" and "This is gonna take a minute" when I really meant hours or years.

On second thought ... my linguistic style sucked even without Kat to drag it into the gutter. I blame it on TV being my only contact with the outside world for most of my formative years.

"What is going on here?" Kat asked, slowly spinning around as we entered the darkened section of hallway. Through the dim light, I could see that these walls had given way to the vicissitudes of time. There was a hole in one which looked out through broken windows onto the quay.

"My best guess is that someone who can control time is holding parts of this place out of the normal flow," I said dryly. "And furthermore, that attempt to preserve the pieces of this place, for whatever reason, is causing some serious fracturing or splintering or—whatever. I'm not a ... who studies the flow of time? Like, what kind of doctor?"

Kat shrugged. "Some kind of physicist, maybe?"

"That seems reasonable," I said, nodding after a pause for thought. "I'm not a physicist, and thus I have no real way to confirm what the hell is going on here. This one is completely new to me, and—oh, let's try this door." And I pushed my way through a door that looked slightly less destroyed than most of the others down the hall.

It rattled, but failed to fall off its hinges. I found myself in a ward, Kat a step behind me now, darkness filling most of the area around us. Old hospital beds were lined up along one wall, mouldering under the same ravages of time as the majority of the facility. The bedding wouldn't have been clean even by medieval standards, but Harry had to go somewhere, so—

"Hey, there's light over there," Kat said, pointing to our left and back the way we had come—or at least along wall that ran parallel to the hallway with the preserved waiting room. There was a light emanating from just above the door that led back to said waiting room.

I frowned. "Why did he just spare that one specific part of the hallway?"

Kat blinked as she came up next to me again. "Maybe something he cares about is over there?"

That made sense. And Akiyama had strode off in the opposite direction, away from there. A feint, trying to lure me from something he hadn't wanted me to see? Smart strategy if so, because I'd been a little too busy trying to wrap my head around the mysteries surrounding me to fully analyze his behavior.

"Of course," I muttered. Kat heard me and looked over. "He was trying to get me to leave, and when I didn't, he wasn't going to lead me to ... whatever he's hiding." I started toward the light, Harry in my arms, Kat a step behind.

"We should be careful here," Kat said, under her breath, head moving around, cautiously looking about. "If he tried to get you away from here once, it's not likely he's just going to let you cruise in this time."

"I'd like to see him try and stop me," I said, tightly, my patience getting my close to its natural end. Or unnatural end, depending on whether you considered stonewalling Japanese time-controlling metas organic or not. It definitely seemed to contain trace elements of hormones and antibiotics ... err ... the metaphorical equivalent, at least.

"I hope you don't get your wish," Kat said, whispering as he we reached the lighted space. There was another door here, a double door, swinging ones, though they were firmly shut. Having been in my fair share of hospitals over the years, I had to guess this was the equivalent of a trauma room, where someone would be brought for major stuff, worked on by doctors, then wheeled off to the ward to our right. The one that was a mouldering wreck.

I eased up to the doors. "Well, I expect we're going to find out one way or another in the next—"

"Dame! Dame desu yo!"

A shout cracked down the hall and Kat was suddenly frozen mid-step, head mid-turn from looking around like it was swivel-mounted. Her hand was out to touch the door ahead, open it for me, but now she was just standing there awkwardly.

Harry had stopped breathing in my arms, no longer limp. Now he was like some kind of fish in ice, unmoving. I tried not to sway him too much in one direction or the other for fear I might annihilate him like I had the paperback on the plane.

I didn't have to work too hard to find the source of the shout; Akiyama was charging down the hall toward me, eyes on fire like he'd looked at the dock, none of that veil of patience and reserve that he'd shown later evident now. He looked pissed enough to do something about my trespass, and I was just about to gird myself for it, maybe figure out what to do with Harry—I was leaning toward just letting him go, because I figured he'd hang in the air until time resumed if I didn't push on him in any direction and just gently extricated myself—when the choice was, literally taken out of my hands by events.

The world around me issued a groaning crack, and at first I thought the entire floor was collapsing beneath my feet. It made me freeze in place, sick feeling rising in my stomach as I tried to find the source.

And then I found it.

It looked as though reality itself were a mirror, and it was cracking. Prismatic views of jagged lines splintered their way through my field of vision, the world developing so many tears, like glass shattering down stress points. Akiyama remained unaffected, though his eyes were a different kind of wild than they'd been a moment earlier—

Then, it had been rage on display.

Now … it was fear.

And as we stood there uncertainly, everything around me suddenly shattered and exploded into a frenzy of light and sound and scent and color, running over my skin like succubus powers unleashed as I was thrust into a realm of glorious madness, all hints of the world, of the hospital hallway and closed door and the mysteries therein—left behind.

31.

Jamal

"Oh my God," Augustus breathed, as the reality of what we'd just seen settled in on us as we sat in the rental car, as though the atmosphere in here had compressed. "There is no way he survived that."

My mouth was hanging open, and I felt like I couldn't breathe, but I turned on my brother as soon as he said it. "No shit, Sherlock. He's in about five pieces over there, of course he didn't survive it. My question is—why didn't you stop it?"

Augustus just shook his head and raised his hand. "Whatever that thing was they threw? It wasn't real rock. It didn't even have any trace earth elements for me to control."

"Well, it sure as shit looks like a rock," I said, pointing at the boulder, which lay on the ground a few feet away from a decent-sized piece of Spiegel's corpse. "And did you notice that they shouted your name just before it hit?"

Augustus's eyes darted. "I did notice that."

I punched the dashboard, lightly enough that the airbag didn't deploy. I wanted to hit it a lot harder. "They just framed us for his murder."

"How?" Augustus asked. "We step out of the car now, we can prove it wasn't me that threw that. I've been over here this whole time."

"Yeah," I whispered, "and I think they know that." I

looked up; there were cameras all over this parking lot. I'd checked them before we parked. "This whole thing was a frame, Augustus. They just smeared you with it."

"Well, I didn't kill anybody," Augustus said. "That stone isn't something I can control. Lab test would prove it ... probably." And now reality was getting to him, too.

"We need to get out of here," I said, pointing at the ignition. "We gotta go."

Augustus just glared at me. "Are you out of your mind? We're innocent. But if we run, we're going to look guilty. They will see us drive off after this. If we stay, we answer questions—"

"It doesn't work like that, and you know it," I said, mind racing. This was never about proving that Augustus killed Ray Spiegel. Hell, they'd have a difficult time making that stick in court, though it was definitely going to mess up our next week or month or however long. "They just tied us to a murder scene. Look at Custis over there. He's hanging around even though he was standing next to a guy when he got killed. The murderer is already gone." I pointed at the roof, then checked the camera angles to be sure. "I guarantee the camera angles are such that there's no visual evidence that anybody was ever up there. So what we have here is a rock flying through the sky, probably a recording on Custis's end—and hell, we have one, too—of them identifying you as the murderer just before it struck." My neck sagged. "Even if you don't go to jail for more than one night ... this is going to play in the press. And it's going to play *badly*."

"But I didn't *do* anything," Augustus said, thumping his steering wheel.

"A reporter just got killed," I said numbly.

"Let's not go exaggerating," Augustus said. "He was more of a blogger."

"Same difference," I said. "The press is going to be all over this. Metahuman attacks on their own? By one of Sienna Nealon's friends? Like I said ... this is going to play. Loud."

"What are we supposed to do, then?" Augustus asked, looking around. "You want us to run? Like criminals? Like cockroaches when the lights come on?" He made a noise of distaste. "To hell with that. I'm staying right here. I'll answer questions."

"We can't do that," I said, shaking my head.

Augustus turned on me. "You know what this is? This is about you. About what you've done in the past. I'ma sit here, because I don't have a guilty conscience, see? You—you probably need to run. They start looking at you here, they might find some things from the past you don't want found. Am I right?"

My face burned. It was a clumsy but cutting reference to the fact I'd killed two men who'd helped murder my first girlfriend. The fact that it came from my brother at a moment of high tension ...

My phone squealed and I felt an electrical surge as someone forced a message through my speaker without my permission. It was like an electrical slap to the face, and a hiss came out as a radio call from the police was piped into our car. "Murder suspects are believed to be Augustus and Jamal Coleman, African-American males, driving a silver Ford Fusion—"

"That legit?" Augustus asked, wide-eyed, staring at my phone as it made that unearthly call.

I sagged and hit the internet, going to the digital record of the DC Metro police radio dispatch calls. There was a transcript there, a little flawed because it was transcribed by a computer program, but I looked through the log and sure enough— "It's legit," I said, putting my head back against the seat rest. "This was a frame. The biggest frame. A Bayeux Tapestry frame—"

"Man, nobody frames a tapestry, you ignorant ass," Augustus said, but he was looking around, clearly discomfited by this news. He hit the start button on the car and it came to life. "They know our vehicle, man."

"I caught that in the APB, yeah," I said, feeling all the life drained out of me.

"Trouble's coming," Augustus said, and for the first time, he sounded numb. He sounded like he used to sound as a kid when we'd done something stupid, and knew that momma was gonna whoop us for it.

"We have to go," I said, my lizard brain reacting in one of the only three ways it could: fight, flight, or freeze. Fighting the cops was crazy and would just lock us into guilt. Freeze meant going to jail. "We have to—"

My phone buzzed as a message was pushed right into it, and I knew it was from Arche:

RUN. RUN NOW.

I stared at for a second, and so did Augustus. His eyes met mine. "That your girl?"

Wordlessly, I nodded.

He flicked the gear switch to drive, looking faintly sick as he did. "We got no choice," he muttered to himself and yanked the wheel to the side as he turned to get us out of the parking lot, away from this scene of destruction.

The destruction of our damned lives.

32.

Sienna

In my relatively short life outside my house and the strict confines of my mother's wrath, certain things remained of her ridiculously overdisciplined training. Outside of my recent brush with alcoholism, I'd mostly remained away from illicit substances. In fact, following my first encounter with booze, I really hadn't indulged much until after I became a fugitive from justice. I preferred to bury my sorrows in work, perpetual and endless, then food, not alcohol or anything harder.

But of course once I lost my job and endured the forever-hell that was Scotland and Rose, booze was totally on the table as a coping mechanism.

That said, the remnant of my mother's training was this: I'd never used a single illicit drug, even marijuana, in the years since I'd come out of my house. Not once.

But as the world shattered around me and I took a tumble through the crazy kaleidoscope of whatever the hell Akiyama had just done to me ... I totally thought I was trippin' balls. Or whatever the drug-addled kids say.

Shocks of red, blue, purple—shit, you name it—they all went flying past me like I was in a tunnel of rapidly changing LEDs. I didn't have time to scream, nor a voice to use. My throat was raw and unworkable, and nothing came out, like someone had sealed my mouth shut with some sort of

TIME

cement putty. There was nothing recognizable in the craziness going on around me, just wild, maddening colors that struck me as something out of a particularly cartoony video game, the kind Reed would probably have played back in the day when he had time for that sort of thing.

The world seemed to snap into focus for a second, and I was in a car next to a woman who seemed awfully familiar—Angel, I think her name was? From the Agency? Miranda's cousin? And the sound of tires squealing filled the background as dark night closed in around us. Her face was set in determination, lips a thin line, and she looked at me for just a second before she said, "Bet you didn't think it'd end like this."

I wanted to say, "No," but instead I was treated to another eye-burning blast of color and light as that brief spell of sanity returning evaporated back into what must have been an acid trip from hell, or possibly someone holding my face extremely close to the Freemont Street Experience in Vegas. More flashes made me think I was soon to discover what an epileptic seizure actually felt like, and then the world slowed for just a second into grayscale, and I saw dingy concrete walls, a confined space—

Coming out of it into more sparking lights, like someone having shot off their entire Fourth of July wad inches from my eyes, I was suddenly in a darker place, looking into the face of a man who was thin, whose face was in shadow, but somehow I knew, as he spoke, that his name—one of them, at least—was Vlad, and he was very, very old.

"This was always to be your fate," he said with incredible gravitas and a hint of something else, as he stared at me, eyes like pools of shadow.

Then the light flashed once more and he was gone ...

I streamed through more places, more sights—endless fields of fire, hot and smoky, fading into the sight of my own face, jaded, tired, drawn, questioning something—woods, sunlight streaming in above me, the sounds of crickets chirping, of bugs in the distance, of a spring or summer writ large all around me, stitching an indelible feeling of peace before I was yanked away, coming out underwater, breath impossible to come by, then thrust into ice, eternal, forbidding and cold, yet strangely appealing. I was dragged, more flashing, more sparking, through cities laid to ruin, smoking holes in the ground, and an infinity of voices parading through my mind as I came crashing out the other side into—

The hospital.

Japan.

With Akiyama standing before me, hand raised, eyes darting about, his perfect composure blown away.

"What ... the hell was that?" I asked, as Kat lurched back into motion beside me.

Akiyama looked me dead in the eyes, and I could see that he was trying to get a grip, but his panic was still too near the surface. "I ..." was all he managed to get out before he descended into stiff Japanese.

"Translation?" I asked, turning to Kat.

She stared at him for a second before shaking her head. "I dunno, he seems kinda out of it. Rambling about control, or something."

"How do you not know what he's saying?" I asked, losing my patience as Harry jerked in his sleep, within my arms. The smell of the decaying hospital was thick in my nose, and the weight of my beau in my arms required me to shift him, especially since he was twitching hard.

"Japanese is a subtle language, okay?" Kat tossed off a shrug. "It's not easy to translate it precisely. Not every concept has a parallel, and I'm not exactly flawless at it, apparently. I'm flying on whatever's left up here, okay?" She flicked her hair, indicating her head.

"Fine, I—" I started to say, trying to speak through Akiyama's rambles. He'd moved during the little time-break interval, and was now standing between me and the door to the room. I was about ready to push past him, but something stopped me.

Harry was spasming in my arms. He wasn't simply twitching in his sleep; he was undergoing a full-blow seizure, as though he'd been exposed to the same lights I had but instead of just being put off eating due to nausea, he'd gone full grand mal.

"Shit," I muttered, trying to get him under control. If a human jerking under the pressure of seizing could cause limbs to fly freely, imagine what a meta with all their muscular power could do. He almost got me in the nose before I turned his arms away, ignoring the stray back kick that numbed my bicep. "I need a place to set him down." I started toward the door Akiyama was now blocking.

"*Dame!*" he said again, pushing himself in front of it once more.

"Dammit," I said, looking him right in the eye, "there is something you are doing here that is messing things up, okay? You either know something or are doing something. Cop to it, and let's fix this together." I looked down at Harry, still spasming. "Before he gets hurt and time ends. Please."

Akiyama just stared at me. "I have nothing to do with your problems. You need to leave."

"My problems are becoming your problems, bub," I said. If I'd had a stray hand, I would have jabbed a well-placed finger right in his face for emphasis. Unfortunately, I was too busy keeping Harry under control to be able to illustrate my point thusly. "Time is ending. That means an infinity of being stuck with the only other person on the planet who isn't affected by the stoppages—i.e, me. You get that?"

"This is my place," Akiyama said, stiff and resolute. "You will leave."

I just stared him down. "I get it. You want to spend this forever frozen time solo. Meditating, maybe, on what you did to break time. That's cool. I mean, not really, but ..."

"I have nothing to do with this," Akiyama said, evincing only a hint of anger, but it was enough to convey how he felt. I smelled denial. "Perhaps you are responsible."

"Yes, me with these time powers I've never felt before now," I said, and an idea occurred to me. "You know how I got the ability to resist what you're doing? You shook my hand. For longer than you should have. I didn't realize it at the time, because death was bearing down on me, but you totally put a shadow of yourself in me, and somehow it made me immune to the flow of time. I don't really get how that works, but ... there it is. *You* did this to me, Shin'ichi. You're the reason why I'm here."

"Lies," Akiyama said. His calm was unraveling, and I realized this was the first time he'd closed his mind to the possibility of what I'd told him before, about our earlier meeting.

"You sent me here!" I shouted, Harry convulsing in my arms. "From your future to my past, so that I would come here now, when you needed my help!"

"You are mistaken," Akiyama said with a hiss through gritted teeth, clearly trying to get a grip on his emotions, which were threatening to barrel out of control.

"Well, a second ago you said I was lying, so I guess we're making progress," I said, staring him down. "What have you done?"

He made a subtle movement to place himself more squarely in front of the double doors to the trauma room. "I have done nothing. This is not your concern—"

"Time's ending, Shin'ichi. Color me concerned."

"Sienna," Kat said, and I looked up at her. Her gaze was rooted at me—no, not me, I realized as I followed her eyes down, down—

To where Harry rested in my arms, unmoving ...

I lifted him up, bringing his face close to my ear—

He wasn't breathing.

I felt everything drain out of me as he hung in my arms, limp.

Harry was dead.

33.

"MOVE!" I shouted, and Kat flung herself out of my way as I put Harry down immediately. I hadn't felt my powers work on him but that didn't meant he hadn't accidentally touched an errant piece of my flesh while convulsing. I put him down as gently as I could while still dropping him like a hot potato, and the best I could manage was to not break anything, like his skull, as he thudded lightly to the floor, legs splayed out where Kat had been standing a second before.

As soon as he was down I tore a band of cloth from my sleeve and pressed it around the tips of my fingers as I thrust them at Harry's neck. I pushed, hard, and was rewarded with a very faint pushback every few seconds.

A pulse.

He drew a low, shallow breath, and I was able to breathe again, if only for a second, taking in the dry, dead hospital air. I felt like all my blood had drained out, and I checked in my head for a faint voice, something to indicate I had somehow done this to him—

But my skin remained cool, no hint of my power having picked up in my hands or anywhere else. It was an unmistakable sensation, hot and wild, bordering on erotic in a way that I desperately tried to ignore whenever I used the power. Damned "succubus = slut" stereotypes. That was a part of the mythology I could have done without.

"I didn't do this to him," I said, removing my fingers from his carotid artery.

"It's the time shifts," Kat said. "It's like they're breaking his brain." She was standing over me, leaning, clear worry in her eyes, too.

"I don't know what to do," I said, looking up at Kat. "I mean ... there's literally nothing I can do."

She gulped. "I don't really love the way you said that."

I closed my eyes. "How do you mean?" I knew exactly what I was getting at. So did she.

"Sienna, I've already used so much power today," Kat said, and I opened my eyes to find her—not exactly shrinking back, but definitely with a breath caught in her throat at the prospect of what might be coming if she used her power to bring Harry back from the brink. "If I do this—"

"I know," I said, cool, quiet. This was not my choice, and I could in no way force her to make it because—in essence—she'd be giving up part of her life, at least as she knew it—to save Harry. Whom she hated.

To her credit, she didn't take a step back, but she did hang her head, putting it in her hands as she made a slight mewling noise. "This is the downside of girl time with you, y'know? All the benefit of getting to play hero and the lovely self-esteem boost you get from being a worthwhile person ... but damn, the self-sacrificing thing? Blech."

"The choices are a real bitch, aren't they?" I asked. I knew exactly what she meant. "And the consequences ... pure hell."

"Yeah," she whispered, and knelt down next to me, over Harry. She looked me right in the eye. "I don't know if the stuff Omega gave me is still working after all these years. And if he's really messed up ... I might not remember you after this is over."

"I'll remind you," I said, feeling a little choked up. "Besides, I think you lose the stuff you care most about first. So ... y'know, you'll forget the name 'Prada'—"

"Sienna," she said, deathly quiet.

I closed my eyes, and felt a little tear stream down my cheek. "I'll remind you. About everyone, if I have to. Remedial Kat education."

"I don't want to be Klementina," she said quietly. "I don't

know what she was like, but ... I don't want to be her."

"If she's anything like you," I said, a really heavy band of discomfort in my throat, "I'm sure she was wonderful."

Kat smiled tightly, then made a fist, putting up to her lips as she breathed around it, sucking in air and letting out tension, her shoulders so tight I thought they might explode. "Okay—"

"You don't have to do this," I said, abruptly, out of nowhere. Who was I kidding? I wanted her to do this. Desperately. Wanted her to make the heroic sacrifice in spite of what it meant to her, and all so I could have my—

My boyfriend back.

"I think I actually kinda do," she said, looking me in the eyes, her faint green ones a little aglow. "I'm not doing this for you." She looked down at Harry. "I feel like I kinda have to do this ... for him." And she plunged her hand down.

"Way to make a girl jealous," I said, and she hiccuped a laugh as she latched onto his forehead with her palm. "Like I wasn't dealing with that already—"

"You were dealing with it poorly," Kat said, and already her voice was strained. Her knuckles were as pale as Harry's forehead, a strange look on the usually bronzed Kat.

"Yeah, well, you know me and emotion," I said. "We're enemies. Forever enemies. Arch enemies. My feelings are like Rose, except I can't kill them. So I just bury them, and we ignore them."

"You should probably stop doing that," Kat said, hoarse. Her expression flickered with pain, and Harry jerked, once, under her touch.

"Yeah, that's something Zollers has warned me about," I said. "I'll get on it—next year. Make a resolution or something."

"Good ... thinking," Kat managed to get out, her breathing picking up, getting labored. "Hey ... Sienna?" And she looked right at me.

"What?" I asked, and I felt a cold trickle of sweat drip down to my lower back, tracing a chilly path along my spine.

She glanced at Harry, then at me. "Whatever you do ... don't ... screw *this* ... up ..." And she lurched, losing muscle control as she fell forward onto him.

"Kat!" I shouted, and started to move toward her. My heart was pounding in my ears as I reached out.

"What ... is that?" Akiyama asked. He was only feet away, but looking around as though something had roused him.

"It's called courage and bravery and self-sacrifice," I said, trying to peel Kat off of Harry before it was too late. Her hand was anchored on his forehead. "You probably wouldn't know what it looks like, what with being stuck up your own ass in denial for—well, forever—"

"No!" Akiyama said, and seized on my shoulder as I pulled Kat free, sending her tumbling off of Harry and onto me. I shoved her off a quarter-second later, my breathing nearly as labored as hers had been. Now it was shallow, like Harry's had been, and he showed no sign of improvement as I listened for—

Oh.

Shit.

"You hear it now?" Akiyama asked, half-kneeling, a hand still on me as I lay on the ground.

Oh, I heard it now, all right. An outboard motor whining in the near distance.

The sound of a boat at the docks.

And then, a voice, crazed, familiar, lashing out across the abandoned island.

"SIENNA NEALON! You—will—kill—me—or I will kill all your friends!"

Prettyboy had joined the party.

34.

Jamal

The sirens didn't fade as we pulled out of the parking lot, still reeling from what had just happened. There was red-spotting in my vision, an afterimage of Ray Spiegel dying beneath the onslaught of whoever had thrown that boulder at him. My blood was pumping, pounding through me, and part of me wished I was at the wheel instead of my brother as we turned out of the parking lot and into the streets of Washington DC.

Rush hour was going all around us, a steady traffic flow down this surface strip of commerce. We were in Alexandria, Virginia, and I had a feeling everyone was going to be looking for us.

"Where do we go?" Augustus asked, clenching the wheel, his knuckles stretching against his skin.

"Just get us away from here while I think this through." I was already working, creating a direct line to someone else. We needed more eyes on this than just me, more people working it than myself and the unreliable Arche, whatever she might be doing.

I sent a surge through the net, creating a direct connection to a phone in Minnesota, my voice exploding out of the speaker as I activated it, the camera, and the microphone all together. "J.J., it's Jamal. I need your help."

"Whoa!" J.J. erupted out of his chair as he nearly tumbled over with it as went over backwards. He was in his boxers, eyes the size of his computer monitor—which was huge, Kerbal Space Program playing on it in the background—as he jerked away from the sudden, unexpected stimulus of his phone roaring to life.

"That's ... a neat trick," Abby said from a little behind him, not nearly so taken aback by it as he seemed to be. He'd almost ended up in her lap, their computers set up at a right angle to each other in a corner of their living room. Her hair was pink again, bubblegum color, and she had on glasses, a tank top, and boy shorts with a pattern only a geek would understand, N7 screen printed down them over and over. "Also, an incredible invasion of our privacy." Her mouth was set in a thin line, her brow furrowed. "I hope you have a good reason to—"

"Augustus and I are in DC and we just got framed for murder," I said, unable to hold it in any longer. "We're running from the cops right now."

Abby just blinked. J.J. was standing there, still, like he thought things would go back to ten seconds ago if he just didn't move. "That's ... a pretty good reason," Abby said, and clicked off the game that had been on her screen. "What do you need from us?"

"The Custis family," I said, channeled right to them. Sirens were still blaring faintly in the real world I was tuning out, and I heard my brother's muttered curse. "We were in a Walmart parking lot, after a meeting with a reporter named Ray Spiegel. We followed him to a meet with Charles Custis and—"

"I thought Reed sent you guys to Ohio," J.J. said, choosing this moment to come back to the conversation and, possibly, life. "What are you doing in DC?"

"Long story," I said. "Well, maybe not that long—this Custis family? We think they have evidence that Sienna's innocent."

"Yeah, that's not a very long story," Abby said, tapping away at her keyboard. "You bullet-pointed it pretty well in like two seconds."

J.J. picked up his phone, which had been sitting in a charging cradle at a slight angle, giving me an impeccable view of the two of them. "So, uhm ... what do you need us to do? You're kind of a wizzier wiz-kid than we are on this stuff."

"I need you to look into how this happened," I said. "They set us up, the Custis family. I think it's the family, anyway. They're all metas like me, Thor-types with data control precision, and they work for some pretty high-juice people here in Washington. We walked right into what they had set up—surveillance cameras recorded us as we arrived, I'm sure. They used some kind of non-earthen boulder thrown by a meta as the murder weapon to make it look like Augustus did the deed." I froze, and something occurred to me. "I bet Charles Custis zapped Spiegel right before it hit, too, locked him right in place with muscle paralysis."

"That's some pretty deep shit you find yourself in," J.J. said, slipping into his chair. "If this family's like you, though—and I mean, a whole family of them ... dude, Abby and I are out of our depth. You, alone, ace us with zero effort. What are we supposed to do against multiples of you?" He frowned. "How many are there?"

"Four, near as I can tell," I said. Augustus cursed again behind me. "Just do what you can. Alexandria cops had our names, description, car info—seconds after the murder. Someone tossed that to them, even though we were across the parking lot. Just work around the edges, see what you can find. Hell, erase whatever you can find that doesn't look good, if you can get away with it—"

"That's a terrible idea, and no," Abby said, spinning around in her chair. "If these people are what you say, there's no conceivable way J.J. and I, with our modest, non-electrical interfacing skills, can possibly permadelete something to the point where you or they couldn't retrieve it. And then they'll have *us* on evidence tampering."

"Shit," I said. She was right. "Okay, well, find what you can and keep out of trouble. You're right, no point in anyone else walking into their bear trap and losing a leg."

Abby stared right into the phone camera. "If the cops are after you for murder, Jamal ... there's a chance you could lose a lot more than a leg."

I didn't want to think about that. "I gotta go. Do what you

can?"

"On it," J.J. said, and he was off to tapping away. "Can you leave the line open? Is it secure?"

"As good as I can make it," I said, "but I'm going to microphone only. Sound and image takes more of my mental bandwidth than I can spare right now."

"Wait ... you were looking at us, too?" J.J. asked as I switched off the visual in my head. "That's ... so rude."

"Sorry," I said, but didn't have the mental juice to mean it much. "And Abby ... good choice. I'm a huge Mass Effect fan."

I couldn't see her, but I could hear the blush in her voice. "Thanks ... I guess. For the compliment. But not for invading our personal privacy. No thanks for that."

Then I was back in the passenger seat next to Augustus, who was threading his way through surface street traffic. "Yo, I could use some navigation here, bro, if you're done with your little confab."

"On it," I said. I switched the next three lights ahead of us green, tripping their cycle and allowing us to build up some speed. I darted into the police dispatch grid, and realized there was a GPS map of all their nearby cars.

Then I cursed. Loudly. Because they were *everywhere*.

And swarming toward us, just blocks away.

"They've got our number," I said, trying to figure out how to muddy the waters. I created eighteen false tips, sending them in twelve other directions via text messages sent directly into the 911 dispatch queue.

Every single one of them evaporated before it even reached the main system. And I watched it happen, powerless to stop it.

"Oh shit," I said under my breath as red lights and sirens flared in our rearview. "You need to up your driving game, bro. Fast."

"I'm on that," Augustus said, slewing past a car on the shoulder, jumping the curb and darting back into the lane. Interstate 495 was ahead, only a couple more blocks. It was hardly a guarantee of freedom, especially since we were being bird-dogged like crazy by the Custis family right now, but ...

TIME

Being on the freeway held a lot greater chance of escape for us than sitting our asses in this traffic, hoping we didn't caught in a line.

"Uhm, this is really bad," Abby's voice came to me. "They've got footage of you in the parking lot, all right. It's in their servers, multiple copies on multiple independent—"

"I had a feeling," I shouted back. "Cops are closing in, team. The Custis family is directing them right to us, probably using traffic cams and maybe satellite surveillance, I don't know. The dragnet's closing on us."

"Dude," J.J. said. "These people ... their hacking skills are like a wall. This is ... it's beyond Grade A."

"Yeah, I had a feeling it was bad," I said, snapping back into the car and the scent of diesel exhaust as Augustus plowed between the lanes, nearly eating the back bumper of a semi trailer before he jumped the curb again. I was gripping tight to the bar and the center console, trying to keep from getting thrown against the window.

"It's bad all right," Augustus said, and then leaned down to look out the front window and up—way up.

A light snapped on from overhead. There was a helicopter on us.

"So this is what Sienna feels like every day of her life lately," I muttered, leaning forward like my brother as he clipped a sign off and jumped a curb as we entered the freeway onramp.

"Yep," Augustus said, focusing on the road ahead as we shot up the onramp and gained speed. He was pushing past seventy already, probably hoping to outrun the cars behind us before dealing with the helo above us. I didn't have the heart to tell him that it was a strategy doomed to fail.

"Bro," I said as we started to merge, the traffic flow coming to a slow, then a stop, "I think it's over." I didn't have the heart to look at him, either.

We came to a stop about ten yards before we plowed into the bumper of a Cadillac ahead, rush hour traffic stacked up hard in front of us. I looked to its natural conclusion using the traffic cameras, and in a flash I saw—

The cops already had a roadblock set up ahead.

Skipping into the opposite lane—which would require us to jump a concrete barricade with a car or steal someone else's ... another roadblock, a mile down. They had traffic sewn up on both sides, five minutes or less after the murder was committed.

And there were enough boys in blue sweeping in around us that fleeing on foot wasn't an option, even with our meta-enhanced speed. They'd catch us with cars, swarm us ...

"Should have just stayed where we were," Augustus said numbly as he killed the ignition, eyes glazed over as he stared straight ahead. "Taneshia is gonna be pissed."

"Yeah, I don't think Momma's gonna be real happy either," I said, and strangely, that was my biggest worry right now.

Augustus looked right at me. "Let's not tell her."

My eyes almost popped out of my head. "Dude, we're about to be arrested or shot, depending on how the next few minutes go. Maybe both. We're known associates of Sienna Nealon, and we're getting clipped for murder. I think Momma's gonna hear about it even if we don't tell her ourselves."

Augustus's mind was racing, and so were his eyes, flitting around the interior of the car. "Oh, shit." Apparently that got him worse than what Taneshia was going to think of all this. "Let's go out in a blaze of glory."

I sagged, looking at him. "Be serious."

His eyes got wide. "I am serious. You want to deal with Momma when she finds out that not one but two of her boys have gotten arrested after she managed to get us out of—"

I smacked him. Lightly, but still. The red and blue lights were drawing closer behind us now. "Death is not preferable to telling Momma we got framed for murder. Now come on," I said, opening the door and thrusting my hands out, straight up in the air. "They're going to be twitchy. So ... don't make any sudden, meta moves, all right?"

Augustus opened his door, putting his own hands out. "We're two superpowered black guys in DC and the cops are about to bust us. What could possibly go wrong?"

TIME

"JAMAL AND AUGUSTUS COLEMAN!" a voice blared over a loudspeaker, the chop of the helicopter prop wash threatening to drown it out. "Place your hands above your head and get down on your knees!"

"Like we ain't seen this enough growing up to know what to do," Augustus muttered over the prop wash, and part of me wanted to laugh at the same time I wanted to cry. He disappeared on the other side of the car as he got to his knees, hands tucked behind his head.

"Drop the phone!" The voice shouted, and I realized with a start they were talking to me.

"Gotta go," I said to Abby and J.J. "We're getting pinched." And without time to hear their reply, I tossed the phone aside and heard it clack on the pavement as it slid beneath a car beside me. I looked up and saw a woman staring out at me with wide eyes from the driver's side door. After a second of looking at me, she glanced at the little lock knob that extended out of her door. It was up. She reached for it, almost comically slowly, and pressed it down, as though locking the door would somehow stop me from getting at her if I was of a mind to.

The voice boomed out of the loudspeaker again. "Lie down on your stomach and place your hands behind your heads! Slowly!"

I took a deep breath, already on my knees, my face burning. I'd been through some shit in my life. Girls hadn't exactly flocked to the short, geeky Coleman brother, and guys hadn't exactly been gentle of their critiques of my non-meta physique growing up. This strength, this power … it was all new to me in the last few years. Being yelled at, degraded, bullied, embarrassed, called out …

None of it matched up to having the cops screaming at me with probably a thousand rounds of ammo pointed in my direction as they told me to lie down and wait to be "dealt with" however they saw fit. Suddenly I had a flash of real empathy for all the people I'd helped arrest this last year, understanding why they tended to fight when confronted.

Because putting your life in someone else's hands when they're yelling at you and you know they could make you literally dead with the stroke of a finger? Was the most nerve-wracking experience of my life. Worse than killing, worse than nearly dying.

It was the feeling of being on a precipice of uncertainty, and being shoved at by unfamiliar hands, by loud voices you didn't know, by people shouting at you to *DO WHAT I SAY*.

Hell, if you had power at your fingertips ... listening to someone yelling at you, when you know they could kill you ...

No wonder most of our prey fought back.

My face was hard against the pavement, the smell of blacktop heavy in my nose. I could hear the footsteps as the cops approached, the reverberations rolling through my forehead and cheek where they pressed against the road. I held as still as I could, my hands against the back of my head, fingers interlaced.

"Do not move," a rough voice came from above me. I could feel them looming there, ominously, knew that they had countless guns pointed at me even now.

"I won't," I said tightly, my throat against the ground, too.

Someone leaned over me, and it felt like eternity before the jab hit the side of my neck.

Suppressant.

It took a few seconds—long, hellish seconds—before I felt the slow euphoria as it started to work. My mouth got dry, my eyes watered a little because that needle sting was not gently done, and it had hit a nerve or two on its way in and out.

Then rough hands grabbed me, and I let out a breath as they pulled me to my feet, my head swimming.

It was already in effect, I realized as a strange emptiness filled me. The cops dragged me along and I didn't fight back, just let them carry me. I saw Augustus getting a similar treatment, woozy-eyed, as they pulled us toward a police van back a little ways.

It was a disorienting feeling, suppressant running through my veins, cops dragging me like I was a misbehaving child.

After all these years ... now ... I felt completely powerless.

Because I was.

35.

Sienna

"I need this shit right now like I need another hole in my head," I said, casting my eyes toward the heavens.

Prettyboy had come to this island. Had called my name. Had threatened death for me and mine, even though Harry and Kat were already at some conjoined version of death's door, linked together through his seizure and her use of powers to try and bring him back. Both were unconscious on the floor around me, and here I was, sitting on my haunches, Akiyama only a step away ...

Like I didn't have e-friggin'-nough to deal with given his ass was about to end time somehow. Now I had this crap to sort through? Some death-wish yakuza nutbag chasing me all the way from Tokyo to an abandoned island outside Nagasaki?

"Who is that?" Akiyama asked, lurking right over my shoulder like a mystified, protective parent asking about the latest trend. Tide Pods, maybe, I dunno. I wished Prettyboy would go eat a case and thus remove himself from my "To Kill" list. Though that probably wouldn't work, unlike with normal morons.

"Some dickhead yakuza Achilles-type with a death wish," I said, getting to my feet. It wasn't likely Prettyboy was going to just go away because I wished real hard that he would, which meant I had to deal with his dumb ass in order to keep him from coming to find Kat and Harry and killing them just to spite me.

"An Achilles?" Akiyama asked, rising as I got to my feet. "With the yakuza?"

"Yep," I said, trying to decide the smartest path out to him. I didn't want Prettyboy realizing which building I was in, in case he got past me. The last thing I needed was him tracing me back to here and slaughtering my friend and my boyfriend while I was stuck in a time freeze or something.

"Madness," Akiyama said, as if trying to figure out why an Achilles would go to work for organized crime. I didn't feel like spelling out for him the appeal to a psychopath of working for a criminal group, so I just stalked off and opened the doors to the hospital waiting area with its frozen fifties décor quietly, taking the route out of here that I'd taken to get in.

"What do you intend to do?" Akiyama called after me, and I looked back to find him following, catching me just as I hit the door to the outside—again, quietly, intending to shut it so that no one would know by the sound of a door closing where I was coming from. Besides, going into a fight with an invincible meta, I needed all the element of surprise I could muster.

I took my voice meta-low and said, "Beat his ass into the ground and kill him if possible. Why?"

Akiyama evinced the hint of a frown. "He is an Achilles."

I shrugged. "I've killed them before." I felt a hard pang; Scotland. Again. Would the damned reminders never cease?

That sent Akiyama's eyebrows up. "You have … killed Achilles?"

"A couple," I said. "They're not actually invincible, you know."

"Hm," Akiyama said, thinking deeply on this. I didn't have time to indulge in thought when asses waited to be kicked, though, so I started back down the path toward the shore. I could hear some yakuza thugs talking down that way. "You must be truly great," Akiyama said as I walked away, "to have beaten so tremendous a foe."

Something about what he said sent a little tickle down my

spine; in our first meeting, he'd called me, "The great Sienna Nealon." Not the sort of thing you forget as a perpetually under-appreciated eighteen year-old.

"If only everyone saw me that way," I said, turning around to show him a tight, humorless smile. Then I was back off to the races. The races, in this case, being a battle with several yakuza and a seemingly invincible man.

There wasn't any way to approach Prettyboy other than straight on down the dock road, so that was what I did, just headed downhill. I saw his little group coming when the road curved and I was about a hundred feet down while he was about a hundred feet off the dock. Past him, I could see a boat at the dock—the same one that had ferried us out here only a little earlier. The captain was sitting at the wheel, a little slick of blood running down his eye, a lone yakuza in a black suit left to guard him. Poor guy.

Nine yakuza in black suits with white shirts waited for me, with their left hands in various states of disrepair. I doubted they had three whole pinkies between them, which suggested to me that either someone hadn't wanted to send the A team out to face me, or else these guys were just a big human sacrifice, meant to prime me for the main event. Because right in the middle of them was Prettyboy.

I looked over the odds. I'd faced worse. If it was just these guys, with their assorted traditional, mostly thug weapons—a couple knives, some clubs—I'd rip through them like a bean burrito through a weak intestinal tract.

Unfortunately, they had an Achilles in their midst. Also unfortunately, none of them had a katana. Because I was better with a katana than probably any of them ever would be. Alas, another disappointment among so many in my life, one that rated just above finding out that Big Bird was just a guy in a suit but below the discovery that being an adult wasn't all sunshine and kittens.

"If you value your lives, get the hell off this island," I said, stalking down toward the motley assortment of idiots in front of me. I didn't expect Prettyboy to turn back, but if I could get a few yakuza out of my way, it'd save me thirty seconds, and right now, every second counted. "I will not be pulling my punches; any of you who come at me will die. I am fresh out of patience, mercy, and anything else good."

"Excellent," Prettyboy said, grinning. Not a happy grin. A psychotic one. Of course.

"Not really," I said, trying to keep my footing as I made my way down the hill without stopping. I was just taking things at a steady walk, and they'd stopped, clearly in anticipation of me charging their formation, which I was doing, albeit slowly. It didn't make sense to just stand back. I needed to get this over with, and it wouldn't make a hell of a lot of difference if I waited for them to come to me, given that the odds here were terrible for me.

The road was bordered on each side by a little block wall about knee to waist high, and to my left it ran uphill into the base of the hospital building. To my right it dropped off in a steep slope down to the shoreline, which was a rocky mess, as I knew from our earlier landing. No beach here, just a twenty-foot drop to pain and agony. My current plan was to send as many yakuza over it as I could manage, not really caring whether they died, so long as they got out of my way for at least a few minutes. And it'd probably be longer than that, given that even if they managed to survive the fall, they'd have to swim back to the dock and climb the damned hill again to get back to me.

The nearest yakuza was a young guy already missing a finger and a half, and with a club in his hand. He had a smile on, too, though his was not nearly as crazy as Prettyboy's. I was unsurprised to see that someone so dumb as to fail badly enough to be forced to cut off that many knuckles before the age of thirty was going to be the first to pay the Sienna price. He started toward me, breaking their calcified little formation, and as I got close. I darted in under his attempted swing of his club, ripped it out of his hand—easier because he was lacking those fingers—elbowed him so hard in the nose that it probably killed him on impact, then kicked him over the embankment and into the water below. A pronounced crack made its way to me a second later, telling me I'd managed to score a hole in one on my first try. Or a corpse-on-rock. Whatever.

TIME

"Come one, come all," I said, gritting my teeth as the yakuza came at me in a rush. One came at me from behind, approaching from the water side. He probably thought he was safe, because he wasn't directly between me and where I'd just thrown his buddy overboard; he had a good twenty foot margin behind him before the embankment tumbled off.

I slammed him in the belly with a blurry-fast sidekick, and it was like I'd shot him in the gut with a cannon. He launched off the ground and flew through the air, and if the stomach trauma didn't kill him and the fall didn't, then with any luck he'd just drown and spare me any more trouble.

While I was kicking him overboard, another guy came charging in close. I whipped a punch at him that caught him in the eye and caused the usual level of damage. He howled, tissue bulging and wrecked goo hanging out of his closed lids as he screamed. Did no one warn these idiots what happened when you fought metahumans? They make pamphlets for asbestos exposure; I felt like they should start printing them, in every language, for "What Happens to Your Body When You Cross Sienna Nealon." Forewarned is forearmed, after all. Or at least you have a chance to not lose your forearm, because my next move was to grab him by his, yank him close, and traumatize his wrist with that club so hard that the radius jutted out of his skin. Then I flung him overboard and listened to him splash below. Missed the rocks that time. Bummer.

Three of them got the wise idea to charge me at once, either by plan or by stupid timing. The first to arrive got my purloined club thrown right in his face. It lodged in the place where his nose had been before it was replaced by hardened wood, and he keeled over, dead or close to death. The other two kept coming, apparently failing to realize that every one of their friends who had come at me had died or been horribly injured thus far. Or maybe they thought they'd be the first to win, I dunno.

Both of these guys had knives, but were slow as frozen shit, so I grabbed the first one by his knife hand, which he led with in a blind, stupid charge—and I fell back into a roll, catching myself on my ass and then onto my back and shoulders. I put one foot in his groin, which took all the starch out of his shorts, put the other in his belly, and launched him after breaking his hand and making him give up the knife, which I caught with my other. He soared into the stratosphere, or at least over the embankment, and I was rewarded for my efforts with both a crunch and splash, leading me to believe that he'd either wrecked his whole rib cage or ended up landing on his head. Either way, he wasn't coming back from that anytime soon.

I rolled back to my feet in time to counterattack the last of this trio of morons, and I wasted no time in opening his throat. In fact, I cut his neck so hard that my stolen knife ran hard against his spine, my hand deep in the gore of his neck. I could feel the tension in my face, my anger coming out as I showed these bastards what the great-granddaughter of Death himself and the granddaughter of the original Valkyrie could do; this was my family trade, after all. Ignoring the shocked, gasping face, I finished taking the bastard's head clean off and headbutted it, launching it into the gut of a guy charging up behind my victim. He let out a gasp as it took the wind out of him. A follow-up kick sent the headless corpse into him, knocking him over and down, pinned beneath the dead weight of a dead guy.

Now I was hitting my stride, and with only three more yakuza to go. Prettyboy was just watching, that sick grin on his face, like he was imagining himself being next and relishing the thought. I was just about to the point of agreeing with him, my patience all spent with people threatening my friends, especially since I felt like I'd lost plenty enough of those lately. The last two standing yakuza came at me in tandem, and I didn't waste a lot of time with them.

One had a club, one had a knife, and I used my superior speed to dart between them as they charged me. From that point, I used my own blade to open up the guts of the guy with the knife, blocked his clumsy thrust, dodged the overhead clubbing attempt of the other, watching it sail home to graze his compadre against the side of the face. I redirected the blade of the yakuza who I'd just gutted, twisting it right into the heart of the guy with the club. He looked shocked, just shocked, that his buddy's weapon had been turned against him to his own fatal detriment.

"Enough of this shit," I said. I elbowed the club guy while kicking the knife guy, and they both went flying from me in opposite directions. The knife guy just about ripped in half where I'd cut him open, his lower body hanging onto his upper body by a thin thread, the smell of guts and no glory filling the air as he smacked against the uphill embankment and came to rest on the wall over the road, head and legs facing in the same direction. He was screaming, crying, in a crazy amount of pain, no doubt, from being nearly bisected, but no one paid him much attention.

The club guy went overboard like the others and was greeted with a *sploosh!* as he hit the water below. Too bad he had a hole of several inches in his heart; the landing sounded like it had been survivable, but unfortunately for him, he'd likely drown before he bled out. Tough way to go.

Prettyboy was the last one standing, and he started to clap, tossing back his black hair as he grinned, applauding my vicious performance.

"I've never seen anyone so happy to watch their friends die and know they're next," I said. Out of the corner of my eye, I could see the last surviving, relatively unwounded yakuza struggling to get out from underneath the decapitated corpse of one of his compatriots, really putting some effort into it. He'd probably be free in a few seconds, I judged, so I tossed the knife into his head and listened to it make a satisfying THUNK! as it penetrated his skull and lodged there.

He remained upright for maybe a second more, then went limp, thudding to the stone road. That was the last of the yakuza, save for the guard on the boat and Prettyboy, who regarded me with some surprise. "You ... threw away your weapon?" he asked in that high voice of his.

"Knives don't do shit to your skin," I said, flexing my fingers and then matching his grin. "But I do. Come and play, little boy. I'm going to make your soul and your powers the cornerstone of my new collection, dickweed."

The grin evaporated from Prettyboy's face. "I will not be made a prisoner of a soul-eater."

"Did you not realize the stakes when you started pissing me off?" I asked, and my face was flaming because I'd just massacred nine hardened, if somewhat stupid, criminals that he'd led here to be slaughtered as his warm-up act. "Did you think—as an Achilles—that coming after a succubus was going to result in a clean death?" I laughed, cackled, even, pouring every ounce of anger I had into my performance. "Dipshit, I'm going to eat you alive and then use your bones as fodder to kill every meta who gives me crap from here on out." I was probably lying about that. As much as I would have liked invulnerability, I wanted this lunatic in my head about as much as I wanted to put a knife in my shoe and run a marathon. He made Wolfe and Bjorn look stable by comparison, because at least they weren't perpetually warring with a death wish.

All of Prettyboy's amusement had dried up. "No. You will kill me cleanly."

I laughed again, salting this wound. "It's cute that you think you get to decide the manner of your death. I'm not Gozer, moron. If you come to me for death, I'll decide the manner of it, and using my skin?" I held up a bare hand. "Just seems the easiest way."

Prettyboy screamed with inarticulate rage and charged at me, surprising me a little. He'd gone from mild simmer to boiling over pretty swiftly, and while I certainly had that effect on some people—okay, lots of people—it usually didn't happen this quickly.

I used an aikido twist against his arm, turning his momentum against him. I tried to force him into a joint lock, but that didn't work. He just let out a furious scream and twisted out of it, joint clearly invulnerable to the pain a normal person or meta would be feeling at having their arm bent at a terrible angle. I didn't fight against it, letting him swing his other fist at me and then catching that, falling back this time into a whole-body roll.

He couldn't really fight against this move; he'd thrown all his weight behind his punch, and when I yanked him down along with me, he got dragged along because he'd overextended himself and didn't have the balance to stop our fall. Pivoting mid-roll, I put a foot in his belly and started to toss him like I had his fellow yakuza.

This, he didn't cooperate with. He rolled off my foot before I could effectively punt him, landing on his back and shoulders awkwardly about two inches from my head. The hard landing would have hurt or stunned a normal person, but not an Achilles.

Prettyboy swiped at me, but I was already moving away from him, rolling sideways. He came after me, coming to all fours, thrusting out a hand at me like a dog pawing at something.

I got back to my feet and assumed a defensive stance as Prettyboy sprung at me. He gave it his all, and I was out of ground, my calves just inches from the wall bordering the road.

He caught me in the gut, and I didn't have a lot of choices. Instinct drove my response, which was to roll, so roll I did.

Right into the wall behind me.

The block wall hit my calves right in the middle, my backward momentum driving me onto the slight embankment behind me. There was maybe five feet of ragged grass before the ground became cliff, and I took advantage of every inch of it, rolling and twisting.

Then I was airborne, Prettyboy beneath me, clutched in my grip, my fingers tight on his lapels—

And down we plunged, toward the rocks and water below.

36.

If you're going to take a twenty-foot drop off a cliff into rocky waters, it's always advisable to have a plan for your landing.

My plan: land on the invulnerable meta who was clutched tight in my arms, screaming(!) as I rode him into a rock below, my knee in his gut.

Prettyboy thudded against a giant boulder as we landed with a splash, his head catching stone and my kneecap slamming into his belly as his back flopped onto seemingly unyielding water. That left me with a pain in my patella that felt like someone had sledgehammered it, but it also caused Prettyboy to fold from either the blow to the skull or the sudden weight applied to his diaphragm. Either way, we lurched into the water with a lot of smacking and cracking of flesh against rock, flesh against flesh, and invulnerable skin against succubus knee.

What a rush.

Also ... ow.

Once the impact was over, sharp, stunning, sudden—we were underwater. I'd had just enough time to draw a breath before I plunged into the chilly deep. The sun overhead shone, rippling across the surface of Prettyboy's face as I held onto him, riding him down a few feet. There were other bodies here, nobody moving, mostly just floating at the surface like chum for the sharks, a little tinge of red in the water, either from the sunlight or their blood. Maybe

Prettyboy's, but I doubted I'd made him bleed—yet.

I held onto my breath like it was life itself, because—well, it kinda was. Water churned and bubbled around us as Prettyboy struggled, and I held onto him and scissored my legs. I'd driven the air out of him on the way down, fortunately, probably mostly out of surprise from the skull-thumping and my knee catching him off guard. I doubted I'd done as much damage to him as he'd done to my knee with his frigging invulnerable skin, but the goal was achieved nonetheless:

Sienna had a lungful of air to work with and Prettyboy was gasping and desperate, sucking in deep breaths of water.

I rode that bastard down to the rocky bottom and he thrashed wildly the whole way, kicking out desperately but without much actual effect. I locked my eyes on his, predator on prey, and he lashed about, not really able to look at me because his drowning instinct had kicked in fully, and he couldn't use anything but his lizard brain. He was grabbing hard at me, not realizing I was doing everything I could to aid in our descent. When we bumped against the seabed below, it was the fulfillment of all my (on the fly) plans and probably not what he'd planned at all.

This is what you get when you mess with me, asshole.

I held him down, bubbles streaming out of his lips, the last of his residual oxygen flooding out. My lungs were tight, like iron, and I kept my breath in as though it were gold and I was the cheapest Midas sonofagun to ever walk the earth. Prettyboy struggled, and scrabbled, and clawed some. I kept my face out of his reach and held him down with all my strength as he bucked and freaked out and generally offered the resistance of an unthinking wild man. Because that's what he was. He didn't have two ounces of conscious thought to rub together, drowning instinct having taken over. All the advantages to being an invulnerable meta, to being able to hold your breath for—I dunno, probably an hour if he'd really tried—were out the window because this dumbass had trod hard on his Boris Grishenko, "I am invincible!" philosophy and never bothered to train for when shit goes horribly wrong.

Thanks, Ma.

It took about three minutes for his resistance to flag. The bubbles had gone to almost nil by five.

And at about seven minutes ... Prettyboy went limp, and his eyes rolled back in his head.

Which was good, because I was starting to get bored.

I looked around for a boulder, and when I found one about ten feet away, I dragged Prettyboy over there and then rolled it on top of him, saving him for later. I knew high powered metas couldn't actually be killed by asphyxiation, but I had bigger fish to fry—like time coming to an end in the next day or so—and figured I'd just deal with his ass in earnest later.

Or never, preferably, since I was fresh out of nuclear warheads with which to scourge off his skin.

Oops. Forgot I was in Nagasaki. My bad. (Too soon?)

I broke the surface by the docks a few seconds later to find myself surrounded by yelling Japanese voices. One of them was the boat captain, sounding quite put out and maybe a little scared. The other was the yakuza who'd been tasked with guarding him, and he sounded put out, too, but for different reasons.

Quietly cutting the distance between me and the fishing boat, I got up to the side, listening to the shouting. It was all in the other direction and sounded like the yakuza was looking up the hill, probably trying to rouse some of the dead bodies I'd left lying there. Which included a guy with a knife through his face, one that was nearly cut in half, and another missing his head, so I'm really not sure what he thought he'd accomplish, but that was the direction he'd chosen to yell, impotently.

I was over the side of the boat and all up in that guy's grill before he knew what hit him. His head came around to face me but his body stayed facing the opposite direction, as I gave him a good twist with my meta strength. If he'd been a stubborn jar of pickles, I definitely would have popped him open. Alas, he was human, so he just died with a GURRRRRK! I tossed the carcass overboard without missing a beat and then looked right at the captain.

"Wait here," I said. "You understand me?"

He nodded furiously.

"Wait here," I said again, then made the finger across the throat gesture. "How long will you wait?"

He burst out in a furious load of Japanese, and I rolled my eyes. "I don't know what that means."

"He said ... 'Forever, if you command me,'" Akiyama's calm voice wafted over to me, and I looked over to find him standing there at the edge of the dock, staring across the water at me.

"Good answer," I said to the captain. "Remember that." And I started hopping my way over the planks back to the quay.

"Did you kill him?" Akiyama asked once I'd landed back on the concrete quay. He seemed genuinely curious, and about as emotionally involved as I'd have been watching a soccer game. (Because soccer is boring, guys.)

"I doubt it," I said, "but he's under control for now. I'll deal with him more permanently after I've solved all these other burgeoning crises that are blowing up in my face."

Akiyama cocked an eyebrow at me. "How ... is he 'under control'?"

"I drowned his ass and put him under a boulder for safekeeping," I said, moving past him and heading back uphill, water streaming out of my clothes and squishing out of my shoes as I ascended. I grabbed my hair and wrung it out, breathing out my impatience and trying to breathe in some serenity. It wasn't going so well.

"I see," Akiyama said, keeping pace with me. "And those yakuza you killed?"

I tossed off a look that probably wasn't that friendly at him. "What about them?"

He seemed to back off an inch or two, and when he spoke again, it was a lot more gently than anything he'd said to me thus far. "You killed them all."

"I'm running a touch low on mercy," I said, "and those assclowns—or some others of their stripe—have been dogging me since Tokyo. I don't have time for all this shit." I put my eyes forward again as I threw open the door to the hospital without regard for how loud it slammed this time. "Apparently the world needs me to save it—again."

"You have ... saved the world before?" Akiyama asked, and now that his reserve was evaporating, he sounded almost a little ... impressed?

"Yeah, I've lost count," I said. "First there was Sovereign—he wanted to kill all the metas and enslave all the humans. Then came Harmon—he was just going to skip straight to the enslavement. Then came Rose—and I mean, there was other stuff in there, too, like the time I saved Chicago from a meteor strike—" I stopped, my shoes still squishing out water on the worn floor of the waiting room. "You know what? None of this matters right now. What matters now is you helping me save time from ending."

Akiyama stiffened, his reserve returning. "I ... don't know what you mean."

I stared him down, and it must have been classic Sienna Grade-A RBF, because he melted back another step, albeit subtly. "You know *exactly* what I mean," I said, not giving an inch. Then I turned, and pushed my way through the door into the decaying hallway, where Harry lay next to Kat, both pale and pasty, but breathing, I noted—

Then I turned toward the doors beyond, and made a beeline for them.

"Wait!" Akiyama shouted, and came after me with his hand raised. "Do not—"

"I'm here to save the world," I said, slapping his hand away and causing him to spin slightly off balance. "If I don't have time for the yakuza's shit, how much do you imagine I have for your ceaseless denials?" Akiyama caught himself against a half-wall to the ICU ward, raising his head to look at me with alarm. "I can't control time, Shin'ichi," I said, hoping my use of his first name would get it through to him that I was fresh out of patience for his stalling, obfuscating bullshit. "I have to work with what I have, and in this case—it ain't much. So forgive my rudeness," I said, and back-kicked the door to the trauma room open.

"NO!" Akiyama shouted, thrusting out his hand as if to stop me. I turned, before he could reach me, and strode into the room he'd tried so hard to keep me out of.

Strode in ...

And froze. Not literally.

And my jaw hit the floor. Also not literally.

But I did stop. And I did stare. And I did wonder how the hell I could have missed it.

Because there, in the midst of a hospital room, was a scene frozen in time.

A doctor.

Two nurses.

And the patient ...

Was a Japanese woman on a bed, legs in the classic pose of childbirth ...

And based on the scene before me, I knew ...

This woman was either dead or close to it.

And somehow I knew, just by looking, that the baby ...

Was probably soon to follow.

37.

Jamal

They put us in the same cell, because why not? We were powerless as normal people, me probably even more so than my brother, who still had the physique from his football days. It was dark, only one working light for illumination, and the walls were poured concrete, the kind that might have stopped me even if I'd had my meta strength. Not a single power socket, not that it mattered without my powers, and I'd lost my phone.

Which was everything.

I was wearing an orange jumpsuit for the first time in my life. So was Augustus, and by his silence, he was taking it just as hard as I was.

"Bet you didn't think us trying to prove Sienna's innocence was gonna end in us ..." I whispered, acutely aware that without meta hearing, we couldn't speak meta-low, and thus avoid the microphones that were surely listening in in hopes we'd incriminate ourselves.

"In jail ourselves?" Augustus asked, voice dead. "Naw. I didn't see that coming. I'd call it delicious irony, but I'm kinda choking on it at the moment."

"I hear that," I said, ass glued to my cot. It was uncomfortable, but it was something to sit on. And at least we didn't have company in here. They probably figured we were more likely to discuss our recent spate of crimes among ourselves if we were alone. I was a little insulted at how little they thought of our combined brainpower, and I could tell Augustus wasn't any more disposed to chatting about criminal activity than I was. I raised my voice, figuring I'd deliver again the same message I'd been shouting since we got here, "Yo, I want my lawyer!" It echoed in the small space, but once again, no answer came.

"We ain't even got a lawyer, bro," Augustus said, head against the concrete wall, staring out toward me. Our cots were on either side of the square room, up against the walls. He was facing me, I was facing him. And we were still trying to do everything we could not to look at each other, probably because it'd just reinforce the reality of the situation.

"I honestly thought ..." I let my voice trail off.

Augustus's eyes met mine for a moment, and we understood each other. "You figured once we got out of the Bluff ... we were done having to worry about ending up in jail, am I right?"

I nodded slowly. My eyes were burning a little, but I didn't want to show it.

"You can take the boys outta the hood ..." Augustus said, dark amusement laced with a little acrimony.

I didn't have anything to say to that. What could I say to that? He'd nailed it; I thought we were free and clear of this shit. Even me, despite what I'd done.

But no. Here we were, trying to help a friend, and end up stumbling our dumb asses into a good old-fashioned frame-up. Fresh meat for the grinder.

Augustus shoved off the wall, standing, and moved over to me, plopping down next to me on my cot, pushing his face up to my ear, presumably to defeat the microphones. "What have they got on us, you think?"

I thought about it a second, then moved my lips up to his ear and matched his low whisper, cupping around my mouth so it'd mute the sound and letting out my breath before speaking so it'd help keep me from hissing. "The anonymous tips. The cameras put us at the scene. Local towers pinged our cell phones at that location. And we were the last to meet Spiegel before Custis—before he died. So they've got a lot."

"Circumstantial," Augustus said, twisting to speak into my ear, taking the same precautions.

"We had the means—or so they'll say," I whispered back, "we had the opportunity, because we were there and you had the powers."

"What about the motive?" he asked, still keeping low.

I shrugged. "I don't know. If they have a record of our talk with Spiegel, they can probably come up with something. It wasn't exactly a polite chat, y'know?"

He nodded. "This is the thing I don't get, though ... unless they got something else major, can they even tie this to us? I mean, really, in court?"

I licked my lips, not really happy with how I had to answer this. "Maybe. They could switch evidence easy, with their access and powers. Put a real boulder in place of the murder weapon. Do some digital touchups to conversations to make things sound worse. Be tough for anyone to prove, you know? Because they got the power to erase any digital fingerprints at the 1's and 0's level. But even if they don't ..."

"What?" he asked.

"Think about it," I said, still whispering, still blocking around his ear to keep my words muffled, for him only. "Court cases take years to settle out. And during that time, let's say we ran across the evidence we were looking for ..." I could see my brother tense. "Who's going to believe it if it comes from—"

"Two dudes on trial for murder," Augustus finished, sounding as sour as a lemon head. "This wasn't just a frame—this was an execution of our credibility." He sagged and leaned back, head against the wall on my bunk now, like he didn't have the will to fight anymore, not even enough to make it back to his own.

I nodded, and pulled away from his ear, settling back next to my brother. "Yep. Now ... we're out of the game."

38.

Sienna

"Oh, geez, Shin'ichi," I said, rubbing my forehead, which was filled with the tension of a furrowed brow. Suddenly ... it all made sense. Or at least I thought it did.

"You do not know what this is," Akiyama said, interposing himself between me and the scene of childbirth, as though I were going to walk in and start beating the shit out of these people while they were frozen in time.

"Really?" I asked him, the fully jaded Sienna coming out. "So it's not your girlfriend or wife dying in childbirth?"

He paused, and I saw his mind racing to catch up. "I ... very well, perhaps you do see what is going on here."

"Yeah, I see what's going on here," I said, turning my back on the spectacle. "You're not exactly the first person to try and hold on a little too hard to something they're losing." I opened an eye and cast a look back at the strange tableau. "You might be the first that can freeze time and hold onto the moment, though."

"I only held on to what was mine," Akiyama said, jutting out his chin, defiant. A mote of dust was frozen in his little suspension field, and the place was completely scentless, which I thought was a little bizarre until I realized that basically he'd stopped all particle motion within this room.

"Oh, so this doctor and these nurses are your slaves?" I quipped.

Akiyama's eyes flitted away from meeting mine. "I let everyone else go. The entire island—it was evacuated in the middle of the night after ... this." He swept an arm around to indicate the scene in front of him.

"Why?" I asked, and he cocked his head at me, giving me a funny look. "Not why *this*," I said, sweeping my own hand over to encompass the frozen childbirth scene. "Why did you get them to evacuate the island?"

He took a hard breath, the tension in his shoulders making it look like he was carrying a lot of weight on his back. "I tried ... many times ... to create a different outcome. Roll time forward, do something different—and the same thing happened. Roll it back, months, even ... but nothing fixed ... this." And here he cast a brief look at the scene, then jerked his head away quickly, as though he could not bear to see it. "Even now, I relive it each day. The moments ... before, when hope was like a banquet before me. The future, laid out and gleaming, waiting. I remember every moment, every sensation, as it rolled on ... and they ... and she ... began to slip away." His eyes had a dark, haunted look to them. "I relive it every day, after watching the sunrise. And every day, regardless of what I do ... it happens the same way."

"Okay," I said, wracking my brain. Kat was the immediate solution I came up with, but Kat was pretty damned incapacitated at the moment. If I could get her recovered, she could probably lay hands on Mama Akiyama and boom, problem solved. "I think we can fix this."

Akiyama did not look at me. "There is no ... fixing this."

"Dude, I have a friend right outside who heals with a touch. She can fix almost anything. I say 'almost,' because, you know, there are limits. Broken heart is right out. Torn quilt, probably not in her purview—I don't see Kat as much of a seamstress, but maybe buried under all that millennial bullshit she's picked up, she actually knows how to stitch from the way olden days—"

"Your friend is from these days," Akiyama said, straining to explain the obvious to an idiot—me. "My wife and child are in the past. You can only stand here, in this place, because you have some resistance to my power. To bring your friend in here would be to ..." He waved a hand in frustration, almost uselessly. "... It would upset the timestream."

I looked around, waiting for the other shoe to drop. "I could be wrong, being new to this whole time business ... but I think the timestream is already pretty pissed off."

"Yes," Akiyama conceded, a little more aggravated than I might have suspected. "I have held on to time too long. The tension has built over the decades, and now ..." He shook his head. "We near a snap, for lack of a better word."

"Time itself will freeze completely," I said. "Because you can't just hold onto a piece of it for this long without affecting the whole."

He nodded and all the life seemed to go out of him. "So it would seem."

I tried to gather all my tact for what I needed to say next. "Akiyama ... you've got to let go, then."

Now the tension gathered even tighter in his shoulders, and he looked so stiff I thought he might explode just standing there. "You do not know what you are asking of me."

I took a deep breath. "Look ... I know it probably feels like it right now, but ... you're not the only person who's felt a loss in his life." I closed my eyes, and suddenly I was back in the middle of wrecked Scottish village, the world on fire around me.

And my heart was gone, along with my breath.

"What is this?" Akiyama asked, and I realized he was next to me, that we were actually there, in Scotland.

"Holy hell," I muttered. The flames engulfing the house next to me were frozen in time. I felt like I could reach out and touch them without being burned, so I tried it. Sure enough, there was no heat, because the moment was frozen in time.

"This is ..." Akiyama slowly looked around. "... your work?"

"Geez, man, you've known me for like five seconds and you've already figured out I'm a human wrecking ball?" I looked around the empty streets of the Scottish village. "Yeah, it was kinda my doing. I ran across somebody here who …" I felt a lump in my throat, and couldn't find the words. Akiyama didn't interrupt, he let me think it out, and a couple minutes later I managed to squeeze, "How did we end up here?"

"Time is … fickle," Akiyama said. "And it is fracturing. It drags any who touch it this close to the source of the problem … to moments in their past of great stress and import."

"How the hell does it do that?" I asked, whispering. I could see the highland boob mountains around me in the foggy day. They loomed like hunchback giants in this place I wished I could have avoided forever. "Know what's important to us?"

"I do not know," Akiyama said. "Time remains a mystery to me in many ways. But there is a care, a force behind it, it would seem, guiding those close to it to places such as this." He looked right at me. "You shudder at being here. It takes your breath away." Here, he was composed, as though being removed from the scene of his family's impending death took away all his excess emotion that leaked out. "What happened here?"

"I lost … almost everything," I said, voice a hoarse whisper. "Nearly lost my life. My friends. My family. And I did lose …" I looked at the browned Scottish earth. "I lost people … I cared about. That helped …" There was no temperature, no wind, but I felt a chill anyway. "… That helped define me." I looked back up at Akiyama. "Without them … I still struggle to know who I am, beyond … well, beyond a destroyer or something."

Akiyama nodded subtly, as though taking this in and coming up with a judgment he didn't wish to share. "And if you were given a choice of moments to return to, to relive …?"

I let out a gasping, mirthless laugh that leapt from my lungs. "I would have picked almost any moment but this one, yes."

"Interesting," Akiyama said, and the Scottish Highlands

faded around us, back to the Japanese hospital, and the impending birth and death scene. He grimaced as it all blurred back into view. "And what do you—" He stopped, as though he'd been frozen himself, then lifted a finger and pointed behind me.

"Uh oh," I said, and whirled to find—

Yeah. 'Uh oh' didn't quite cover it.

"I ... find you ..." Prettyboy said, soaked to the skin, his suit torn across the chest, dripping on the floor just outside the door to the waiting room. He wore a maniacal grin and his eyes were—madly—focused on me.

39.

A ripple ran through the room as Prettyboy started toward me, and things seemed to freeze, just for a second, time distorting around him as he leaned forward to charge me. Then he broke through and came at me, one of his yakuza buddies' discarded clubs clenched in his fist.

"Shit! Shit! Shit!" I shouted as he came at me, time stuttering once more as he drew close. It was trippy, seeing him pause, lurch back a step in time, as though someone had hit rewind, then shoot into action again, forcing me to dive to the side to avoid his sudden, high-speed landing.

"Get him out of here!" Akiyama shouted behind me. "He will ruin everything!" I couldn't see his face, but he sounded like he was taking this all so super well, emotions threatening to blow out in every direction like gaskets.

"I think everything is already heading to hell in a handbasket, Shin'ichi," I snapped back, rising as Prettyboy struck at me with a martial arts-inspired punch that I had to parry, "but I appreciate the fact you think it's still somehow all under control."

Prettyboy zipped backward again, his arm returning to his side as he rechambered his punch, then loosed it on me again in high speed. I doubted he had any idea what was going on, time have completely lost its freaking mind or grip on reality or something. I started to get the feeling that Akiyama hadn't been entirely right in explaining what would happen if we brought Kat into this room. Then again, the way Prettyboy was zipping around, caught in the flows of time just at the edge of the birth/death scene, maybe he wasn't too far off.

"I'm really coming to hate this guy," I said, catching Prettyboy's punch the next time he threw it. I had a plan, and it involved sending him airborne, preferably through the nearest wall, where he would plummet out into the water below and have to climb his way back up the tower again to go another round. If I did that to him twenty, maybe thirty times—maybe a thousand, I dunno—perhaps eventually he'd lose interest. Besides, I could rest between rounds while he pounded up the stairs again. And these super tough guys? They always neglected their cardio. He'd probably take forever to climb back up after a couple toss-outs.

My fingers brushed Prettyboy's arm where his sleeve was torn, presumably from an underwater boulder ripping it as it fell off or something. Time froze, then sped up, and suddenly my skin burned all along my digits and my palm. I gasped, and time spun again—

I was standing with Prettyboy on the edge of a cliff at sunset, fiery orange sphere dropping into mountains ahead as we looked out over a green valley and boxy Japanese city. Prettyboy was younger, and crying, tears running down his cheeks. He stepped up to the edge of a several hundred foot drop, put out one foot, and started to tip over—

Another flash, and I was in a tiny bedroom, city view of Tokyo, so massive, shining, behind him. He had a bottle of pills in hand, and was taking them one by one, swallowing them down with a bottle of sake—

Light blazed, and then I was under the water, somewhere, darkness overhead, and Prettyboy was drowning. It wasn't just now, when I'd drowned him, it was another time, and he thrashed madly against death that wouldn't come—

And in a forest, where he was hanging from a noose—

In his yakuza suit, gun pressed to his temple—

I jerked away from him as time stuttered back into motion and I gasped, the horror of seeing so damned many suicide attempts all condensed down into one explosive payload of emotion like a blast that leveled me with feelz. "Aughhh," I said, hitting the wall and making a dent in it.

Prettyboy was partially hunched over, bent at the waist, staring at the ground. "What ... was that ...?" And he rose, flipped the dark hair out of his eyes, and looked at me. The manic grin was gone.

"Shit is getting real around here, Prettyboy," I said, pushing off the wall and watching him warily. I saw Akiyama, lurking between us and his family, doing a little hunching himself. He looked about two seconds shy of taking a knee, as though something were straining him. Or maybe he was just finally losing his grip on time. "I don't have an abundance of patience to deal with your angst just now. Any chance we could reschedule for later?"

"I don't think so," Prettyboy hissed, brandishing the club. "You ... will not escape this fate. You must help me ... to end this."

"I'm not really into assisted suicide," I said, taking a ragged breath. "I'm not gonna say 'You have so much to live for,' because I'm not a damned liar, but—seriously, if I can't work with this other guy to resolve his problem, we're all going to get stuck in the end of time."

"End?" Prettyboy asked, and the grin started to return.

"I shouldn't have said it quite like that," I tried to correct. "If time ends, it's really more of a freeze, which means you will be stuck feeling like this foreve—"

I didn't even get it out before he jumped at me. He hit a time stutter and sped up, and socked me in the head with the club. I saw stars, like they'd come streaking down out of the sky to wipe me out, and I hit the ground. A strong hand gripped at me, hauling me up. The disorientation of being blasted at high speed upside the head skewed my sense of balance, and I couldn't tell which direction was up until I was hanging there, in Prettyboy's grasp as he held the club high, threatening me. "I will let time end, and it will end me with it," Prettyboy said, and I couldn't quite form the words to tell him he was oh so wrong.

"Akiyama," I slurred out instead, looking over Prettyboy's shoulder to see Shin'ichi, now down on one knee, still between us and his family, "I hope you didn't lie to me. Much."

Prettyboy cocked his head at me, about to ask what the hell

I meant, but I landed a foot on his chest and shoved as hard as I could while simultaneously reaching down and twisting his arm, then shredding the front of my shirt to escape his grasp. It wasn't tough; I wasn't light, and he was hanging onto clothes not meant to support that much weight. Amateur move, really.

My shove with my foot managed to send Prettyboy back a few steps, and as I landed, I exploded off my feet as quickly as I could. I hit Prettyboy in a football tackle, my shoulder to his gut, which was like sledging my shoulder into a garbage truck. The difference being Prettyboy didn't have nearly the mass of a garbage truck, and so when my feet got traction, I was able to rip him off the ground and carry him forward in my charge.

"No!" Akiyama shouted, but I was already committed. Prettyboy, clenched in my arms, got plowed forward toward the time freeze around Akiyama's family. He jerked and stuttered, but didn't really do anything because I realized, when I was about two feet from colliding with Akiyama and seven or so from plowing into one of the nurses next to the bed …

Prettyboy was frozen in time.

I let him loose, and he just hung there, mouth slightly open, limbs askew from where I'd yanked him off his feet. I took a step back, rolled my neck around, popped my joints a few times, cracked my knuckles—

"What are you doing?" Akiyama asked, and he was sweating furiously, now down on his haunches. I didn't think he was going to last much longer in holding on to all the shit going on in his bubble.

"Achilles are supposed to be invincible, right?" I asked. "Iron skin? But I have theory about this, see—I think they're invulnerable up to a point. I've dropped garbage trucks on someone with that power, and it hasn't really hurt them, per se—but there's got to be a logical limit to that. Meaning, they can take, say, a 747 crashing into one of them full force, but could they survive being thrown into the heart of black hole? I think not."

"… What?" Akiyama was seriously showing the strain,

sweat beads popping on his forehead.

"If Prettyboy is frozen to me," I said, putting up my fists, "every hit I land is magnified in its strength, because my speed and momentum are off the charts relative to his complete lack of both. It's going to be like delivering a freight train to him every time I land one." I punched the air a couple times experimentally. "So ... let's see how much he can take, shall we?"

"Wh—" Akiyama started to say, but didn't get it out.

I went to work on Prettyboy like he was the heaviest heavybag I'd ever practiced on. Each punch felt like I was hitting concrete. My knuckles were bleeding in seconds, but I didn't care. I'd burst through concrete block before, pounded hard enough to bend steel, punched sandbags built to withstand my fury—

Hitting a semi-solid substance like Prettyboy? Hell, the biggest challenge was that every time I struck him, he moved a little and I had to keep up.

Akiyama was speaking, but I couldn't hear him over my breathing and the flurry of punches I was throwing, adding the occasional kick just to spice things up. I imagined Rose's face over Prettyboy's, imagined long red hair instead of black, thought about everything she'd taken from me, everything she'd done to me. I poured all my hate, all my anger, all that pent-up frustration and fury—

The press hated me.

The world hated me.

Every government on the planet was after me for crimes I didn't commit.

I let it all out in the hardest workout session I'd had in years, my knuckles busted wide open as I lit into the near-motionless Prettyboy while he hung there and took every hit. I gave him so much juice I thought if time snapped back into motion he might hit orbit when all the momentum and force I'd directed his way came crashing in at once. To counter that, I circled him, trying to stick and move so that he'd feel it all over his entire body when he came back to normal time.

I didn't know if I was doing any good, if I had the ability to even really hurt him, but I gave it all I had anyway. And when I'd finally had enough, I collapsed, my breath coming in hard gasps, my hands a bloody pulp, soaked in crimson up to the elbows. Prettyboy's clothes were covered with a thousand bloody knuckle prints.

"Do you ... feel better now?" Akiyama gasped from behind me.

"A little," I conceded, falling over onto my back, staring at the ceiling above. "I don't know if that did any good, but it sure felt good."

"I think ... you will find out ... in a moment ..." Akiyama said weakly, and I turned my head to look.

He was on the ground like I was, like he was about to kiss the floor.

A grunting squeal came from in front of me, and I lifted my head to see Prettyboy hit the ground, landing on his feet. His face was curiously pinched, and I stared at him. He did not seem to register me.

He opened his mouth as if to say something, but didn't get anything out. It stayed open for a moment, then flapped once—

Then blood spurted out in great red sprays, running down his lips and chin, soaking into that already coating his drenched white shirt.

He keeled forward motionless, thumping down next to my knees. I didn't waste a lot of time; I sat up and plunged fingers into his neck, trying to do the wise thing and assess the status of my quarry while simultaneously getting my only effective weapon remaining—my touch—queued up and ready to go.

I didn't need it, as it turned out.

There was no pulse, and Prettyboy was leaking gallons of blood out of his mouth, his nose, his ears, his eyes, his fingernails ... he was crying blood, and he was not taking so much as a breath. There wasn't even a weak pulse.

I kept my fingers on his skin for a few more seconds, but there was nothing going on there.

"I give you ... peace," I said, and collapsed myself.

Sienna: 3, Achilles-types: 0.

Bow to the champ, bitchez.

40.

Jamal

Time slowly ground away, hours and minutes, like a pencil in a sharpener being slowly reduced to wood shavings. Augustus and I didn't dare speak until we heard a click in the lock, and both of us sat up, human speed, as the door swung open with a squeal to herald the arrival of ... someone.

"Get up against the wall," a guard said, holding a baton in his hands. "Once you're in position, we'll come cuff you."

Augustus moved to follow his command. "Where are we going?"

The guard looked like he was going to spit out a nasty reply but instead said, with only a little irritation, "Your lawyer's here to see you."

We shared a look as we both put our hands, palm down, against the wall. They cuffed us, not gently, chained our legs, and then led us out of the dim, grey cell into a more brightly lit hall.

It was almost blinding at first. Three guards were around me, one at each shoulder and another at my back, baton thumping into his hand inches from my spine, like a thinly veiled warning. Augustus was a few paces behind as we were escorted through concrete halls and into a brightly lit room where someone waited.

"Miranda," I breathed as we came in.

Miranda Estevez rose as I entered, her long brown hair

with its highlights gleaming in the dim light. Miranda was a cool lady, and she didn't give much away. "Remove those chains, please, so I can consult with my clients."

"We didn't chain their mouths shut," the lead guard quipped, but after a leaden glare from Miranda, he nodded and they started to unlock us. "They're due for an injection of suppressant in the next hour."

"The US Attorney is coming in to talk with us in the next few minutes anyway," Miranda said. "I'm sure we'll be done before the hour is up."

The lead guard looked like he wanted to say something to that, but whatever it was, he must have buried it because he and the others left without a word. Once the door clicked shut and the lock turned, we were alone with Miranda.

"Well, this isn't where Reed sent you," Miranda said dryly, eyes evincing not a glint of amusement at our current predicament.

"Yeah, yeah," Augustus said. "We wrapped that up this morning."

"And ended up in jail in DC by night. Well done." She slow-clapped a couple times for mocking effect.

"We obviously weren't aiming to," I said. "We got framed."

That made her raise an eyebrow. "So says every criminal."

"You think we're criminals?" Augustus asked, and the heat was rising in his tone.

"No," Miranda said. "But it doesn't matter what I think. I'm your lawyer, I'm in your corner no matter what."

"Does Reed know we're here?" I asked, mouth a little dry from hours without a drink.

"Of course," Miranda said, like, duh. "J.J. and Abby called him first. He was the one who flew me to get here." She ran a hand through her hair, which did look just a little windblown. "He's outside, waiting. And you should know—he's not happy."

"Well, we're sitting in jail, so ..." Augustus said. "You can let him know I'm not exactly jumping up and down and singing show tunes all up in this place."

"That's good," Miranda said coolly, "because I'm pretty

sure that you'd hit those high notes like a bird on a window."

Augustus got an offended look but someone rapped on the door, and he shut his mouth. Miranda called out for them to enter, and a few seconds later, a glasses-wearing, disheveled, middle-aged white dude popped in the door. His hair was dark, but thin at the top and heavily combed over. He came over to the table as Miranda scooted her chair around to sit on the side to Augustus's right, and this new guy, who introduced himself quietly as "Martin Browning," sat down pensively across from us.

We all sat in silence for a few seconds while Martin Browning appeared to gather his thoughts. I was no lawyer, but wasn't it usual for detectives to interview you before a US Attorney came in?

"We seem to have arrested you gentlemen in error," Browning said, clearing his throat. "Based on anonymous tips. But, uh ..." He reddened a little. "We, uh ... don't have any evidence that you guys were actually involved ... at all ... in this crime. In fact, just the opposite appears to be, uh ... showing up in the evidence." He smiled, rather weakly.

"That's interesting," Augustus said flatly, and thrust his chained hands out. "Because here I am, chained up like a criminal, jabbed in the damned neck by a needle, my powers suppressed—and for no damn reason?"

I was surprised how quickly my brother moved from relieved to belligerent. I was still sitting here trying to turn over in my head how they'd lost all that evidence. I had a theory, of course, but the pleasant rush of relief at the prospect of getting the hell out of here clouded all clear thought about how it might have gone down.

"Sorry about that," and Browning motioned toward the window. The door clicked open, and a couple of the guards came in. They looked about as surly as I might have expected, faces down, just doing their jobs, as they unlocked us. "We have to follow what evidence we have, you understand."

"I—" Augustus started to say.

"My clients understand, of course," Miranda said, rising, "but I hope you'll have them processed for release immediately?"

"Of course," Browning said, nodding furiously as he rose with her. "We are sorry about the ... misunderstanding, and we want to make sure we get your clients out of here ASAP, especially given the, uhm, profile of ... them." And here Browning nodded at us once, didn't even bother to shake our hands—which was probably quite smart given how much Augustus was seething—and bolted for the door, the guards hanging around.

"Come on," one of them said—the same guy who'd been kind of a douche to us on the way here. "Let's get you cashiered out."

"I'll wait for you guys outside," Miranda said as we started to follow the guards out of the room.

"Along with Reed, I'm sure," Augustus said tightly. He sounded like he was wound so tightly he might just blow up.

"I'm sure," Miranda said coolly, and we were off, back into the labyrinth of the jail—and hopefully on our way to getting the hell out of here.

41.

Sienna

I came back to myself as time unfroze and stuttered around me, the sound of people speaking Japanese coming through somewhere over my head. I rolled to my belly and looked, and sure enough—

Akiyama's little still life had sprung to actual life, first swiftly and then slowing down to regular time. I could hear the elevated concern in the doctor's voice even though I couldn't understand a word he was saying.

I got to my feet, stumbling a little as I rose, my knuckles still bleeding from lack of healing. They ached, the bones were probably cracked, and if I needed to do any punching, my only advantage would be the numbness in both of them.

But I had feeling ... it was more of an ass kicking I was going to have to deliver here, at least of a type.

Akiyama was watching the scene unfold, stoic again, though he showed faint signs of strain in the lines of his forehead. "This ... is where I remember ... first getting the feeling that things were going wrong."

I came up next to him where he had pulled himself up on both knees. He must have sensed me through the sudden burst of activity around the table, though neither doctor, nurses or the patient so much as glanced my way. I was a spectator for this, and I felt utterly out of place.

The doctor shouted something, startling one of the nurses,

TIME

who dropped the tray she was holding. She scrambled, hurrying for a drawer across the room, and as she did ...

Akiyama's wife passed out, neck going limp, head lolling back.

That prompted another cry, this time from the other nurse, one echoed with a grunt from the doctor.

"I can't imagine what you're going through," I said, blood dripping from my knuckles. I felt like I'd gone twelve rounds with a heavyweight, not the equivalent of a heavybag. Either way, it was a lot of punching, even for me.

"Every day," Akiyama said in that choked whisper. "Every day I relive this."

"Shin'ichi," I said gently. "This isn't healthy. You know that old saying about 'time healing all wounds'? Well, it doesn't really work that way if you keep re-wounding yourself over and over." I knew a thing or two about that these last few months.

Scotland still felt ... so close. Like yesterday.

And yet ... a million days past.

Like my mother's death. It felt like we'd just talked, even though I knew it had been seven years.

"I don't want to heal," Akiyama said, voice rising. He looked at me, and his eyes were dark. "I want to live this. To live before this—"

"You have to let them go," I said, turning on him. "This isn't good for you, and it's wrecking the world—"

"To hell with the world," he said, rising to his feet. "To hell with all of you!"

"Hanging on, keeping them in this perpetual loop of torment," I said, not backing off, "it's not doing you or *them* any good! You can't move on with—"

"I WILL NOT MOVE!" Akiyama bellowed in my face, and here I took a step back. The world seemed to crack a little around me, little mirror threads breaking throughout the room, time splintering. The scene before me sped up in some of the panes, slowed down in others.

"I ..." Didn't know what to say to that. I didn't want to throw a punch at him, because—hell, he had to sleep some time, and apparently he could maintain his control on time through that. Knocking him out presumably wouldn't be any more effective.

The bitter conclusion was coming fast—if I couldn't reason with Akiyama, his death seemed to be the only solution.

But how could I kill him if he was going to travel back and help me kill Weissman?

"I don't have time for this," I said, shaking my head, taking a step back.

Akiyama laughed bitterly. "Time ... is all I have anymore."

I looked at him as he sagged back to his knees, watching the fracturing of time as the scene played out in front of him. I eased out of the room and found Harry moaning softly, his eyes moving about like a feverish man who was seeking water or solace.

Dropping back down, I seized his arm above the sleeve, careful not to touch him. "Hey," I whispered as he looked at me.

"What ... happened?" he croaked, turning his head to indicate Kat, who, although pale, was still breathing.

"Totally awesome things," I said, lifting a bloodied hand and making him grimace away from it. "I killed Prettyboy, who showed up without an invite. Also, some—okay, all—of his yakuza friends. So, there's that." I chucked a thumb behind. "And I got the door open to Akiyama's secret sanctum, so ... yay, me. Things are moving."

He stared up into my eyes, frowning lightly. "Time ... it's coming to a quick end, Sienna. Sooner than I predicted. And it—" He cringed, eyes pinching tightly shut. When his pain passed, he opened them again. "It's ... bad." He turned to look at Kat. "What happened to her?"

"She tried to save you," I said, a little tensely, maybe a touch reluctantly.

He stared at me, and the corners of his mouth moved just a little. "Huh. Really?"

"Try not get too excited about your baby mama doing you a solid," I said, a little snippily this time.

His eyes floated, then locked on me. "I'm ... in love with you. She's not ..." And he passed out again, going limp in my arms.

"The hell, Harry?" I started to say, but time went and did its inside out, wildly psychotic colors act, and I found myself in another Japanese hospital room, standing behind Harry again, and over Kat, who had that baby on her chest once more. The nurse spoke, in Japanese, and Kat started to say something—

And just as quickly I was back, holding onto Harry's arm, rolling my eyes so hard I thought they might spin out of my head. "Choice timing, universe," I muttered, rising to my feet. "Really rub it in right after he said—what he said."

I moved over to check on Kat. Her breathing was steady, pulse was fine, but when I pinched her finger, she fluttered her eyes. Lack of pain reflex would have been mildly concerning, but since I didn't have a ton of time to be concerned at the moment, a little relief washed over me as she raised her head, blinking at me.

"Sienna? What happened?" Kat asked, sounding pretty groggy.

"Good news," I said, actually relieved for real, "you didn't forget me."

"No," she said, looking utterly bewildered. "Why would I forget you?"

"I dunno," I said, settling back on my haunches. "I figured, what with you being a modern day, meta-equivalent of the Kardashians, the first thing you'd forget would be the little people, like me."

She just stared at me. "What's ... a Kardashian?"

"You forgot that?" I asked, laughing. "I think I speak for most of the world when I say, 'Lucky you.'"

"Oh—okay," Kat said, and sat up, a bit unsteadily. "What's ... going on with Akiyama?" she asked, nodding at the open door.

"He's got a trauma going on in there," I said, "which makes sense, cuz it's the trauma room, right? But ... yeah ... he's holding on to the past in a big way, and it's causing time to snap back, hard. Or stop, I guess."

"How does that work?" Kat asked, still sounding really sleepy. Her eyes were only half open, and she was blinking furiously.

"Have you ever seen me pop out of a flying Delorean with wild, white hair, wearing a white lab coat and—why am I bothering, you probably don't even remember—"

"I remember *Back to the Future*, okay?" Kat rubbed at her head.

"So far it's looking like it's all big wins in the memory department for you," I said. "Anyway, near as I can tell without being Doc Brown, Akiyama has held onto this moment in time so long that if he doesn't let go soon, the rest of the world gets ... well, cocked up because his hold spreads. Or something. I think."

"Lot of qualifiers there," she said, getting to her knees. "Okay. What do we do to make Akiyama let go? Knock his ass out?"

"I don't think that's going to do it," I said, rising with her. "And the answer to the first question is, I dunno. I have enough trouble letting go of my own issues and past traumas, so I'm probably the last person who should be in charge of coaching others on this—what?"

Kat was just shaking her head, lips curled in a smile of unmistakable amusement. "You're the first person who should help, given all the shit you've been through."

"I'm not a counselor, Kat," I said, "and I'm not sweet. I took a pass at it just now, and—I'm telling you, he's dug in. A bomb could not dislodge Akiyama from his current course of action."

"Why not?" she asked, hobbling over to the door to the room. "What's so important—" She stopped, staring in at the scene, which was frozen again, at least temporarily. "Oh."

Akiyama was on all fours again, staring at the paused time.

"Hey," I called in, "any chance you've reconsidered letting g—"

"I CAN'T!" Akiyama drowned me in fury as he shouted over his shoulder at us. Then he turned back to the scene, which, apparently prompted by his outburst, spun to life again.

"See?" I turned to Kat.

She stared into the room, then shook her head. "I don't think I can do anything. I don't even think I could manage to walk over there right now, so unless you want to bring him over here for a heart to heart—" And she sagged against the door frame.

"I don't think he'd be amenable to that," I said, catching a glimpse of him in profile. Beads of sweat were rolling down his face, and he was taking in the horrifying scene as it played once more, for probably the millionth time. It made my stomach twist, looking at his face with each viewing.

However many times Akiyama had seen this ... the pain was just as fresh as the first.

Kat looked up at me from where she'd collapsed once more. "Then I think ... this one's on you. Again, Sienna. No pressure. World in your hands. This is old hat for you by now." She forced a smile that could only be described as encouraging, and then shut her eyes.

"But this sucks so much," I said, letting my own emotions flow, "putting this all on me, like I haven't just lost—" I shut up. "He won't heal, Kat, because he doesn't want to." She didn't stir. "He can't let go." I pictured that village in Scotland, the one I'd seen in my dreams for the last few months, and a chill broke out over my skin. "I know how he feels. God knows—I know exactly how he feels, because sometimes I wish I could just forget—"

The emotion overwhelmed me, crawling up my throat, threatening to spill out in word and—other ways. Weepy ways. But that wasn't why I stopped talking in the middle of the sentence.

"Oh," I said. Because I got it. Finally.

I knew what the service was that I had to perform for Akiyama. And with a last look at Kat, who was peacefully out, and a worried one at Harry, who twitched in his sleep like he was having a fever dream, I crossed the threshold into Akiyama's trauma room ... to do the only thing I could for him.

42.

"Shin'ichi," I said quietly as I entered the room. He didn't turn, but I saw him stiffen as he watched the scene unfold again, his wife screaming in pain. I must have missed this part before, but it was an agonizing cry, the sound of labor, or maybe labor gone terribly wrong. It was a wrenching note, and I wanted to cringe away from it.

But I couldn't. Not any more than he could.

"I won't let go," Akiyama said, still on his knees. He was watching from a few feet away, staring at the event—the scene—like it was the last thing on earth that he cared about. Because it kind of was.

I came up behind him slowly. "I know," I said. The screaming had stopped, and she'd gone limp on the table. Her stomach bulged, and the doctor started to talk furiously, yelling at one of the nurses.

"I have lived here for so long," he said, as I slipped down to sit next to him. "I cannot imagine a life without … her." He had a single tear tracing its way down his cheek. "I lived as a god before I met her, and I gave it all up to be here, with her, after but a chance look." He glanced at me. "I saw her in a line after the bombing. The country was a smoking ruin … but when I saw, her, I saw … beauty amid the ashes, like a cherry blossom on a lifeless tree." He turned his gaze toward her again as the scene snapped back to the beginning. "We were together for over a decade, but … it was longer, of course. I would relive the good moments, over and over. My life with her was ..." His voice trailed off, breaking, before he composed himself, "... perfect."

"I wouldn't know what a perfect life feels like," I said, the hard floor biting into my ass as I sat patiently and listened to the doctor give commands in Japanese. "But I know what life feels like—and it's not supposed be just the same moments on repeat, forever." I looked at him, he looked at me. "Once upon a time, I might have thought you were fortunate to have the power you do, cuz ... control of time, it's a pretty cool one. But this ..." I shook my head at the spectacle before, the reheated torment that Akiyama consumed every day like a poison that would never actually kill him, only make him wish for death. "I don't think the reason you have this power is so you can torture yourself until you break time."

"What do you know about power and the reasons for it?" Akiyama threw at me, anger burning through his tone.

"I know that when we have these time flashes, it always seems to be critical moments from our lives and not just a random Tuesday where you're clipping your toenails," I said, thinking of the village in Scotland. "Now maybe that's just the default setting for a cold and indifferent universe that doesn't give a damn about us, but ... to me, it seems like the sort of thing that's ... not so much random."

"What does that matter?" Akiyama asked. "What does that have to do with anything?"

"Nothing," I said with a shrug. "Everything, maybe. But I guess it doesn't do much for you at the moment." I looked right at him. "I can't let you wreck time."

His gaze hardened. "You can't make me leave."

"I don't want to *make* you do anything," I said, taking a deep breath as I stared into his dark eyes. Now I could see it, now that he was so close to the edge. "I want to help you. Time ... may not be able to heal this wound of yours, but only because you won't let it." I put a hand on his shoulder, gently, and he started to flinch away, but controlled himself, staring at it suspiciously.

"I know time better than anyone," Akiyama said, tearing his gaze from my hand on his shoulder to look at me, directly. "The idea that it, on its own, has some magical healing property—is laughable. Time does not heal anything; your pain only diminishes the further you get from its infliction. It fades, at best, a remedy of the forgetful." He looked at the scene as again, his wife let out the last shriek and passed out as the doctor began to panic in earnest. "I don't wish to forget. Ever."

"I know, Shin'ichi," I said, raising my hand from his shoulder ... to the side of his neck. "And that's the problem."

He turned his head, slowly, to look at me, baffled at my placid agreement. I let my fingers stay on the side of his neck, kneading into the muscles. He looked at my hand briefly and said, a little tautly, "I don't know what you're trying to accomplish, but it won't—"

The first strains of my power must have hit him just then, because his face fell, and I could see the wheels turn as he tried to assess where the dull burn was coming from.

"I'm sorry," I said, moving to clamp my other hand on his cheek, holding him tight so he couldn't wriggle free, not that he had much strength left to do so at this point. "But this is the only way." I looked him in the eyes and saw panic rising, the fear, as the pain grew where my skin touched his. "Your pain is so great, you'd stop the world in its tracks to keep drinking deep of your own torment. These memories are like poison, Shin'ichi, but they won't just kill you—they'll ruin everything and everyone."

I stared down at him, and he started to jerk, feebly, in my grip. "So ... I need them. At least ... some of them."

My power propelled me into his mind, and I tried to decide how deep I needed to excise. Performing memory surgery was something I'd done more than a time or two, and while I'd never exactly relished it ...

Now? After what Rose had done to me?

I hated it more than ever before.

"This isn't about taking your past," I murmured, the words squeezing out into the real world as I existed in the blue flashes of Akiyama's memories. "It's about making sure that you—and everyone else—has a future."

TIME

To that end, I locked onto a certain point in time, in his memory, and entered the very moment when everything had gone wrong for the first time.

Akiyama stood at the side of the scene. The doctor had shouted, and Akiyama had burst into the room from the waiting room, hearing it through his meta hearing.

"This," I whispered, seeing Akiyama's face frozen in fury, in anguish. "This is the moment."

And I took it, as I always did when viewing someone's memories from within them.

There were a few more, all from after that point. Moments of high emotion, all of which tied back to this one, where he made the decision to lock his powers on a single space of time, and never let go.

I could feel the threads of his will slipping away as he let go, the emotional ties to keeping up his nigh-eternal war against its passage in this room, in this place unbound one by one by my removal of the memories that bound him here.

With a last gasp, I pulled my hands from him and fell over, the heat of my power burning through my flesh like fire in my blood, a little too titillating to make me feel good about experiencing it in semi-public. I thudded to my back, staring at the ceiling, which was black with the decay of time.

"I am sorry, my—" And here Akiyama said something in Japanese, something I hadn't absorbed through the memories I'd taken. He was sitting there, that tear still streaking its way down his cheek.

But his wife ... and the doctor ... and the nurses ...

And the baby, the one that had never drawn so much as a breath ...

Were all gone.

In their place was a broken wall, a trauma room ravaged by time and ruin, and a sky that looked out on the setting sun over the empty sea.

"I'm sorry, too, Shin'ichi," I said, but he did not move, did not look at me, did not even acknowledge my presence, "but it had to be done."

43.

I left Akiyama sitting there, staring into the sunset, motionless, speechless. He seemed like a vegetable, for all intents and purposes, and I would have felt bad about leaving him as such except I didn't want to disturb him, either. I was pretty sure he knew, in general, what I'd done to him, and poking the bear after you've ripped apart his memories? Didn't seem like either the smart or the kind move.

"Man, my head feels like someone decided to have a hell of a bender," Harry said as I walked back into the ruined corridor outside the ward. He was sitting up now, looking at Kat, who was similarly sitting up, leaning against the doorframe to the trauma room. "Makes me sorry I missed it."

"The only thing that got bent was time," I said, trying to disguise my relief that he appeared to be more or less back to normal. Play it cool, that's the Sienna way. Or at least play it cool until you get pissed, then unload a vengeful rain of hell upon your foes. That's maybe more the actual Sienna way.

"So ... is time all better, then?" Kat asked, looking around. "Did it get ... fixed? In the non-pet, spaying/neutering sort of way?"

"Time remains intact, so far as I can tell," I said, looking around for any of those obvious fractures that Akiyama had produced when he'd gotten overly emotive. "It certainly seems to be chugging along normally—"

Of course I shouldn't have said that, because tempting time was apparently as smart an idea as tempting fate. The world went psychedelic around me, and once more I found myself in that other Japanese hospital room, with Kat on the bed, baby laid atop her chest, and Harry's broad shoulders stooping over her.

"Why the hell did I have to go and open my big yap?" I mumbled, standing just outside the little family circle, over Harry's shoulder. "Because of course I've now got to be treated to a nice dose of jealousy-inducing flashback to the time when my friend Kat was schtuping my current boyfriend—"

"What should we name him?" the man was asking, and I realized, with a little bit of a chill—

That was *not* Harry's voice. It wasn't totally dissimilar, but it wasn't Harry.

"Harrison," Kat said, staring in obvious, googly-eyed glee at her newborn baby joy. "Harrison Aleksandr Graves." She looked up. "I want to name him after my brother."

"Holy shit," I said, as the kaleidoscope of colors blew past me with a fury once more, and I was deposited back at the entry to the trauma room in the present day. I hit my knees, totally from the passage of time travel and the flashback and not at all from the touching tribute to my friend Aleksandr, now lost, that Kat had performed some sixty years ago.

"Holy shit, indeed," Kat muttered. She did not seem that taken aback; a little smile perched on her lips.

I stared at her, she met my gaze evenly, and I caught a hint of knowing in her eyes. "You remember?"

She nodded, once. "The stuff Omega gave me, before I was 'retrieved' by the Directorate? Whenever I use enough of my powers to trigger memory loss ... some old memories come bubbling back up. I kinda recalled this, but now that I've seen it, in living color ..." Her voice drifted off, and she looked at Harry, who was staring back at her in a very restrained sort of way ... "I remember you ... Harry."

Harry choked back a little sniffle. "Good," he managed to get out. "That ... that's good. What all do you, uh ... do you remember?"

Kat settled her head back against the wall, as if drifting back into a pool of soothing memory, a peaceful smile on her face. "I remember raising you around the world. I remember spending a winter in Smolensk. I remember a summer in Oslo ... a year in Yokohama." She opened her eyes, and her smile turned sad. "I remember losing your father in Ulaanbaatar." Now the smile faded. "And almost losing you in Prague."

Harry sniffled. "That was where, uh ... where you used your powers and—"

"And forgot you," Kat said, and her eyes were full. "I'm so sorry, Harry. I tried to save your life and—I forgot you."

"You did save my life," Harry said, nodding, but not looking up. "You did. I would have died if you hadn't. And because of what you did ..." He threw his arms wide and forced a smile. "Here I am. Alive and kicking. Still moving about the world. And—"

"Sleeping with Sienna," Kat said, and her lips tightened together.

Oh.

Oh, shit.

Whoops.

"Hey, I totally did not know he was your kid," I said, finally inserting myself into this blissfully sweet and tear-filled family reunion. "I mean, I don't know that it would have stopped me, especially at certain, uh ... junctures ... of our relationship, but still ... didn't know."

"I'm just ragging on you, Sienna," Kat said, shoulders shaking with amusement, her smile telling me that she was totally busting my ass. "He's a big boy. Older than you." She turned her gaze to Harry. "I'd tell you to find someone your own age, but ... I don't think you could do much better than her."

That sounded like a compliment. Or maybe an insult to Harry. "Thanks," was all he said, and it was kinda strained.

"Need a hand?" I asked Kat, offering her one.

"Sure," she said, and seized my arm up the sleeve in order to lever herself up with my help. Once she was on her feet, she leaned against the wall. "I'll be back up and running here in just a minute. I think."

"Take your time," I said, looking around a little warily as I made my way over to Harry and helped him up. I kept a hand on his elbow as I walked him over to the wall next to Kat. They kept their eyes on each other the whole time, as I leaned him to next to her, and I reflected ...

Oh, what a difference a few minutes made. If they'd been looking at each other like this before that last little flashback ... I'd have been pissed.

Now, it was hard not to be happy for them, because ...

Well, hell. How could you not want to see a sixty-plus-year reunion between ... uh ... my boyfriend and ... geez ... his mother, my good friend Kat.

Man, my life was weird.

44.

Jamal

"Nice to see you fellas without orange jumpsuits and steel jewelry," Reed said as Augustus and I exited the jail with Miranda trailing behind us. He'd been leaning against a wall, arms folded, not looking too pleased or impressed with being called out to Northern Virginia in what was getting to be the middle of the night. "It wasn't a great look on you when I saw it on the news earlier."

"Well, you know, the steely handcuffs don't really offer enough pop against my skin tone," Augustus snipped at him, adjusting his shirt like it was too tight, or had itching powder in it. Something.

I was powering up my phone, trying to give Reed a pass on his hard snark. Who could blame him for being pissed that he had to drop everything and cross the country to bring us a lawyer to bail our asses out?

Lucky for us, Miranda hadn't had to do much. My phone buzzed as it came back to life, a text message already waiting for me from Arche.

Sorry about that.

I sent right back to her, or at least her number, avoiding the traditional message routes and delivering it direct with 1's and 0's of electrical energy to the point of origin. I felt a little touch from her own exploring, probing, digital fingers, and for a second it was like talking direct to her, no devices between us.

"Did you know this was going to happen?" I asked, seeing a flash of a digital avatar that looked like her.

"No," she said, voice garbled and digitized. "If I had known how stiff the opposition was, I would have warned you. I didn't mean to send you into the lion's den unprepared. Those weren't my orders."

"Orders ...?" I asked. "Care to tell me who you're working for?"

Her avatar showed the hint of a smile. "No. You're a smart fellow. You'll figure it out."

I tried not to show my disappointment. And here I'd been hoping she was helping me out of the goodness of her heart or our prior association or ... other ... reasons. "Well, thanks for getting us out of it."

"They didn't see me coming—this time," she said. "Be careful if you go after these people again. They're more dangerous than I thought they'd be. More prepared."

I thought about it for a second. "You know I can't just leave them alone."

I caught a flash of that smile again. Arche never looked ... happy, exactly, but there was a certain amusement in what I saw here. "I know. Best of luck, Jamal."

And then she was gone, her digital footprint vanished from my phone like she'd never even been there.

"... just trying to figure out what you were thinking," Reed was saying as I popped back into the real world.

"Phones out, everybody," I said, and they all looked at me questioningly. "Never mind," I said, and a little bolt of electricity lanced out from my hand, finding their phones with a tiny trickle of blue to each of their bodies. I switched off every one of their phones and did a quick search, manually deactivating every single microphone, camera and transmitter so that I'd physically have to power them up again once we were done. "Okay, Reed—take us up."

If Reed didn't know what I was doing, he made no display of it, instead following my request and shooting the four of us into the sky. Miranda gasped, but Augustus and I both managed to control our surprise as the ground fell away and the wind carried us a thousand, then two thousand feet straight up, and brought us together in a tight little circle.

"A little warning next time might be nice," Miranda said, the legs of her pants flaring like bell bottoms.

"We're well out of range of most listening devices, if you've switched off the ones we carry with us," Reed said, looking straight at me. "So ... what is it you didn't want to talk about with anyone else around to hear it?"

I traded a look with Augustus, and he answered for me. "We were chasing evidence that Sienna was defending herself in Eden Prairie."

Reed stiffened visibly. "Say what?"

"Last year," I said, taking up the story, "when Sienna and I worked with ArcheGrey1819, that superhacker? She told us there was video proof that Sienna was innocent in the Eden Prairie explosion. That the local cameras had recorded her getting her ass beat by those prisoners, and that she blew up in self-defense."

"Of course she did," Reed said, still stiff. "We all know that the Eden Prairie incident was just a pretext for Harmon to sic the dogs on her."

"Right," I said, "but the problem with siccing the dogs on her was, after Harmon died, there was no one willing to call them off. Most people didn't know she was innocent—but some do. And they're hiding the evidence, maybe at Harmon's behest, maybe for their own reasons at this point. But we got ... pointed in the direction of the supposed custodians of the proof."

"And they're a metafamily that works in IT for a whole lot of congresscritters," Augustus said. "Powers like Jamal and Arche to affect the digital flow of information."

Reed's brow furrowed. "So you're saying that ... there's an active conspiracy to keep Sienna on the run? It's not just Harmon's dead hand and bureaucratic momentum keeping it going?"

"There's probably some of that at work," I said. "I mean, the press that was there, that was mind-controlled and attacked her, they'll probably swear till their dying days that she's evil and came after them, but ..."

"But they were basically the only witnesses and they were under the influence of that meta with the feral whatever powers," Reed said, working it out for himself. He took a deep breath and stared off into space for a moment before looking back at us. "How long have you been on this? Trying to prove Sienna innocent?"

I traded a look with Augustus, and he answered for us both. "Since just after we rolled up that Revelen Serum cartel. Right when Guy Friday joined us."

"That's a long time to be working this under the radar." He looked at Miranda. "I trust, given your history with Sienna, you can keep this secret?"

Miranda let slip a ghost of a smile. "I've kept much darker secrets for Sienna than the fact she's innocent. And she had me working on this on my own, anyway, so ... to borrow one of her favorite phrases," she looked at each of us, "'Welcome to the party, pal.'"

"I knew she was innocent," Reed said, pensive, "but I never dreamed there'd be a way to prove it. This is ..." And he smiled. "I want this done. More than anything." Now his eyes flashed danger, though. "But these people, this family you're talking about? They damned near put you in the same boat as her with only a couple moves."

I nodded. "They're dangerous, no doubt. And now they know we're looking. The game's afoot fer realz."

"We'll need to watch our step, then," Reed said, and he seemed to come to a decision. "But ... at least now we know something, too. We have a first step."

"The Custis family," Augustus agreed.

"They're protected by power," I said. "Their own metahuman abilities—but also friends, I think. These people—they're asses we can't just kick, or we'll find our own kicked back even harder."

"That's all right," Augustus said, and his tone sounded different than it had when we'd started this day in Ohio, charging into trouble. "We've got time. We do this slow, if we have to. Tie 'em up. Get it right. Keep a watch on 'em—and wait for them to make a mistake, because everybody does, sooner or later. And now that they know we're after them ..."

"They'll be moving," Miranda said. "Before, they were probably just standing still on this, or acting behind the cloak of anonymity. Now that we know about them ..."

"Yeah," Reed said, and a smile broke over his lips. "We know who holds the cards. Now ... we just have figure out how to get them."

45.

Akiyama

The sun was rising over the island, and Shin'ichi Akiyama felt ... strange.

His memories of Akiko were still there, still keenly felt, and yet ...

There was a distance between them, now. A veil that had been drawn over those most strongly felt, a strange divide ...

"Time," he decided, as the orange glow lit the sky in the east.

He sat here, in this room, now open to the sea by the slow weathering of time, and had a vision of things being ... different here. It was just a vision, though, bereft of strong emotion, only traces of sadness lingering like dampness in the streets once the rain had stopped. He felt it drain through his soul, and ...

He smiled wistfully. The good times were still there, in his memory, ready to replay, but all else ...

Had faded.

Akiyama rose to his feet, taking a last look at the sunrise. How long had he been here? He scarcely remembered, but it felt like forever, like a sentence in that American island prison, Alcatraz. He furrowed his brow as he stared out over the sparkling waters.

There were visitors here now, and he'd barely talked to them, but ... he'd seen enough. Remembered enough, to know of them.

To know ... her.

She'd done something for him that he never could have done for himself, and for that ...

"I have accrued a debt," he whispered.

Akiyama turned his back on the rising sun, felt the slow build of his power in his fingertips again. It had felt strange for some time now, as though an anchor were dragging his abilities down. He had only the vaguest recollection of what he'd done—again, as though looking at the last sixty years through a veil of sorrows—and now he found himself thinking of a most curious thing, something he had not contemplated in quite some time ...

The future.

Leaving the decaying room behind him, Akiyama walked out the door.

Somehow, he knew would never return here again.

And with that knowledge came the strangest sense ... of relief.

46.

Sienna

Akiyama came down the road to the dock at a slow walk, taking his sweet time. The fisherman was still waiting there on his boat, clearly still too terrified of me to consider disobeying my directive. Kat was on her cell phone, speaking in crisp Japanese, in what sounded like a grateful tone, while Harry ...

Harry was leaned against me, and I against him, just watching the sun come up as Akiyama shuffled toward us at a glacial pace.

"The plane's going to be in Nagasaki in a couple hours," Kat announced as she hung up. She took in Harry and me intertwined with each other, using each other as support columns, and smirked a little. "They'll refuel and be ready to go an hour or so after that."

"Can we sneak aboard?" I asked Harry. He nodded. "What about customs on the other side?"

He nodded again. "No problem."

"Nice to have you back," I said, and he sparked a little smile at me.

"Yeah," Kat said, with a lot more meaning. "It's nice to have you back, Harry." And they shared a look of their own.

"I do have one question for you, though," I said, trying to get this last one in before Akiyama arrived. "Why not just tell us that Kat was your mom?"

Harry rolled his eyes. "Have you met the no-memory Kat? How do you think she would have reacted to that unprompted revelation? 'Hey, it's me, your son. I know I look and act older than you, but you totally are my mom. Gimme a hug'?"

Kat laughed. "That's legit." Her smile faded. "I was so driven to be ... not Klementina. There's no way I would have accepted ... any of that."

Harry adopted a pained smile. "I know. Besides ..." He shrugged, and the pained part of it left. "I knew it was just a matter of time before the truth came out on its own terms."

"Saw that in the future, did you?" I asked, poking him in the ribs. He did not avoid my move, laughing instead. "Even through the cataclysmic crashing of all of time?"

"Yep," he said, taking my pokes with a good-natured laugh. "I knew that if time survived, that'd all work out. But of course time surviving was kind of touch and go there for a while ..."

I tried to put aside my amusement as Akiyama arrived, cutting off our laughs and infusing our little group with a drift of seriousness. "Shin'ichi," I said, a little stiffly.

"Sienna," he said, bowing to me. "Thank you for what you did."

"Yeah, about that ..." I said, feeling a little remorse for ripping his memories of loved ones out of his head. "I know I had to and all ... but I'm still sorry."

"Your apology is unnecessary," Akiyama said, back to that steely reserve. "You did what needed to be done. I do not feel any regret for your conduct. You helped me in the only way that you were able ... and that is enough for me." He paused, taking a long breath. "Now ... I believe I owe you something in return."

I felt my muscles tighten. "Yes. Well."

Kat was suddenly at my side, and she pulled me a step away, holding up a finger to Akiyama. "Just a sec." She only dragged me about a foot or so, and spoke in a normal voice everyone could hear, so I had no idea what the hell the point of this apparent aside was, since we had no privacy. "Sienna ... you could get your mom back."

TIME

I blinked at her; surprise flooded through me.

Mom?

"I am sorry," Akiyama said, shaking his head. "If her mother has already died ... there is no changing that. It would ... break time far worse than what you saw here to try and change that part of the past."

That breath of hope I'd felt for just a second—the idea that my mom could come back—died just as quickly as it arrived, and my shoulders fell subtly. "That's all right," I said, though truly I felt like it was anything but. "You know me," and I did a little smile-forcing of my own. "I'm not much for looking back or living in the past, and that ... well, it was a long time ago."

Akiyama stirred. "Or ... very soon to come, in my case." He gestured toward the boat. "I will need to make my way to ... where we are to meet, if I'm to do this."

Kat just stared at him, eyebrows pushing together. "Can't you just ... teleport there?"

Akiyama smiled. "I can move through time, not space."

"I'm sure we can get you a ride to Minneapolis," I said, looking at the boat, waiting for us. Harry stirred into motion first, skipping carefully over the unsteady boards to show me the way to follow. I did, and Kat followed me, with Akiyama bringing up the rear, and soon enough, the fisherman was throttling up and we were pulling away from the dock.

Akiyama gave the island a last look; it was tough to tell from just his face what he was thinking, but I felt like there was an element of relief there, like some weight had been lifted from him. Finally, he turned to me and, speaking under Kat's chatter to the fisherman as she apparently tried to smooth over all that poor guy had been involved in over the last couple days, Akiyama said, "So."

I glanced at Harry, who waited, on the seat next to me, supportive, listening. He nodded, and brushed my shoulder. It wasn't like I needed his reassurance, but after all I'd been through ... hell, my whole life ... it was nice to have it anyway. "Yes?" I asked, turning back to Akiyama.

Akiyama smiled, again, this quicksilver thing. "Tell me ... about our first meeting."

47.

We got Akiyama booked on a flight to Minneapolis and left him to experience the wonders of the modern world, all the things he'd missed in being out of circulation for so long. Harry said he'd be all right, and I believed him, which left me to follow his lead once more, and about half an hour after we'd arrived at the Nagasaki airport, I found myself standing on the tarmac with Harry and Kat as the ground crew finished refueling the waiting plane.

"You sure you don't want to come with us?" I asked Kat, who was once again wheeling her own rollerbag like a champ and totally not an entitled, elitist reality TV superstar.

She smiled. "I need to do a little cover and damage control here, I think. We didn't exactly leave things in flawless condition on our way to Nagasaki. Harry says I need to talk to the cops and clear the air a little in order to take the heat off myself—and you."

"Thank you," I said, truly meaning it. The sun beat down from overhead, but it was a pleasant, dry morning, with a spring tinge to the air. "For everything, Kat."

"Yeah, you kinda owe me a lot more than I thought," she said, eyes gleaming with mirth, "since I made your current boytoy."

"Mommmmm," Harry said, closing his eyes and sounding a lot like a teenager who'd just been embarrassed by a parent. "Please."

Kat got serious. "Take care of him for me, will you?" Then

she looked past me. "And you—I want to see you again, soon. Over sixty years without a card or a call—it's too much, Harrison."

He rolled his eyes. "You literally forgot I existed."

"Well, now I remember, okay?" Kat wagged her finger at him. Whatever else that Omega serum had done, she seemed ... different. I was guessing other stuff might have come back, too, because while she still had the same Kat effervescence ... there was a certain mature quality to her look, and the laughter, the joy she usually carried ...

Looking in her eyes, it felt more ... muted than it had been before.

"Be careful, Sienna," Kat said, and she grabbed me up in a hug before going after Harry for the same. He didn't shrug away, either; he took it gracefully, willingly, and put his head down and closed his eyes on her shoulder like he was just ... soaking it up. And he probably was, given it had been something like five decades since he'd gotten a hug from his mother.

One sympathized. It kinda felt that long to me, too. And it stung all the more, thinking back to the conversation I'd had with Kat only hours earlier.

Time. She sure was an unyielding bitch.

We made our way into the plane without further ado, and sat in our seats, across the little aisle from each other. There was no flight attendant on this trip; Kat had ordered none in order to give us the minimum number of witnesses to figure out Sienna Nealon was onboard. Harry had blessed the idea, saying it was our only chance, and so we found ourselves in an empty plane save for the pilot and co-pilot up front, the cabin door already secured and the cockpit shut.

Harry was looking out the window to where Kat waited, watching the plane, all alone on the tarmac. She waved at him, and he raised his hand, waving back.

"I'm glad it all worked out with ... uhm ... your mom," I said, still feeling really weird about how that was Kat. My Kat. The thoroughly unserious Kat I'd known for years.

But then again ... she'd lived for over a hundred years before I met her, and only remembered a few of them.

So, really ... did I know Kat—the real Kat, Klementina Gavrikov ... at all?

"I'll see her again," he said, and turned to look at me before stealing another glance at her. He waved again, and I could see her doing the same.

"Lucky you." I turned to look forward once more as the plane's engines started up with a gentle whir, ready to take us away from this place and spirit us back to the US.

48.

"Where to?" I asked as we lifted off into the air, the plane fighting against the force of gravity and triumphing again, as always. It was a brisk and liberating feeling, when you thought about it, kicking the ass of nature's directives and spitting in its face as you did whatever the hell you pleased, directionally.

I missed being able to do it all by myself, without engines or planes or anything but the whisper of a soul in my head.

"Las Vegas," Harry said, still staring out the window. "There's a convention going on that's got McCarran airport all abuzz, plus a fight on Saturday that's highly anticipated. We'll be able to slip through easy in the hubbub, pick up a car and ..." He turned and smiled to me. "Disappear."

"Good," I said, though I probably sounded uncertain. Because that was how I felt: uncertain.

Harry was still looking at me. I knew ... he saw it, now that his future sight was restored. He could see right through me, knew everything I was going to say, but still he sat there, patiently, just waiting ... for me to say it.

"Time heals all wounds," I said slowly, like I was speaking profundity instead of trite words.

"Mmhm," he said, watching me with those warm eyes.

"But ... I'm still wounded, Harry," I said, flicking my gaze down to the plane's creamy beige carpet.

"I know." Soft. Soothing. Totally Harry.

"But ..." I said, keeping my voice steady, "it's getting

better. And I feel *guilty* ... that it's getting better." I dared to look up at him again, and in his eyes I saw ...

Sympathy.

"They gave their lives for me ..." I said, my voice breaking, "and I don't want to forget them the way your mom forgot you ..." My voice was shuddering now, unsteady, like we'd hit turbulence that affected only my throat. "But—but I've forgotten *so much*, Harry—so many holes in my mind ..." My first sob split the quiet cabin.

He was still here, this time. Not that he had anywhere else to go.

"It's going to be okay," he said, and suddenly he was there, and it reminded me of how, just a few months earlier, in a field in rural Illinois, he'd taken me in his arms and let me cry it out.

This was what had felt like it was missing the last few months—from me, from *us*. And I realized, as I sat there, crying again on Harry's shoulder, that the reason he hadn't been around for any of these times ...

Was because until now ... I hadn't been ready for him to be.

I hadn't wanted him to be.

But all that had changed now, and Harry's arms wrapped me up tight, taking care to keep our clothing dividing our skin from each other lest I drain him dead. But still, it was enough, plenty enough, to feel him close against me as he repositioned himself, taking me down to the floor with him, and I leaned against him and felt his breath in my ear, his chest move up and down beneath my arm as I sobbed.

And I let him hold me, warm and safe and complete, for the first time in a long time, as we flew off into the east.

Toward home.

Sienna Nealon Will Return in

DRIVEN
Out of the Box
Book 20

Coming June 1, 2018!
(Or more likely somewhere around May 15, 2018, if I hurry.)

Author's Note

Thanks for reading! This is, believe it or not, the twenty-ninth book featuring Sienna Nealon. Let that sink in. I hope you're still finding these as fun as I am, because as long as I keep enjoying myself and people keep buying, I'll keep writing them. They continue to be a real thrill for me to work on, so...expect many more. The moment they stop feeling fresh, I'll drum every ounce of imagination I have left and we'll call it quits before they start to get stale. (Mileage may vary – some people already feel this way, according to reviews I've read, but most seem to enjoy them, so...on we go!)

I know you're probably grabbing these on or before their release dates (yay for pre-orders!), but on the off chance I don't set one up, if you want to know immediately when future books become available, take sixty seconds and sign up for my NEW RELEASE EMAIL ALERTS by visiting my website. I don't sell your information and I only send out emails when I have a new book out. The reason you should sign up for this is because I don't always set release dates, and even if you're following me on Facebook (robertJcrane (Author)) or Twitter (@robertJcrane), it's easy to miss my book announcements because...well, because social media is an imprecise thing.

Come join the discussion on my website:
http://www.robertjcrane.com!

Cheers,
Robert J. Crane

ACKNOWLEDGMENTS

Editorial/Literary Janitorial duties performed by Sarah Barbour and Jeff Bryan. Final proofing was once more handled by the illustrious Jo Evans. Any errors you see in the text, however, are the result of me rejecting changes.

The cover was once more designed with exceeding skill by Karri Klawiter of artbykarri.com.

Thanks to Jennifer Ellison and John Clifford for being my first readers on this one.

The formatting was provided by nickbowman-editing.com.

Once more, thanks to my parents, my in-laws, my kids and my wife, for helping me keep things together.

Other Works by Robert J. Crane

The Girl in the Box
and
Out of the Box
Contemporary Urban Fantasy

Alone: The Girl in the Box, Book 1
Untouched: The Girl in the Box, Book 2
Soulless: The Girl in the Box, Book 3
Family: The Girl in the Box, Book 4
Omega: The Girl in the Box, Book 5
Broken: The Girl in the Box, Book 6
Enemies: The Girl in the Box, Book 7
Legacy: The Girl in the Box, Book 8
Destiny: The Girl in the Box, Book 9
Power: The Girl in the Box, Book 10

Limitless: Out of the Box, Book 1
In the Wind: Out of the Box, Book 2
Ruthless: Out of the Box, Book 3
Grounded: Out of the Box, Book 4
Tormented: Out of the Box, Book 5
Vengeful: Out of the Box, Book 6
Sea Change: Out of the Box, Book 7
Painkiller: Out of the Box, Book 8
Masks: Out of the Box, Book 9
Prisoners: Out of the Box, Book 10
Unyielding: Out of the Box, Book 11
Hollow: Out of the Box, Book 12
Toxicity: Out of the Box, Book 13
Small Things: Out of the Box, Book 14
Hunters: Out of the Box, Book 15
Badder: Out of the Box, Book 16
Apex: Out of the Box, Book 18
Time: Out of the Box, Book 19
Driven: Out of the Box, Book 20* *(Coming June 1, 2018!)*
Remember: Out of the Box, Book 21* *(Coming August 2018!)*
Hero: Out of the Box, Book 22* *(Coming October 2018!)*
Walk Through Fire: Out of the Box, Book 23* *(Coming December 2018!)*

World of Sanctuary
Epic Fantasy

Defender: The Sanctuary Series, Volume One
Avenger: The Sanctuary Series, Volume Two
Champion: The Sanctuary Series, Volume Three
Crusader: The Sanctuary Series, Volume Four
Sanctuary Tales, Volume One - A Short Story Collection
Thy Father's Shadow: The Sanctuary Series, Volume 4.5
Master: The Sanctuary Series, Volume Five
Fated in Darkness: The Sanctuary Series, Volume 5.5
Warlord: The Sanctuary Series, Volume Six
Heretic: The Sanctuary Series, Volume Seven
Legend: The Sanctuary Series, Volume Eight
Ghosts of Sanctuary: The Sanctuary Series, Volume Nine
Call of the Hero: The Sanctuary Series, Volume Ten* *(Coming Late 2018!)*

A Haven in Ash: Ashes of Luukessia, Volume One *(with Michael Winstone)*
A Respite From Storms: Ashes of Luukessia, Volume Two* *(with Michael Winstone—Coming April 3rd-ish 2018!)*

Southern Watch
Contemporary Urban Fantasy

Called: Southern Watch, Book 1
Depths: Southern Watch, Book 2
Corrupted: Southern Watch, Book 3
Unearthed: Southern Watch, Book 4
Legion: Southern Watch, Book 5
Starling: Southern Watch, Book 6
Forsaken: Southern Watch, Book 7* *(Coming 2018!)*
Hallowed: Southern Watch, Book 8* *(Coming Late 2018/Early 2019!)*

The Shattered Dome Series
(with Nicholas J. Ambrose)
Sci-Fi

Voiceless: The Shattered Dome, Book 1
Unspeakable: The Shattered Dome, Book 2* *(Coming 2018!)*

The Mira Brand Adventures
Contemporary Urban Fantasy

The World Beneath: The Mira Brand Adventures, Book 1
The Tide of Ages: The Mira Brand Adventures, Book 2
The City of Lies: The Mira Brand Adventures, Book 3
The King of the Skies: The Mira Brand Adventures, Book 4
The Best of Us: The Mira Brand Adventures, Book 5* *(Coming 2018!)*
We Aimless Few: The Mira Brand Adventures, Book 6* *(Coming 2018!)*

Liars and Vampires
(with Lauren Harper)
Contemporary Urban Fantasy

No One Will Believe You: Liars and Vampires, Book 1* *(Coming Early 2018!)*
Someone Should Save Her: Liars and Vampires, Book 2* *(Coming Early 2018!)*
You Can't Go Home Again: Liars and Vampires, Book 3* *(Coming Early 2018!)*
In The Dark: Liars and Vampires, Book 4* *(Coming 2018!)*
Her Lying Days Are Done: Liars and Vampires, Book 5* *(Coming 2018!)*

* Forthcoming, Subject to Change

Made in the USA
Monee, IL
15 November 2020